ONE
of
US

DAVID GREGORY

ONE
PRESS

Katy, Texas

One of Us

©2024 David Gregory Smith

This book is a work of fiction, depicting the events recorded in the four New Testament gospels in a modern setting. Any resemblance of the characters or events in the book to modern characters or events is coincidental.

Cover design by Jun Ares
Interior layout by Sandra Jurca

Published by One Press, Katy, Texas

www.FreeWithGod.com

Trade paperback ISBN-13: 978-0-9675141-7-8

9 8 7 6 5 4 3 2 1

Printed in the United States of America

PRAISE FOR *ONE OF US*

"*One of Us* is a masterpiece that grabs your soul and doesn't let go. David Gregory brilliantly crafts a tale that brings Jesus into today's tumultuous world. Both daring and compassionate, it's a must read for anyone seeking hope and clarity in our chaotic times."

> —Dr. Andrew Farley, bestselling author, lead pastor of The Grace Church, and host of the nationally syndicated call-in program, *The Grace Message*

"*One of Us* achieves something almost impossible these days: a truly fresh and unique retelling of the greatest of all stories. It crackles with excitement, jumping off the page with vigor, passion, immediacy. This is Jesus up close and personal."

> —Mike Mason, bestselling author of *The Mystery of Marriage* and *The Blue Umbrella*

"Both utterly fresh and thoroughly biblical. It was like I was reading the gospels for the very first time. This is the story we'd all like to read."

> —Robby Angle, CEO, Trueface

"Wow. What a gift to my faith journey. The more pages I turned, the more I settled into my own story with Jesus. *One of Us* is transformative."

> —Janet Newberry, author of *Education by Design, Not Default*

"*One of Us* is both brilliantly conceived and amazingly executed. I loved it!"

> —Ralph Harris, author of *Life According to Perfect* and *God's Astounding Opinion of You*

Also by David Gregory

FICTION

Dinner with a Perfect Stranger:
An Invitation Worth Considering

A Day with a Perfect Stranger

Night with a Perfect Stranger:
The Conversation That Changes Everything

The Last Christian: A Novel

Open: Get Ready for the Adventure of a Lifetime

The Next Level: A Parable of Finding Your Place in Life

Patriot Rules: A Novel

NON-FICTION

The Rest of the Gospel:
When the Partial Gospel Has Worn You Out (with Dan Stone)

If Jesus Loves Me Why Isn't This Working?

Beyond Rules: God As You Never Imagined

Awesome: Praising God Straight from Scripture

To Truett,
a man of story, and of faith

One

After all the country had been through, little had changed. All the protests, the violence, the voting, the economic crisis, the calls for revolution, the calls for restoration—people's deepest hopes had not, in the end, been realized. The rich and powerful were richer and more powerful. The poor and weak were poorer and weaker. The search for meaning, the spiritual hunger, remained.

Few trusted the government. Few trusted the media. Few trusted the institutions that had always held society together. Neither political side trusted the other. Increasingly, the ruling class tightened its control over the population. They knew the danger that widespread powerlessness could bring; above all, they sought to insulate themselves from that threat.

Then an unassuming man waded into the Rio Grande.

I'd known Juan Carlos all my life. Though in recent years I'd lost touch with him, we'd grown up together—not in the same town, but close enough that our families visited a lot. He and I were like brothers. He was always a radical kid, different—kind of like me, actually. Over the years, he'd done things people considered a bit strange. So I wasn't surprised when he disappeared for a couple of years. Nor was I surprised when one day he showed up again in the middle of the Rio Grande.

Juan was in his mid-30s, Mexican, dressed in jeans and a

blue-checkered laborer's shirt. He entered the river from the Mexican side halfway between McAllen, Texas and Rio Grande City. The border patrol spotted him and took no notice. Many were still crossing daily. What was one man?

But he didn't wade across. He stopped halfway and started speaking. Loudly. Mostly in Spanish, partly in English, to anyone within earshot.

Few heard at first. A couple of fishermen on the American side. Some teens on the other. But every day, around noon, Juan Carlos would wade out and begin speaking.

"God is going to completely change things up," he announced. "So get ready. Change how you think about God. Believe what he's about to show you."

Word got around. A few more people started coming down to his spot along the river.

"Another realm is about to be introduced. God is fulfilling what he promised. For the first time, you're about to be connected to him."

The small crowd grew. Dozens of people sitting every day on both banks, listening. Someone started posting videos.

"God is completely changing how your lives are going to work," he proclaimed. "A bigger change than you ever imagined. A new government is right around the corner. God's government. A new system is coming! A totally new arrangement! The bulldozers are already on the way."

That got people's attention. A hundred people a day started showing up. Then several hundred. Then a thousand, mostly poor, from as far away as Monterrey and San Antonio. Some came out of curiosity. Some came for guidance. Most came for hope.

"Get ready!" Juan implored. "Prepare yourselves for what's coming!"

He began inviting the crowd, one by one, to wade out into the river to him from either side, confess their sins, and admit their need for God. He would then dunk them in the water—"baptizing," they called it. At first it was just a person or two. Within a month, long lines had formed and Juan was baptizing nonstop from mid-morning until dark.

People beyond the Rio Grande Valley started taking notice. Opinion makers began commenting on social media. Some religious nut was attracting followers in South Texas, they said, now several thousand a day. He was calling for the government to be overthrown. He needed to be silenced. The last thing the country needed was to add religious conflict to its already fraying social fabric.

Those in power in Washington, in corporate America, in the media, and in Silicon Valley were watching as well. They didn't mind protests, of course, if they advanced their cause. But a religious rabble wouldn't be under their sway. Especially one led by a man unafraid to say to some local politicians who ventured down to the river, "You snakes! You come down here, pretending all of a sudden to be religious, but everything you do is just for show. You claim to support the poor, but you're in the pocket of special interests. What makes you think you can fool God? The good citrus trees—those who respond to him—God will keep. The bad ones he'll uproot. Respond to God!"

I knew, of course, that Juan wasn't starting just another religious movement. He was introducing something far beyond that, something that would transform not only individual people's hearts, but, eventually, the entire planet. Those in power couldn't see that. All they could see was the threat to their rule.

They were right to be afraid.

Thousands of years before, God had promised to bless the whole world in a way no one expected. And he had promised to send someone to make it happen. An Anointed One.

But a messiah had never come, and most people no longer expected it. Many centuries had passed, and as the influence of the Hebrew scriptures spread far, especially to the West, people had settled into comfortable religion. They tried to live good lives. They tried to keep the Ten Commandments. They prayed occasionally. They went to worship house. Or they just stayed home. After all, society was far more secular than it used to be.

Nevertheless, for many, the hope of a messiah remained. No one admitted to that in polite, well-to-do company. But among the poor, and the religious (which, in the Rio Grande Valley, were largely synonymous), there was this underlying belief: El Único, The One, would one day come and set everything right. God had promised it.

Now, speculation metastasized across the Valley. Had anyone ever come here quite like Juan Carlos, calling people to God, defending the poor, proclaiming the truth even to the point of making enemies in high places? Was he the fulfillment of the promise? Was he El Único?

Conjecture reached a fever pitch, until one day Juan Carlos, standing in the middle of the river, declared:

I am not El Único! But he's coming. In fact, he's already here, among you. Let me tell you: he's far greater than I am, because he existed long before I came along. He's from above. I'm from below. I'm not even worthy to clean his toilet. He's the Lamb of God, the one who takes away the world's sin. I dunk you in this river, but he's going to dunk you in the Holy Spirit, and in fire!

That clip on social media threw gasoline on an already-burning blaze. People became desperate to find El Único.

The powerful did nothing. Yet. They watched, and waited.

I'd been waiting, too. Waiting for the day I'd go to the river myself. Finally, that day had come.

Juan Carlos wasn't hard to find. Late one morning, I drove

from our auto repair shop in McAllen to the river and walked with many others two miles to his spot. A dozen Border Patrol SUVs overlooked the river. Beyond the SUVs, a thousand or more people lined the sloping bank on the American side. An even larger number stood on the opposite side.

As Juan preached, the crowd stood silently, listening and adding an occasional "Sí, señor." When he finished, he invited people to be baptized. They waded out, one by one, first from the south bank, then from the north. Over the course of three hours, I inched along with those around me, until it was my turn.

I waded out to where Juan Carlos stood waist deep in the water. We embraced, and then spoke briefly. He finally nodded, placed his hand behind my back, and lowered me into the river. When I rose out of the water, I saw the heavens being parted, and the Holy Spirit came down like a dove, landing on me. And then El Papá said to me, "Emanuel, tú eres mi Hijo amado; estoy muy complacido contigo." *Emmanuel, you are the Son I love. In you I am very pleased.*

TWO

FBI Special Agent Jason Cuellar pressed the stop-record button on his iPhone and glanced around him. Everyone in the crowd seemed stunned into silence. He wasn't sure what had just happened, but he was sure of this: the Juan Carlos phenomenon had just leaped into a new orbit. What looked like a miracle had just occurred down here. On video. Crowds would probably grow tenfold.

The man Juan Carlos just dunked exited the river on the Mexican side. The crowd parted for him and he disappeared from sight.

Cuellar turned and made his way through the crowd on the American side, back to his Chevy Tahoe. He sat in the front seat and watched the video he had just shot. Unfortunately, it showed what he expected: the man was too far away, and the angle too tight, to identify him. Nevertheless, he had caught the spectacle sufficiently that it would grab attention within the agency. Not that online videos of the event wouldn't do the same thing within a day. He forwarded the video to his supervisor, the head of the McAllen field office, with a simple note:

Brad, from the river today. You're going to want to look at this.

THREE

Two days later, I was in the Sierra del Carmen mountain range of northern Mexico. The Holy Spirit had led me to this high, arid, desolate landscape—one of the most remote places on earth. Save for the occasional javelina, gecko, or rattlesnake, I was alone. On one mountainside I found an outcropping of rock next to a tiny stream. There I stayed, without food. I grew gaunt, my skin parched, my lips cracked. I met with El Papá and listened.

After forty days, my hunger pangs, which had long since passed, returned. My body was breaking down, consuming itself.

At that point, Satan came.

I knew he would. He had to. I was the one threat to his rule over earth, and all of humanity. He'd been trying to eliminate that threat since before I was born. My mother was intensely pressured to abort me. That's what pregnant high schoolers in the Valley often did. No one knew who the father was, and she never said. An old man at the worship house had even predicted that because of me, incredible pain would come her way. She could avoid all of that so easily.

"No," she always replied. "Dios ha hecho grandes cosas por mí. Y me ha dicho que este niño será grandioso." *God has done great things for me. And he has told me, this child will be great.*

After I was born, she had to flee into Mexico, to relatives in Monterrey, when her life, and mine, had been threatened. She never told me why. As I grew older, I came to understand. The catalyst behind it had not been human at all.

She met my dad, an Anglo, in Monterrey, and married. They returned to the Valley when it finally seemed safe, but they were never entirely sure.

There was nothing Satan wouldn't do to derail my mission. And now he appeared to me in person to accomplish just that.

He was loathsome. Not his physical appearance, of course; his beauty knew no parallel. But I was repelled by what his whole being cried out: his utter opposition to everything he was created to be, to God's entire created order. Yet, even in his hideousness, his allure was undeniable.

When he appeared, I regarded him from the rock where I sat, but said nothing. He stood some distance away, scrutinizing me. He knew that my body screamed for nourishment. Finally, he stepped toward me and motioned with his head toward the rocks at my feet.

"Since you are God's Son, tell those rocks to become a meal."

I knew exactly what he was trying to do. Dominion of the earth had been lost by the choice of man. Humanity had willingly given earth's title deed to Satan. And only a human could reclaim it. I was that human. And, as a human, I had to choose what the first man had failed to choose: to be one with God, to live in continual union with the Creator, to draw my life from him only.

But I had to do it completely as a man, not as God. I was who I was—the I AM—but as a man I'd laid aside my right to operate as God. If Satan could get me to act independently, and use my ability, *as God*, to provide for myself, he had me. He would win. If he could get me to respond to him as God instead of as man, my mission would fail. I would not regain what humanity had lost. And now my body screamed for me to do just that.

But Satan knew nothing of me, and what I was really about. For 35 years I had lived in unbroken oneness and communion with El Papá. He was my very life. I was indwelled by him—the first of my kind. I lived, because he lived in me. I spoke to him. He spoke to me. I listened. He taught me. He showed me the things he was doing.

The only thing I wanted to do, every moment, was to love him. To do the work he had sent me to do. Every day, he was my supreme joy, and pleasing him was my supreme joy. Doing what he wanted was never a burden; it was a delight. I couldn't possibly be happier than doing his will.

The desire of my heart overrode that of my body. I glanced up at Satan and simply replied, "God has said, 'People can't live only on food, but on every word that comes out of God's mouth.'"

I was transported away from the rock, away from the Sierra del Carmen entirely. I found myself standing on top of the dome of the U.S. Capitol, overlooking Washington, DC. Satan was standing next to me. The wind whipped around us. There was nothing to hold onto, only the Statue of Freedom to lean against.

"Since you are God's Son," he said, "throw yourself down from here." He floated a step away from the ledge we were standing on, out into mid-air, and smiled at me—a ghastly smile. "After all, didn't God say, 'He will command his angels to hold you up with their hands, so your feet aren't hurt by a single stone'?"

This time, he wanted me to presume upon my relationship with El Papá, to assert my own will, to force El Papá into having to rescue me and prove his care for me. I refused to take the bait. El Papá didn't have to prove himself to me. I knew fully who he was, and he knew fully who I was. I was his.

I shook my head. "God also said, 'You shall not put the Lord your God to the test.'"

A moment later, I was standing on the roof of a tall building. I glanced at the landscape: skyscrapers, almost as far as one could see. Below me, in a long arc, flew the flags of over 200 nations. I was atop the United Nations building in Manhattan.

"You see all those flags down there?" a voice said behind me. Satan peered over the edge of the roof. "The nations those flags represent—I will give every one of them to you. I will make you leader of them all. You will rule the whole earth. They've all been given to me, and I can give them to whomever I wish. All you have to do is fall down and worship me."

He was offering me what would one day be rightfully mine. This was the easy route. The instant route. The painless route. I could bypass everything I would soon have to face, and in a single moment achieve the utmost.

But despite the lie Satan told himself, it wasn't the utmost. Not for me. Not compared to being one with El Papá.

I looked at the flags and saw what Satan could not: all the earth's peoples were meant to be one with El Papá, too. El Papá was meant to live in them. They were meant to know him, and his love, and the joy of having their hearts aligned with his. That's what I had come to give them.

Satan could never offer me that. And there were no shortcuts to it. I turned back to him. "God said—"

The scene changed. I was standing on a high bluff, overlooking water surrounded by a sprawling metropolis. I recognized the outline of San Francisco Bay. And down below us, Silicon Valley.

Satan stood in front of me, gazing at the panorama. "Whoever controls what you see here—the internet, social media, the AI revolution—controls the world! You can get people to believe whatever you want them to believe. Get them all to believe in this God of yours. If you simply bow down—"

"Go away, Satan! God said, 'You shall worship the Lord your God, and serve him only.'"

We stood glaring at each other. He had lost.

I found myself back in the Sierra del Carmen, next to my out-cropping of rock. The trial was over. For now. He would be back.

The sun pressed down upon my face and neck. In the shade,

under the outcropping, sat an Igloo cooler. I smiled. I didn't realize angels used Igloo coolers. I opened it, took out a bottle of
fresh water, wrapped some beans in a tortilla, and ate.

The next day, I drove back toward the Rio Grande Valley,
so filled with the Spirit's power and with joy that I could barely
contain it. The time had arrived to accomplish what I'd come to
earth for: to connect people to El Papá. I was ready.

FOUR

I returned to a Valley that had changed. Videos of my baptism, and the Holy Spirit descending on me, had gone viral. Some people claimed the whole episode was a hoax. An AI-generated illusion. The fact that, oddly, none of the videos of the event recorded a clear image of me added to the confusion. One thing was certain: everyone had been trying to figure out where this unknown man had disappeared to.

Crowds coming to hear Juan Carlos had doubled overnight, then doubled again. Over 10,000 a day were showing up, hoping for something else miraculous that might happen, searching for meaning.

Juan kept telling the crowd, "The one who told me to come here and baptize, he said to me, 'When you see the Holy Spirit coming down and landing on someone, he's El Único.' He's the one who is bringing a new system—a new government!"

Despite enormous pressure, Juan Carlos had refused to identify the man he had baptized. "That's for him to reveal, in his own time," he said.

Two days before I returned, Juan was arrested, accused of crossing the border on the American side illegally. I knew the charges were false. So did the crowds.

Undoubtedly, officials believed arresting Juan would dissipate the throng. They were wrong. People kept coming, now to protest and demand Juan's release. Rocks were thrown at border patrol agents. Arrests were made. Texas's governor threatened to call out the National Guard. The rolling chaos that had enveloped the country not too long before had finally come to the Valley.

I crossed back into the U.S. at Nuevo Laredo and drove three hours to my apartment in McAllen.

The next morning, a Saturday, I attended the worship house nearby. I usually drove back to San Isidro, where I grew up, and went to worship with my mother. But this particular morning I had a message to deliver in McAllen. I needed to pick up where Juan Carlos had left off.

Splits had developed in many worship houses over Juan. Most attendees thought he was doing God's work. Most worship house leaders weren't so sure. Most in the religious hierarchy, above them, were sure. Juan Carlos was a nut. They wanted nothing to do with him.

Though religion's influence had been waning for decades, more than a third of Americans still attended worship every week. Three-fourths believed in God. People were accustomed to the religious system. They could count on its stability. The hierarchy wanted to keep it that way.

Worship services were fairly uniform from place to place. During the service, at a designated time, anyone could stand up, read from the Hebrew scriptures, and say a few words about what they read. I stood that morning. The worship house leader acknowledged me.

"Manuel," he said.

I opened the scriptures and read:

"Behold, I send my messenger ahead of you,
      Who will prepare your way,
The voice of one crying in the wilderness:
      'Make ready the way of the Lord,
      Make his paths straight.'"

"This is talking about Juan Carlos," I said to the crowd. "Heed what he's been saying!"

I glanced over at the worship house leader. He was already frowning.

"The time is fulfilled," I continued. "God's rule is near. In fact, it's right here. It's time for you to change your mind about God, how you think about him, and how you respond to him. He wants you connected to him in a way you've never imagined!

"Let me tell you how valuable being connected to God is. It's like an investor who finds a stock that she knows will shoot through the roof. Few people know about it yet. She sells every stock she has so she can buy ten thousand shares of it."

The people were perfectly quiet as I spoke.

"Being connected to God is like a pro baseball scout who gets a tip about the next superstar, an unknown 15-year-old kid from Honduras. The scout doesn't wait. He drops everything to fly down immediately and sign him to a contract. It's like a geologist who figures out there's oil under some worthless land a hundred miles west of here. He cashes in his retirement accounts, sells his house, even sells his car and buys up every acre of that land while it's still available. That's how much being connected to God is worth."

I sat down and could hear whispers across the crowd. "Could he be right?" "Is that passage really talking about Juan Carlos?" "How do I get connected to God like this?"

That evening, I threw on a suit and headed north to Delta Lake to fulfill a long-standing obligation: attending the wedding of a young family friend. Arriving at the old converted ranch house, I hugged my mother, brothers, and sister, and then my friends Pedro, Sebastian, and Justin. I had known the three of them for several years, since a good rancher friend of mine, Tim Wright, had hired the water well operation they crewed. It had taken the four of us about five minutes to bond.

"Where you been, man?" Pedro asked. "You've been gone forever."

"I was with El Papá." They were used to me talking that way.

Justin prematurely loosened his buttoned collar. "You heard what's been happening around here?"

"It's been crazy since that—whatever—happened at the river," Sebastian said. "And then Juan Carlos being arrested ..."

"That guy Juan dunked," Pedro said. "Some people are saying he may have looked kind of like you."

I shrugged. "Yeah. Well ..."

My mother stood in the front doorway and called to us. "Why are you men still in the parking lot? It's time! ¡Apúrense!" *Hurry up!*

We went inside and witnessed a beautiful wedding. Afterward, everyone drifted outside to the pavilion for the reception. The live band started playing, people began dancing, and everyone stuffed themselves with guisados, chicharrones, chicken fajitas, and rajas con queso. Until the power went out.

"Ohhh!" the crowd moaned.

Cell phone flashlights appeared.

"Isn't there a generator?" someone asked.

"Unfortunately, no," a voice answered.

Someone shined a light on a man who walked to the center of the pavilion—the venue's manager. "Sorry, amigos. Our backup generator went out two weeks ago. It's not yet fixed." Another groan from the crowd. "Give us a few minutes to see if we can get the power back."

Five minutes later he returned. "I have bad news. Power's out all over the area. There's nothing we can do."

The bride burst into tears, her father trying to comfort her.

My mother stepped toward me. "Can you do something?"

I smiled gently at her. "Do I look like an electrician?"

She raised her hand and patted my cheek. "Yes, actually. Except your hands are usually greasier."

"It's not quite my time," I replied. But I knew I couldn't let the most important night of the young couple's lives be ruined.

My mother ignored my comment and walked over to the manager. "My son can help."

My glance fell on the suddenly hopeful eyes of the bride's father.

A minute later the manager, two employees, my three friends and I were standing at the circuit breakers out back.

"Flip the top switch," I told the manager.

"We already did that half a dozen times."

"Flip it again."

One of his employees flipped it. Some indoor lights went on.

"Whoa!" the manager said. "What happened?"

"Flip all the other ones."

Switch by switch, the power returned to the main house, the outdoor lights, the sound system, everything. The crowd roared its approval.

The manager laughed. "Well, that's a surprise. I guess miracles never cease."

The band started blaring again. Pedro, standing next to me, glanced across the lake. "Hey guys ... we're the only ones with power."

The men scanned the darkness along the shoreline.

"Then how did we get it back?" one of the employees asked. They all slowly turned toward me.

Just then the bride ran up, tears of joy running down her cheeks, and threw her arms around the manager. "Thank you for saving the reception!"

Seeing her face, I couldn't have been happier.

I glanced again at my friends, who were looking at me oddly. That was a good thing. It would help prepare them for our next encounter.

FIVE

On Sunday morning, I took care of several transition items. I'd given a sixty-day notice on my apartment before I left for Mexico. Now I needed to sign final papers on selling my share of our family's auto repair shop to my brothers and sister.

It felt strange, the thought of leaving our auto repair business. I started working there after school when I was 12, learning from my dad. By age 16, though too young to be certified, I was as a practical matter a fully trained mechanic. Eventually, he taught me to run the business end as well, which I'd been doing since he passed. I still enjoyed getting my hands greasy, though.

I met my siblings at a notary's office.

"What are you going to do for a living?" my brother Felipe asked.

"El Papá provides."

He shook his head, "El Papá?" My family never had gotten used to the fact that I referred to God in a way no one else did. "You're just going to trust God to provide? That's crazy."

It seemed crazy to him, for sure. For me, my Father's provision was as certain as the Rocky Mountains still standing tomorrow.

I gave some of the business's proceeds to my mother, saved some for upcoming travel expenses, and with the rest ordered a full-sized, used van which I would soon need.

Late Monday morning, I hopped in my pickup to run a few errands. As I approached the light at a freeway underpass, I saw a young woman standing at the corner. Like most people in the Valley, she was Hispanic. Mid-twenties, unkempt black hair. Her face was dirty, her clothes worn. And she was pregnant.

She held a cardboard sign that said,

Will do anything for food.

I'd seen plenty of such signs before, though not quite that brazen. That's just the way McAllen is—how the whole Rio Grande Valley is, really. Poor. Rough. A place where, for a lot of people on both sides of the border, life is mostly about survival.

I rolled down my window. "You hungry?"

"Duh."

Whether she was or not didn't matter, I knew. She would have said yes regardless.

I glanced at the McDonald's on the other side of the street. "I'll buy you some breakfast over there." The light changed. "See you in a minute."

"No, I just—" she started to reply.

I drove through the light, circled around, parked in the McDonald's parking lot, and looked across the street. She was still standing there.

"You coming or not?"

She shrugged, put her sign down, and walked across.

"I wasn't asking for breakfast, you know."

"I know what you were asking for."

"What's that supposed to mean?"

I didn't answer. We went inside and she glanced up at the menu. "I want pancakes."

I ordered each of us two egg and sausage burritos and juice.

"I said pancakes."

"Your baby needs protein."

I so wanted to break through her hard exterior. Dictating this one meal choice might not help that, I realized, but she needed to start learning to choose for two.

She frowned at my order, but didn't decline it when it came. We sat at a booth and she gulped some orange juice and dove into a burrito.

"Está rico," she admitted. *It's good.* She quickly had another bite. "But I need more than one breakfast, you know." She looked at me, as if uncertain about my response.

"Tell me what you need."

She glanced at the large Walmart across the street. "A shopping spree over there wouldn't hurt."

I downed a bite of burrito and opened my orange juice. "How many?"

"How many what?"

"How many shopping sprees?"

She stared at me, taken aback. "What—you like the ultimate sugar daddy?"

I had another bite before replying. "No. But I can provide you more than one of them could."

"For real?" For the first time, she seemed to let down her guard just a little. "How?"

"If you knew who I was, you'd ask me, and I'd give you something worth more than a thousand trips to Walmart."

She scoffed. "Yeah, right. Driving that old pickup? What could you have, man?"

I looked out at two men and a woman sitting with their duffle bags and grocery carts under the freeway, near where she'd been standing. One of them had a dog. "I'll tell you what," I said, "after we finish here, why don't we go over to your boyfriend over there and I can tell you both."

She looked toward the underpass and then back at me. "Oh, neither of those guys is my boyfriend. They're just—we all just hang out there together."

"You're right," I replied. "In fact, your boyfriend left when he found out you were pregnant. And neither your mother nor your sister will take you in, because you're still doing drugs."

The young woman's eyes dropped. Tears welled up and began rolling down her cheeks. "I … I know it's bad for the baby. But I just …" She stopped talking and wiped her cheeks, but she couldn't keep up with the tears. In a moment she looked up at me, her eyes much softer. "How'd you know all of that?"

"I didn't know. El Papá knew."

She grabbed a napkin off the plastic tray and wiped her cheeks again. "You sound like that guy Juan Carlos keeps talking about, the one who's going to make everything right."

"I am that guy."

We simply beheld each other for a moment.

"What's your name?" I asked her.

"Rachel."

"Rachel, normally I wouldn't ask this, but would you mind if I placed my hand on your belly?"

She shook her head. "I don't mind." She scooted off her bench and stepped toward me, her shirt covering her slightly distended tummy. I put both of my hands gently on it and spoke toward it.

"Be whole, little one."

I removed my hands and she looked down at her belly. "What did you do? I felt something happen inside me."

I smiled at her. "Your baby will be fine, Rachel. She's no longer damaged by the drugs."

"She?" Her face broke into a huge smile and the tears began to flow again. "She?"

Six

The next day I returned to the underpass. Rachel's face looked radiant, just as it had after our encounter the day before. She introduced me to her friends. I sat on the concrete incline next to them and asked about their lives.

Ramon had come from Mexico three years earlier, Carmen twenty. She'd worked in the citrus groves for years before she tore something in her shoulder. She couldn't afford proper medical care, and it didn't heal right. Miguel was from the Valley. He dropped out of school when he was 16. Maya had been in community college after high school but a boyfriend got her hooked on drugs. It was downhill from there.

"None of you thought you'd be here under this bridge every day," I said. "Life didn't exactly turn out as you expected."

"Es la neta," Miguel replied. *It's the truth.*

"But that's going to change. I came to give you a full life, a rich life."

"I could take rich," Ramon commented.

I smiled. "El Papá blesses the poor, you know. Would you like to know how?"

They all nodded.

"I'll tell you. When you're desperate, you're ready for El Papá to take the reins of your life. That's true whether you're poor or rich. Being poor just gets you there more quickly. El Papá comes to you when you've lost what you hoped life would bring—like all of you have—and he embraces you. When you finally realize how much you need him, then you end up gaining everything."

My eyes met Miguel's. He chimed in. "You're saying that if you're really hungry for God, he'll satisfy you."

"Exactly."

"But that's not going to feed us lunch," Ramon said.

"Well, it's a package deal. El Papá provides." I glanced over at the Walmart. "How about if you and I go get something for everyone?"

Fifteen minutes later Ramon and I returned and made peanut butter and banana sandwiches. Everyone dug in.

Rachel looked at me. "Protein?" she asked.

I grinned at her. "The peanut butter."

I looked around at them all and picked up where we had left off. "Here's what it's like being in El Papá's family. You care deeply about each other, and you see how deeply you yourself are cared for." I turned my gaze to Maya. "You want El Papá more than anything, and he shows himself to you." And then to Ramon. "Your heart is right with God, Ramon, and so you can see him in everything around you."

"But how do I get my heart right with God?" he asked.

"You can't," I replied. "But he can. And he will."

The following day I brought all of them tacos and spicy tater tots for lunch. I was glad to have brought extra, because two more people had joined the group.

I loved these people. Their lives had fallen so far short of everyone's expectations—especially their own—that they were almost completely without pretense. I was sorry they'd ended up under a bridge, but I knew El Papá was using that for their good. Hugely for their good, in fact.

When everyone had finished their meal, I walked across the street and threw the trash in a bin.

"Look," I said to them all after I walked back, "I know you've been discarded by the world, like garbage in that bin. The world doesn't think you're worth much. Let me tell you how much you're worth to El Papá."

I sat down next to them again. "Suppose some guy came by here and said to you, 'I bought a lottery ticket yesterday and I won $10 million. But I accidentally threw the ticket away in one of those bins. Can you guys help me look for it? If we find it, I'll let you have half a million each.' Now, what do you think you'd do if you found it?"

Carmen laughed. "We'd throw the biggest party this underpass has ever seen!"

"Right," I answered. "That's exactly the way El Papá feels when he finds you. Heaven throws the biggest party you've ever seen."

They all looked at one another. "But we're nobody," Maya objected.

I shook my head. "That may be what you think of yourself right now." I motioned over toward the cars at the light. "It may be what those people driving by think. It's not at all what El Papá thinks. He'd give everything he has just to have you."

We sat and talked for a couple of hours. From time to time, I glanced at two police officers near the corner, who seemed to be listening. Clearly, sound under the bridge carried.

When I finally got up to leave, I looked at Carmen. "Stand up for a minute," I said to her. She stood. "Show me how far you can raise your right arm."

She raised it about ten degrees above parallel to the ground. "That's all I can do," she said.

"Would you like me to restore it?" I asked.

"I … how can you do that?" She regarded me for a moment. "Yes, I would."

"Step toward me."

She did, and I laid my hand on her right shoulder. "Be restored," I said. I stepped back from her. "Now, raise your arm."

She raised it until her arm was touching her ear. "¿Cómo le hiciste?" she exclaimed, beaming. *How did you do that?* "¿Cómo le hiciste?"

I grinned at her. "El Papá can do anything." The two officers nearby caught my eye again. I nodded to them.

The next day six more people joined us under the freeway. Word was getting around the underpass community. I taught them again about the family of God. As I was finishing, one of the two officers I'd seen the day before approached us. I glanced at my groups of friends. He made them nervous, I could tell. I took several steps away from them, toward him.

"I've been listening to you teach about God," he said. "And I saw what you did yesterday with that woman. My son is sick." He paused to gather himself. "Actually, he's dying." He looked me in the eyes. "Could you please heal him, too?"

I could tell in a moment what a tender heart the man had. "I will come. But don't tell anyone—not yet." I wanted at least a few more days of relative privacy to accomplish what I needed to. But the policeman held his hand up toward me. "No, it's OK. You don't have to come to my house. Just speak it here and I know it's done." He motioned toward the area surrounding us. "I have authority here, in this realm. You have it in a greater one."

I was amazed. How did this man have such great faith? I nodded to him. "Let it be as you've believed, then. Your son is healed."

The man stuck out his hand and we shook. As he turned and left, I couldn't help but marvel at him. I walked back over to my underpass friends.

"What did he want?" Ramon asked.

"He wanted to exercise faith."

Thursday afternoon I drove to the UT-Rio Grande Valley campus. El Papá had prepared someone specific there. It was Cinco de Mayo and I expected students would gather for speeches at the outdoor University Commons. I was right.

I sat on a three-foot-high brick wall and listened to speeches decrying racial oppression, American imperialism, and white supremacy. Some students sported Mexican flags, others "La Raza" flags. A speaker drew loud applause calling for "La Reconquista"— the reconquest of the American Southwest.

Things got heated when a small group of white students walked silently past the wall I was sitting on, holding American flags and wearing "Come and Take It" T-shirts with a cannon barrel pictured across a Texas flag. They were roundly booed, screamed at, even spat on, but they passed without violence breaking out.

Some distance to the side, I noticed five students sitting on the grass, praying. Like the crowd, they were Hispanic. I walked over and joined them. When the last of them had stopped praying, I prayed. When I finished, they were all staring at me.

"You pray like you actually know God personally," a young woman said.

"I do," I said. "You will, too."

"What do you mean?"

"God is doing something new. Have you read where under God's new arrangement with people, he says, 'They will all know me, from the least of them to the greatest'?"

They all shook their heads.

"Then prepare to be surprised."

"Are you an instructor?" one of them asked me.

I smiled at her. "Not officially."

At that point I realized that the crowd was no longer a hundred feet away. Numerous of them had walked over, not to join us in prayer, but to aim their ire toward us. They closed in and encircled us.

"No more religion!" one of the young men exclaimed to the crowd. "It's a tool of oppression." He started chanting, "No more religion! Tool of oppression!" The crowd joined him. "No more religion! Tool of oppression!"

I glanced at the students I'd been praying with. They were afraid. "It's OK," I mouthed to them silently.

"No more religion! Tool of oppression!"

I stood up and joined the group in their chant. "No more religion! Tool of oppression! No more religion! Tool of oppression!"

One by one they stopped chanting, until I finally stopped as well.

"Hey, man, how can you say that?" one of them asked. "You were here praying with these dudes."

"Leave them alone," I said. "They aren't oppressing anyone. They're doing a beautiful thing. But you're right. Religion often is a tool of oppression. It keeps people weighed down. It keeps them bound up. It doesn't free them to be everything God created them to be. That's about to change. When the Son sets you free, you really will be free."

They had no idea what I was talking about. That was OK, for now.

"Do you know who was the first warrior for justice?" I asked them.

"Who?" a young woman in front of me responded.

"God," I answered. "Here's what he said to his people a long time ago:

'Free those who are wrongly imprisoned. Lighten the burden of those who work for you. Let the oppressed go free, and remove the chains that bind people. Share your food with the hungry, and give shelter to the homeless. Then your light will break forth like the dawn.'

"Does that sound like oppression to you?" They all remained silent. "God is making all things new."

"Starting when?" someone demanded.

I looked around and spotted the questioner, a young woman wearing an old Black Lives Matter T-shirt. I immediately liked her. She cared, she was passionate, and I could tell her heart was open. "Starting now."

SEVEN

By Friday, I knew that my time of relative anonymity was about to end. Videos of my encounter with the students at UT-RGV were no doubt circulating online. People would put two and two together.

Losing my anonymity didn't bother me. I came to reveal El Papá, not to the few, but to the many. Being in the limelight wasn't something I sought, but neither was being in the shadows. I was perfectly content either way. I felt incredible joy simply going through every day with El Papá, and doing his will. The rest was simply … circumstances.

That night, I went to a birthday dinner at the house of Pedro's mother-in-law. She lived in the tiny town of Encino, an hour north of McAllen and twenty miles from anything else on the map. Once you get away from the counties bordering the river, South Texas is pretty empty.

Pedro, his wife, Marta, and her mother, Isabella, had invited a bunch of friends and relatives to celebrate Isabella's 50th. But when I got there early to help with preparations, something was wrong.

"Isabella has a fever," Pedro told me. "A bad one. It just started an hour ago."

"What's she sick from?"

"No idea."

"Where is she?"

He led me to the back bedroom. Isabella was lying on the bed, eyes closed, sweating profusely. The sheets were already soaked. Marta, sitting next to her on the bed, worriedly glanced at us as we entered.

"It's up to 103," she told Pedro. "I think we should take her to urgent care."

"Wait," I said to her. I motioned for Marta to get up and I pulled a wooden chair next to the bed. I took Isabella's limp hand in mine and I put my other hand on her burning forehead. "Isabella," I said to her. She opened her listless eyes and looked up at me. "Levántese." *Get up.*

Vitality returned to her eyes. She squeezed my hand and then sat up in bed.

"Mamá!" Marta exclaimed.

"She's fine," I said.

Marta stepped forward and put her hand on Isabella's forehead. "It feels normal," she said, and then she looked at me. "What did you do?"

I smiled and rose from the chair. "El Papá made her well." I turned to Pedro. "Do you need some help with the grill?"

Isabella swung her legs off the bed.

"Mamá, you can't get up yet!"

She waved Marta off. "I feel fine. Let's go fix dinner."

After the guests arrived, word got around. People kept glancing over at me. I didn't mind, although it hadn't been my intention to distract from Isabella's birthday. That was unavoidable, though.

After dinner, cake, ice cream, and presents, we all learned how unavoidable it was. Someone from the group must have leaked word of what happened. Around 9:00, there was a knock at the door. A young mother was there, holding a child whose legs dangled beneath her knees.

"Rosario," Isabella said. "Is everything OK?"

"Armando is running a fever and has a bad sore throat. I think he may have strep." She looked past Isabella into the living room where everyone was sitting. "Would your friend be able to …"

I got up from the couch. "Of course," I replied before Isabella could answer. I walked to the door and looked at the child, who swallowed in pain. "How old is Armando?"

"He's four."

I smiled at him. "He's a big boy for four!"

She nodded and managed a slight smile back. "His father is tall."

I placed my fingers against the boy's throat. "Armando," I said firmly. "Be healed."

The boy looked at his mother, swallowed normally, and grinned. "Mamá, I'm all better!" He squirmed out of her grasp and headed for the kitchen table. "Can I have some cake and ice cream?"

"Of course," Isabella answered. She looked over at me and our eyes met. "Thank you," she mouthed.

Ten minutes later the doorbell rang again. A woman with lupus. Within half an hour, a line had formed down the front walk. I stayed until 1:30 in the morning, healing everyone who showed up. Afterward, I slumped into a kitchen chair, reached for a fork, and had the last bite of birthday cake: a bit of leftover icing on the edge.

Pedro and I walked outside for a little fresh air and looked up at the stars. I loved how you could see them so clearly here, away from the city lights.

"Can I ask you a question?" Pedro finally said.

"Sure."

His gaze turned from the stars to me. "Who *are* you?"

Isabella invited me to spend the night, since it was so late. I refused her kind offer. I knew perfectly well that first thing in the morning, if not before, her house would be besieged with even more people. I didn't want to burden her with that.

Life, as I expected, had changed. My anonymity was over.

I drove south and caught a few hours' sleep on the couch at the auto shop. When morning came, I drove to my home worship house in the tiny town of San Isidro. My mother was visiting her sister, so I knew she wouldn't be there. It was just as well. I wasn't sure what kind of reception I'd get at the worship house.

I soon found out. I walked in and people all over the building—people I'd known since I was a kid—started staring at me. Word of what happened at Isabella's had clearly spread. Here, where people had known me for years, they didn't know what to think.

After the service started, I stood and read from Isaiah:

The Spirit of the Lord God is upon me,
Because the Lord has anointed me
To bring good news to the afflicted;
He has sent me to bind up the brokenhearted,
To proclaim liberty to captives,
To set free those who are oppressed,
To proclaim that the time of the Lord's favor has come.

"Right now, this scripture is being fulfilled before your very eyes," I said. A murmur passed through the small crowd. I could make out some of the comments.

"I always knew he was going to be special."

"Where is Maria? She would be so proud."

"Was that Manuel at the incident at the river?"

"Did you hear what happened last night in Encino?"

But not everyone responded graciously. Loud enough for most of the room to hear, someone said, "Wait a minute, we've known Manuel all his life—how can he be the one to fulfill this?"

Then from the back, a man stood up and said, "If you're who you say you are, why don't you prove it?"

I wasn't surprised. Of course some would respond this way. They'd known me since I'd been playing T-ball. How could I be the Anointed One?

I looked at him, and then at the people. "You know," I said gently, "a prophet is never welcomed in his home town."

"But you're not a prophet!" someone objected.

I continued. "I realize that some of you will say to me, 'Do here what you did over in Encino.' God has done miracles before among people who didn't even know him. He's going to do that now as well."

Mr. Sanchez, a grizzled old grapefruit farmer, stood up and glared at me. "We're not going to let you do here what Juan Carlos did all over the Valley. Causin' arguments. Dividin' people. Gettin' 'em riled up, protesting, arrested."

Mr. Muñoz, the worship house leader, followed him. "We're not going to turn this place into a circus. If you want to do that, do it on some other day, at some other place."

Ms. Gilbert rose to her feet. "But what if Juan Carlos was right? What if Manuel is El Único?"

At that point the whole place erupted.

"How could he be El Único? My kids went to school with him."

"Juan Carlos is a lunatic! That's why he's in jail."

"Is he saying God is going to bypass us and bless heathens? That's not how God works!"

By now most people were standing, arguing with each other, their voices raised. Above the din, a man shouted, "Get him out of here!"

Several men came toward me to do just that. They pushed me out the back of the worship house. I didn't know what they planned to do. I'm not sure they did, either. People followed us out back, shouting. We were heading toward a large gravel pit 50 yards behind us. The situation seemed precarious, but I was at peace. My time, I knew, was not even close. El Papá had something else in mind.

Then someone in the front parking lot laid on their car horn. Loudly. Everyone stopped and looked through the open back doors. A girl, maybe seven or eight years old, stood in the wide front doorway of the small worship house, crying, cradling her left arm. The car horn finally stopped. A woman got out of the car and joined the girl. I walked through the silent crowd toward the front of the building.

"I think my daughter broke her arm falling off our tire swing," the woman said. "Can you help her?"

I knelt down, eye-level with the girl. "Can I look at it?"

She nodded, still crying.

I could see where the arm was broken. I placed my hand on her head. "Be whole," I said.

Her crying stopped. Slowly, she stretched out her arm. Then she shook it gingerly, and then more forcefully. She looked at me, wide-eyed, and then at her mother. "It's gone, Mom! It feels OK."

I took her hand and placed it in her mother's, who now had tears in her eyes as well.

"She'll be fine," I said to her.

I turned and glanced briefly at the people behind me. Then I walked to my truck and drove toward McAllen.

EIGHT

My phone was going crazy as I drove back to McAllen, vibrating with texts. It had been at the worship house, too. Finally, I pulled into a Whataburger parking lot and glanced at them. One from my brother Felipe caught my eye:

Whats going on? Two reporters here at the shop waiting for u. Plus people in the parking lot.

It had begun. I texted Felipe back.

Tell them I won't be at the shop today. Thanks.

I called Marcus, my car dealership friend. Could he do me a huge favor and have my used van ready at his house instead of at the dealership? No problem, he said. Half an hour. It was a small precaution, but that way his employees wouldn't see me driving off with it. I wanted a day or two before people recognized the van as mine.

I went through the drive-thru and ordered a breakfast sandwich. The young lady at the window did a double take when she handed me my order. She pulled her phone out of her pocket, glanced at it, and then turned back to me.

"Hey, aren't you—"

"I am." I held up the sandwich bag. "Thanks for the breakfast."

Twenty minutes later I pulled up at Marcus's house. The van was out front. We exchanged car keys and shook hands.

"Good luck," he said as I walked toward the van.

"Don't need it," I answered over my shoulder. "I have El Papá."

I drove an hour and a half north to southern Duval County, just east of Hebronville, passing miles of flat terrain covered with citrus groves that gradually turned into eight-foot mesquite trees. I had friends to be with. I talked to El Papá on the way. And in my spirit, I heard him talking to me.

Pedro had told me where he, Sebastian, and Justin were crewing the water well they were currently drilling. I turned off the highway and slowly drove down a dirt road. When I got to the site, the three of them were sitting at the rear of the truck, having lunch.

"New wheels?" Sebastian asked as I got out of the van. "Chido." *Cool.*

"New for me. You guys are working hard, I see."

"We drilled 150 feet this morning," Pedro answered. "Supposed to have hit water by now. But nothing."

Justin stood and handed me a hard hat. "Pedro told us what you did at Isabella's last night. The internet is going crazy over it, you know."

I smiled. "Why do you think I came to be with you guys in the middle of nowhere?"

They finished their lunch and the supervisor came out of the cab. "Let's go. Another 50 feet."

They drilled for two more hours. I sat against a tree, watching them and talking with El Papá. Finally, they reached 200 feet.

"Shut it down!" the supervisor called out to them. "Shut the whole thing down!"

He and I had barely been introduced, but he looked at me and said, "Just lost 40 percent of our fee. We drill another one, we can recoup. But then it's lost time." He shook his head. "Either way, it's a loss."

I looked at Pedro, who had stepped over. "Drill down another 16 feet," I told him.

He stared at me, a bit incredulous. "¿Mande?" *What?*

"Drill down another 16 feet."

"We were supposed to hit at 150. We already drilled down another 50."

The supervisor turned to Pedro. "What, is your friend here a geologist?"

"Sixteen feet," I said to Pedro again.

Pedro pulled the supervisor aside for a moment. A minute later he walked back and said to Sebastian and Justin, "Another 16 feet."

"What did you tell him?" I asked Pedro.

"I told him you were the guy who healed all those people in Encino last night."

"And what did he say?"

"He said, 'Maybe he should lay his hands on that drill!' Then he said, 'Fine, another 16 feet.'"

They drilled 16 more feet. And then the water came gushing.

"¡No manches!" Pedro exclaimed. *No way!*

The guys all let out whoops and high-fived.

The supervisor simply smiled and nodded. "Great job guys. Let's see if we can wrap it up before nightfall." He looked at me and stuck out his hand. "I'm not sure what just happened, but thank you."

Sebastian and Justin started pulling casing off the back of the truck to secure the well. But Pedro took me aside. "Manuel, how did you know there was water down another 16 feet? Water wells never go that deep here."

"I didn't," I answered. "But El Papá did."

Pedro looked down at the ground. "I don't get it. Why are you even bothering with me?" He looked up again at me. "You know I'm no good."

I put my hand on his shoulder. "Don't worry, Pedro. From now on, you'll be drilling down into the hearts of men."

I stopped at a roadside fruit stand on the way to McAllen and bought a pink grapefruit. It was good to sit quietly by myself at a picnic bench and eat. I talked to El Papá some more. But mostly I listened. Where would he and I be working next?

I texted Pedro before getting back in the van.

You guys meet me at Los Asados tomorrow at 11:00 for lunch.

They had the day off, I knew.

Ur gonna draw a crowd.
  I know.

I slept that night at the mobile home of Victor, who used to work at the auto shop, and Raul, his brother. The next morning, I invited them both to Los Asados. On the way, I stopped off at the underpass and picked up Rachel and her friends.

Pedro had secured a table for 14. We were early enough that the place was empty. Despite the online buzz the last two days, the hostess didn't recognize me, although she did do a double take at the underpass folks. At our table, everyone small-talked for a few minutes until Raul brought up a question a number of them no doubt had.

"Manuel," he said, "how did you heal all those people two nights ago in Encino?"

"By faith."

Two wait staff approached to take our orders. Raul turned to me again after the waiters left. "You didn't really answer my question."

"Yes I did."

"How?"

"By faith." I looked around at them all. "We walk by faith. With faith, nothing is impossible for you." I reached for a salt shaker, poured a tiny bit into my hand, and placed one grain at the tip of my index finger. "Here's the truth: if you have faith as big as this grain of salt, you can say to that convention center next door, 'Be moved across the street,' and it will be moved. Of course, I suggest asking the people on the sidewalk over there to move first."

"But nobody lives that way," Victor objected.

"I do." I dipped a chip in some salsa and looked at him. "And you will, too, Victor. This is how God's family works. It's what you were created for—a faith walk with El Papá. Life is so much more than this"—I picked up another tortilla chip—"this material … stuff."

After everyone's food had been served, I said to them all, "Let me tell you what the family of God is like." I talked, and they asked questions. Half an hour later, the restaurant was beginning to fill up. Patrons were watching us. People had gathered in the entryway, waiting, it appeared, for me. Word as to my location had clearly gotten out.

I reached into my wallet and pulled out enough cash to pay our table's bill and handed it to Pedro. "This is for all of us. I'll meet you across the street in the park after I tend to these people. You know where the hill is at the outdoor theater?"

"Sí."

"Let's all meet on the backside of that hill."

"To do what?"

"To tell people that El Papá is adding to his family. They are meant to be included."

NINE

When I was a kid, I used to love rolling down Westside Park's big hill, which formed the rear seating of the park's outdoor amphitheater. Kids still did that, I discovered. Several were on their way down as I approached.

Fifty or so of us gathered at the hill. More would soon arrive, I knew. From the hill, we could hear cheers from the nearby softball fields. I turned to the gathering and said, "We can stay here a while and I'll teach, or we can go watch softball."

"Here!" several people responded.

"Softball!" a girl of about ten said right in front of me.

We all laughed.

"Maybe," I said to her, "your family and I can go over after a while and watch. I like softball, too."

I invited everyone to have a seat on the sloping grass.

"Until now," I said to them all, "you've had commandments from El Papá that you were to keep."

"Eso es cierto," someone said. *That's true.*

"So, you've experienced El Papá mostly as a law-giver, correct?"

Most of the group nodded.

"And despite the religious rituals you've done—some of which he instructed you to do—you haven't really known him, have you? Known him personally, I mean."

Many of them shook their heads.

"Well," I said, "that's about to change. The time has come to think about God, and how you relate to God, in a totally different way. A long time ago, he promised a completely new arrangement between people and himself—a Spirit-based relationship, not a rules-based relationship."

A loud cheer went up from one of the softball fields. Perfect timing.

"The time for God's new arrangement," I continued, "is now. I've come to make it a reality. El Papá is calling you to respond to the good news."

"But how do we respond?" a middle-aged man asked.

"By doing this: believe in the one he's sent."

More people had joined us. I stood so everyone could hear me. "It's like this. A Texas real estate developer has money to invest, so he buys land. But some of the land turns out to be swampy, not stable enough to build on. Some of the land is arid. He builds houses on it, but they don't return a profit, because no one wants to live there. Some of the land looks good, but it's poorly zoned."

"Must be in Houston," someone commented.

I smiled. "Maybe so. Anyway, he builds a new subdivision, but then a noisy factory gets built next door, so he can't turn a profit. But some of the land he buys is perfect. It has nice, rolling hills, lots of green trees, and several small, beautiful lakes. He builds a large subdivision and makes a mint.

"So here's the deal: God is investing the good news in people's hearts. Which property does he want you to be?"

Probably a hundred and fifty people were on the hill by now. I recognized some of them. A female police officer from near the underpass. The young college BLM woman who now sported a "Social Justice Warrior" T-shirt, whom I was thrilled to see. And a face I knew only from local TV commercials: Dan McElroy, a personal liability attorney.

I taught for another 20 or so minutes and then glanced at

the time on my phone. In a sound-bite world, people's attention spans were limited.

"OK, let's pause it there," I said. People stood and started moving forward. I held my hand up. "I know some of you have come for healing. I'm glad you came. But before we do that, I have another commitment for just a little while."

I looked at the ten-year-old girl. "Would you and your folks like to get some cotton candy and watch some of the game?" She looked up at her parents. They smiled and nodded. "Great," I said. "I haven't had cotton candy in ages."

The crowd waiting for me after the game numbered several hundred. Plus video trucks from two local TV stations. I started tending to people's needs. Many more people arrived. We stayed until the park closed.

"I'll be in town somewhere tomorrow," I told them. "Just check social media, I'm sure."

I dropped my underpass friends at the various places they happened to be sleeping, and then I drove an hour north to the ranch house of Tim and Eileen Wright, good friends of mine who had opened their house and two guest cabins to me. I'd invited my three friends to spend the night there, since their latest worksite was nearby. They were waiting for me when I arrived.

"Social media's going crazy over you," Justin said. "I thought you wanted to be under wraps."

"How did you even make it here alone?" Sebastian asked.

"That was El Papá's doing. He's giving us a little space." I looked at Justin. "And no, I'm no longer under wraps, that's for sure. I have to go where people are. That's the only way to show them El Papá."

Ten minutes later, I collapsed onto one of Tim's guest room beds, not even bothering to turn down the covers.

TEN

David Patterson glanced at his watch as he exited the top floor elevator of FBI headquarters. *6:25.* Despite rigidly adhering to his early morning routine, he was running ten minutes late. He'd have to shorten his prep for an 8:00 meeting with two Justice Department officials. As he passed through his office door, he glanced at the nameplate. "Deputy Director." A slight irritation welled up within him. Again. *When am I going to get my actual name on this door?* He knew the answer: the moment he went from being "acting" to "permanent." Whenever that might be.

He pulled up his emails first thing, as usual, to review whatever may have come in the night before. One of them caught his attention. Why was Brad Dempsey, head of the field office in McAllen, sending him an email at 5:10 a.m. Texas time? At Patterson's direction, after the Juan Carlos thing blew up, Dempsey had started sending him reports directly, but those had slowed considerably.

Patterson opened the email, and then its link to a local TV news report from the night before. He watched the clip, leaned back in his chair, and thought for a moment. Then he shot off a message to the Director.

We need to meet this morning.

SAN MATEO, CALIFORNIA

Three hours later and three thousand miles away, Eric Urbanski sat at a conference table, sipping Hazelnut coffee and admiring San Francisco Bay as his team assembled for its weekly staff meeting. Like numerous ex-CIA and ex-FBI officials, Urbanski had migrated to Silicon Valley for a senior position in trust and security—misinformation management.

His team ran through its usual recounting of issues from the previous week and activities for the current week. Urbanski sat and listened, asking an occasional question. He believed in delegation and had largely trained the team to lead itself. When the briefing ended, he put his coffee down and leaned forward.

"Is everyone aware of this thing happening in South Texas? With this new guy?"

Everyone nodded. The traffic online had been impossible to miss.

"Good. I've been asked this morning to keep an eye on it."

His team knew that "I've been asked" meant one of two things: a request from the CEO, or a request from Washington. Or both.

Urbanski continued. "The instructions are to keep this from becoming another Juan Carlos situation."

The team had learned something else a while back: due to his tenure in government, their boss excelled at speaking in the passive voice, constantly attributing actions and intentions to a nebulous "they." In this case, the meaning was clear: another mass protest movement on behalf of a charismatic religious figure was unacceptable. Their job was to do everything within their power to make sure it didn't happen.

"So where do we start out with this guy?" Urbanski asked. "Does he have any social media accounts?"

Heads shook around the room.

"None at all? Instagram? Facebook? X? A YouTube channel?"

More head shaking.

"So, he does nothing online. Other people just post videos of him."

Nathan Swift, the most senior analytics manager, answered. "So far, yes. Everything from third party postings."

Urbanski nodded. "OK. Well, that makes our job easier, at least for the time being. Nathan, you head this up. Just monitoring for now." He looked around the table. "But keep him on a short leash. Anticipate. Be proactive on this one, not reactive. I want us framing this narrative. He's an extremist. He's a demagogue. He threatens democracy. What people think about this guy should come from us. Understand?"

A young woman at the table put her latte down. "I'm confused. Why are people worried about him? He's not the only preacher out there. I mean, there's a shelf life to these guys. Hasn't the Juan Carlos stuff died down?"

The analyst across from her answered. "Because according to a local TV report last night, he's not just preaching. He's healing."

"Who?"

"Everyone around him."

"Of what?"

"Everything. Literally."

Urbanski leaned forward and addressed them all. "Do you see the problem? If this is actually true, there are no limits to the following he might attract. Or the power he could wield."

ELEVEN

I spent time with El Papá early the next morning. He'd been making it clear that the time for me to start assembling a small group of trainees was close. These would be responsible for carrying on the message after me. Now that time had come.

"I have a proposal for you guys—an invitation," I said to my three friends as we helped ourselves to a mountain of pancakes that Tim and Eileen had made for us. "Whether you accept is up to you. El Papá is doing something completely new, and I'm the one he has sent to do it. Life isn't exactly like it was a few days ago."

"We noticed," Justin said.

"It's going to change more, not less. El Papá's scope isn't just the Valley. It's the world. He's going to fulfill what he promised for the whole earth. So, here's the deal. I'm asking each of you guys to come be with me, to learn from me, to be a part of this thing with me."

"I'm in," Sebastian said.

I grinned at him. Sebastian was just the type to leap into something with half the facts. "OK, hold up. You need to realize up front, life will completely change for you, and it won't ever be the same. You won't be drilling water wells anymore. You'll be trusting El Papá to provide for us. And you're not going to be home much, at least for a while."

"I'm still in," Sebastian said.

"Me, too," Justin added.

They looked at Pedro. "I'll have to talk to Marta about it." They had just married a year earlier, so this was a bigger leap for Pedro. A much bigger leap.

"Of course," I responded. I looked around at them all. "Now, just to make sure I'm being clear: this is going to demand your all. You're giving up everything to be part of what El Papá is doing."

"I'm down," Justin said.

"OK, then. Pedro, I'll wait to hear back from you. You other two better give your notice at the rig."

They all headed to work. I followed them out the gravel road in front. At its end, on the other side of the gate, a man stood next to a parked car. I got out of the van and stepped toward him. Interesting, how El Papá had enabled this one man to figure out where I was.

"Señor," he said, "my son is very sick. He's 13. He has leukemia. The doctors, they didn't know if he would make it through the night. I was at the park where you were last night, but …" His voice trailed off. A look of despair filled his eyes.

"Where is your son now?"

"He's at home. The doctors said there was no point keeping him at the hospital."

"Tell me your name."

"Pepe."

"Pepe, I will follow you there."

We headed back toward McAllen. After twenty minutes, he pulled over along the side of the road. I stopped and walked to his car. He was slumped over the steering wheel, weeping.

"They … they just called. Jaime died." He broke into a wail.

I placed my hand on his forearm. "Pepe."

He slowly composed himself and turned to me.

"Don't be afraid, Pepe," I said. "Only believe. Take me to him."

Half an hour later we pulled up to a small frame house. A police car was out front.

"They called the duty funeral director, but he hasn't shown up yet," Pepe said as we got out of our vehicles. He'd been crying more along the way, I could tell.

Pepe led me inside the house. Half a dozen friends and relatives were already there, tears in their eyes, comforting a woman on the couch who was evidently Jaime's mother.

I stepped toward her. "Jaime will be OK."

One of the women standing there glared at me. "What do you mean, he'll be OK? Jaime's gone!"

I turned to Pepe. "Where is he?"

Pepe led me to Jaime's bedroom.

"What is he doing?" someone commented from the living room.

"Who is that?" someone else said.

Pepe's wife followed us in and closed the door behind her.

"Pepe ..." she said, confusion in her eyes.

"Lena, just wait," he said.

He looked at me, as if to say, "Go ahead."

I sat on the side of the bed and took Jaime's lifeless hand in my own. "Jaime, I say to you, wake up."

The boy opened his eyes and looked at me, then at Lena. "Mamá," he said.

Lena fainted. Pepe shouted and threw himself toward the bed, smothering Jaime in an embrace. "Jaime! Jaime! Hijo mío! Estás vivo!" *My son! You're alive!*

Relatives tried opening the door, which Lena partially blocked. "Lena! Is Lena OK?"

I knelt beside her and put my hand on her arm. She revived and slowly moved away from the door.

"She's fine," I said as I helped her to her feet.

The relatives entered and saw Jaime sitting up in bed. Another woman fainted. A man screamed. The policeman appeared in the doorway. "What's going on in here? The funeral director just—" He looked at Jaime and froze. "¡Dios mío!" *My God!*

Within a few minutes, Jaime was at the kitchen table having some lunch.

"I can't believe it," Lena remarked. "I haven't seen Jaime like this in two years. He looks completely healthy."

I looked over at Pepe and our eyes met. "He is completely healthy," Pepe replied, beaming.

"Before everyone hops on their phones," I said to them all, "can I ask you a favor? Please don't tell anyone what happened. At least not yet."

"You don't want people dragging you to cemeteries," Pepe's brother, Jose, said.

I smiled. "Something like that, yes."

"I'm not sure how I'm going to write this report," the police-man said, and everyone laughed.

I hugged Jaime, Lena and Pepe, said my good-byes, and headed back toward the underpass. I wanted to spend more time with my friends there, and with anyone with me the night before at Westside Park.

TWELVE

The eastern sky was still dark when I awoke the next morning. I crept to the front porch and sat in a rocking chair. Half an hour later, I heard the screen door open behind me. It was Justin.

"What are you doing out here so early?" He made sure the screen door closed quietly behind him.

"Listening."

Justin sat in the other rocking chair and looked out toward the first light of dawn. "To what?"

"Papá."

He sat silently for a moment. "What's he saying?"

I paused, and listened. "He says that he loves you, the same way he loves me."

"No, he doesn't. There's no way."

I looked over at him and smiled. "But he does."

We sat quietly for a few moments. Finally, Justin spoke. "Can I ask you a question?"

"Of course."

"How do you do these things?"

"What things?"

"The miracles you do."

"I told you all the other day at lunch."

"I know, but … run it by me again."

I started rocking gently. "I don't do them, really."

"What do you mean, you don't do them? I see you do them."

"I know. But it's not really me doing them. It's El Papá. He's in me. I'm in him. He and I are one."

He looked out over the front of the ranch. "It would be nice to have that kind of relationship with God."

"You will."

He turned toward me. "What do you mean? I couldn't—"

"Justin, a day is coming—soon—when you'll be one with me, and one with Papá. Just as he and I are one. That's the whole point of all of this. I came that you might be joined to us. He and I will live in you, just as he lives in me. And we will live through you, just as he lives through me." I turned to face him. "Do you understand what I'm saying?"

He shrugged. "I'm … not sure."

I smiled. "Soon you will be. When that day comes, you'll have no doubt we've come to live in you."

Late that morning, Justin, Pedro, Sebastian and I took the van to Harlingen, 35 miles east of McAllen. I wanted to start taking the message to the other cities in the Valley. Pedro sat next to me on the way.

"I talked to Marta," he said. "I'm in."

I glanced over at him. "You're sure."

"I'm sure."

"And she understands what this'll mean for her."

"I'm not sure I understand."

I smiled. He was right. None of them really understood.

"But she's willing," he said.

I nodded. "OK. That's real faith on her part." I looked at Pedro. "And yours."

We spread out a lunch at Victor Park on the southeast side of Harlingen. A crowd started to gather. TV crews showed up. Phones taking videos popped up like dandelions. I went to a slightly raised spot, taught for a while, and then invited questions.

A middle-aged Latino man near the front asked, "I'm curious: what would you say are the greatest commandments?"

"The greatest are love God with all your heart, soul, mind, and strength, and love your neighbor as yourself."

"You're right," he replied, smiling. I could tell he thought he was fulfilling those commands just fine. Which, of course, he wasn't. Nobody was—or even could.

"But I have a follow-up question," he said. "Who's my neighbor?"

I took a sip from a bottle of water and thought for a moment. "I'll tell you. A Latino Ph.D. student at UT-Austin was about to turn in his dissertation. His whole career depended on it. The day it was due, however, his laptop crashed. He didn't have it uploaded to the cloud, and the final version wasn't saved anywhere else.

"'Help me recover my file!' he asked a fellow Latino student from his study group.

"'Sorry, I'm too busy with my own stuff today,' the student replied.

"He phoned another Latino friend. 'Help me recover my file!'

"'I'm going hiking with my girlfriend,' he answered.

"But there was an Anglo student in the next cubicle. He had always held a grudge against Latinos, because his father blamed migrants for taking away his career in construction. The Anglo student stood up, looked over the cubicle wall, and said, 'I can help you.' And he recovered his file.

"Now," I said to the man who had raised the question, "which guy was a neighbor to the Ph.D. student?"

"The white guy."

"You're right. Go love people like that young man chose to."

While I was speaking, I noticed a couple of familiar faces in the crowd. Dan McElroy, the young attorney, was there again. So was the young woman who had worn the BLM T-shirt. After I stopped teaching, I walked through the crowd and leaned close to her ear.

"What are you looking for?" I asked her.

I held my face close to hers and our eyes locked as she regarded me. "Where are you staying?" she asked.

"Give me your phone," I replied.

She handed it to me and I entered Tim's address. "Come tonight and see."

I stayed at the park healing people until 8:00, and then we headed back to Tim's ranch. A train of cars followed us, but a red light separated us from them shortly before we had to make a turn-off. El Papá was still giving our group a little breathing space at Tim's before the crowds swamped us there, too.

Half an hour after we got to Tim's, at 9:45, there was a knock on the door. Pedro opened it. I glanced over and smiled.

"Gentlemen," I said, "An honest young woman. Come in, Kiara."

She hesitated, and then walked toward the dining table, her brow furrowed. "How did you know my name? Did God tell you?"

"No, I saw it on your phone."

She looked around at all of us. "What exactly is this little group doing?"

Pedro motioned toward me. "He's changing the world, and we're following along."

"I saw you actually healing people," she said to me.

I nodded. "You'll see greater things than that." I pulled a chair out from the table. "You're welcome to join us."

She sat and reached for a piece of banana bread that Eileen had baked. "You're crushing it online, you know. You wouldn't believe all the videos online already from Victor Park. How did you even make it out here without that whole crowd following you?"

I took another slice of the bread myself. "El Papá provides."

We all chatted until almost midnight. Underneath her hard exterior, one thing became clear: Kiara wanted what I'd come to offer.

Thirteen

The next day I went to the law offices of McElroy and McElroy. Dan McElroy's father, Darren, was universally despised by local small businessmen as the worst ambulance chaser in town. In their opinion, whenever Darren McElroy showed up, your life savings were about to be destroyed, whether you'd done anything wrong or not. Dan, his son, had supposedly followed in his footsteps.

"I'm here to see Dan McElroy," I told the receptionist.

"Do you have an appointment?" she asked.

"Not one that you have recorded, no."

"Well, we don't—"

Dan came around the corner into the reception area and froze, staring straight at me. "Manuel!" he said. He glanced at the receptionist, then back at me. "Mr. ... uh ..."

"Gonzales."

"Yes. Come right on back."

We walked into his office and sat down. "Well, this is a surprise. What brings you here?"

"You do."

"You need legal help."

I shook my head. "No. I'm here for you. Personally. I want you to come be with me."

"Be ... with you?"

"Yes, to accompany me."

"In case you need legal help."

I smiled at him. "No. To learn from me. That is what you want, isn't it?"

He regarded me for a moment, seemingly unsure how to respond to someone who had seen right through him.

"Well, yeah, I mean, I'm interested, for sure, and I like coming to hear you, but ..." He looked around at the piles of folders and papers on his desk. "I couldn't possibly get away now. Not until things slow down a little."

I eyed the papers and folders and then looked straight at him. "Let those who want to fight over money do their own fighting. You, come be with me." I reached for a slip of paper and a pen on his desk, wrote on it, and walked to the door. "I'm at that address."

Late that afternoon there was another knock on Tim Wright's front door. It was Dan McElroy. He'd come straight from work in his pinstripe suit. He glanced at what must have looked like a motley crew sitting in Tim's expansive living room.

"This is your group?" he asked.

"You could say that," I answered.

His gaze paused on them, and then he looked at me. "Maybe this would be good for me."

I grinned. "You have no idea."

Two nights later, Dan threw a huge party at his house for me and the group. All of his attorney friends were invited, with their spouses and significant others. The food was piled high and the alcohol flowed freely. One by one, he took me around to his friends and introduced me. They seemed genuinely happy to meet me, though I could tell many weren't quite sure what to make of me.

Dan finally tapped on a wine glass and got everyone's attention. "I'm so pleased that you joined Tiffany and me along with my new friend, Manuel Gonzales, and his friends." He held his wine glass up toward me. "A toast to you, Manuel. We're so honored to have you with us."

Everyone toasted and drank. I looked at Dan and smiled. "I'm delighted to be here with you." I looked around at everyone else. "With all of you."

The crowd clapped its approval. Then Dan stepped toward me and said in the hearing of everyone, "When I first heard of you, and saw what you were doing, I was sure you'd only be hanging around religious people. But ..." He glanced around at the crowd. "I guess not." They all laughed.

"How much time do you attorneys spend representing people who don't have a problem?" I asked them all.

There were some snickers from the crowd. "Not much." "Zero." "Nada."

"Well," I said, "I'm the same way. I came for those who realize they're missing something, and want it."

I got back late to Tim's that night. Justin and Sebastian were sitting in the living room, engrossed in some cable news show. I grabbed a glass of water, guzzled half of it, and walked toward them. "What are they talking about?"

"You," Sebastian answered.

"Oh."

I was about to take my glass back to the kitchen, but Sebastian filled me in. "Two of them don't believe in faith healers. One of them wonders if the online videos are fake. And the other one thinks this country could use a religious revival."

They watched for another minute before the topic changed to something else. Sebastian looked up as I returned from the kitchen. "Can you believe this? People talking about us—you—on one of these shows? What do you think?"

"I think," I responded as I made my way toward the stairs, "that the commentators can stick to their business, and I'll stick to mine—what El Papá has given me to do."

FOURTEEN

Early the next morning, I went out to one of Tim's guest cabins and spent the day talking with El Papá. It was time to finalize the rest of my trainees and start functioning as a group. After discussing it with El Papá, I spent the next several days going to the people he directed me to, all of whom I had either known previously or had met in the prior couple of weeks. Everyone eagerly came on board. We ended up with twelve:

Pedro, age 26, his brother Sebastian, 24, and Justin, 23, the water well drillers

Diego, 19, a mechanic from our auto shop

Maya, 22, one of Rachel's underpass friends

Ana Victoria, 28, one of the police officers near the underpass

Kiara, 20, the social justice warrior and UT-RGV nursing major

Jorge, 26, an equity analyst at the investment firm Tim used

Mike, 25, the assistant manager at our auto parts supplier

Sofia, 19, one of the praying students from UT-RGV and a social media whiz

Dan, 29, the personal liability attorney

Emma, 23, a young marketing professional and Tim and Eileen's daughter

All but Pedro and Dan were single. Marta, of course, had already given Pedro her OK.

"Is Tiffany on board with this?" I asked Dan.

"She's fine with it," he said. "She likes her space." She'd get plenty of that in the coming months, for sure.

We had a home-cooked brisket dinner that Saturday at Tim's, with baked beans, sweet corn, salad, and two delicious Dutch apple pies with vanilla ice cream. We sat around the table talking and laughing as we finished dessert and had coffee.

"Hey, we need a name for our group," Sebastian suggested.

Jorge, the movie buff among us, chimed in. "We'll call ourselves The Fellowship of El Único!"

Everyone raised their coffee cups and toasted, "The Fellowship of El Único!"

I sipped my coffee. "I was thinking something more like … Manuel and his friends."

They all looked at me and smiles began crossing their faces. Kiara slowly raised her cup. "Manuel and his friends."

Everyone toasted. "Manuel and his friends."

STATE OF NUEVO LEON, NORTHERN MEXICO

That night I told the group to make sure they had their passports.

"You paying for a cruise?" Jorge asked.

"No, you guys are paying for a cruise; the speaker goes for free." I grinned at him. "Seriously, it's time to cross the border. People on the other side need to hear."

Two days later, we all (except Maya and Justin, who didn't have passports) packed up, piled into the van, and headed for the border. Everyone in the group spoke fluent Spanish, except Mike. "I'll manage," he said.

"Where are we heading?" Sebastian asked.

"Monterrey, to start."

"You need a vehicle import permit to drive that far in."

"We have one."

"You need Mexican liability insurance."

"Have that." I turned and looked back at him. "I grew up here, too, you know."

He laughed. "Sometimes, it's easy to forget. You're not exactly … normal."

We crossed the border and stopped on the other side of Reynosa at a roadside taqueria for lunch. We put two picnic tables together out back and sat to eat tortas and burritos. I was at one end; Sebastian was at the other.

"Sebastian," I said. "What you said to me earlier, about me not being normal—you've got it backwards, you know. I'm actually the one that's normal."

"What, with all the miracles and stuff you do? Come on, man."

I got up, walked over to a wolfberry tree a few feet away and snapped off a small branch. "Here's what you guys are seeing when you look at me. I'm a branch. El Papá is the tree. I'm connected to him, as connected as someone can be, just like this branch was as connected as it could be to that tree. What you see me doing, it's El Papá living through me, just like that tree bears fruit through its branches. This is how people are designed to live. It's not extraordinary. It's normal. You guys are going to live exactly the same way."

I could tell this was a stretch for them, at this point at least. "It's like this. If I put this little branch on the table"—I set it down—"how soon will it produce a wolfberry?"

"Nunca," Sofia responded. *Never.*

"Why not?"

"Because it's not connected to the tree anymore."

I pointed at her. "Exactly. On its own it can't produce a thing. It has to be connected to the tree. People are disconnected from El Papá. They're born that way, because of sin. But they were meant to be connected to him, to be one with him. He in them. They in him. One spirit. That's the only way his love, and his life, can flow to them, and through them."

I looked at each of them. "You may not have realized this yet, but that's why I'm here—to reconnect you to El Papá. So you can become one with him."

We drove on to Monterrey and parked at the bottom of Mirador Asta Bandera (Flagpole Viewpoint), a tall, green hill near the center of the city with a 100-foot Mexican flag atop a 330-foot flagpole. Overlooking the entire city, the top of the hill could hold hundreds of tourists at once. We hiked the path to the top. The ten of them sat on a circular three-foot wall and I started teaching in Spanish. Sofia translated for Mike.

"Let's talk about priorities," I said to them. "Don't make it your goal in life to increase your bank account, your retirement fund, your stock portfolio."

Mike immediately interrupted. "Stock portfolio? Who has that?"

Everyone's eyes turned to Jorge. "Hey," he said, "just because I work at an investment firm doesn't mean I'm rich."

"Yeah, right," several of them replied.

"Besides, Manuel didn't say money is evil."

"That's true," I said. "But loving money brings all sorts of evil. You can't love both God and money. You'll love one, and hate the other in comparison. You can't serve both.

"What I'm saying is this. Don't invest your life, and your heart, in things that disappear. This life isn't all there is. Invest in El Papá. Your treasure in heaven will never disappear. The stock market drops by 50 percent—which it does sometimes—and there goes your retirement. Inflation hits 10 percent, and your money loses half its value in seven years."

"Rule of 72," Jorge said.

Several people had wandered over to listen. One by one, they took their phones out to take videos. Word would get out in no time, I knew.

"It's like a guy who makes millions running a hedge fund in

New York," I continued. "He's not really producing anything for people. He just shorts stocks that he thinks will fall. He spends every minute of his life doing that. He makes millions, and then someone comes along and buys out his company, and he makes $100 million.

"But instead of taking that money and actually doing some good with it, he says to himself, 'Just think how much money I can make with this $100 million!' But God comes to him that night and says, 'You fool! Tonight is your last night on earth. Now who's going to get that $100 million that you invested your soul to make?'

"Understand this," I said to them all, "I'm not talking about rich people here. I'm talking about everyone. You may not have much in your bank account—you may not even have a bank account—but you can still be completely invested in this world. El Papá didn't create you for that. There's nothing in this world that will ultimately satisfy your heart. Only El Papá can do that. Be rich toward him."

Soon a crowd of several hundred blanketed the top of the hill, listening. Little kids were running all around, laughing. I spoke for a little while longer until a policeman made his way through the crowd and leaned close to me.

"I just wanted to let you know that the parking lot below is full and they've closed the park to any more people. I think someone's coming up to tell you that you can't have a scheduled event here."

"But this wasn't a scheduled event," Dan objected. "We just came up here and Manuel started talking to us."

I held up my hand toward him. "Dan, it's OK." I turned to the policeman. "Why don't you tell them we're wrapping up now."

The policeman nodded. "By the way," he said softly, "thank you for coming."

He stepped aside and got on his radio. I turned to the crowd. "OK, we're going to have to wrap it up." The crowd moaned.

"Where are you going to be after this?" someone asked.

I looked at Diego, who was from Monterrey. He shrugged.

"Not sure," I answered. "But we'll be close enough tomorrow."

At that point three little kids ran near me. They had been dashing in and out of the crowd, playing tag, and creating quite a distraction. Jorge and Pedro grabbed two of them by the arm.

"Oye," Jorge said to one of them, "¿No te das cuenta de lo que está pasando aquí?" *Hey, don't you realize what's going on here?*

"Jorge, Pedro," I said to them, "let them go."

The kids ran to their parents. I stepped toward them. "May I be with your children?" I asked them.

"Of course," they said.

I sat on the ledge and put the children on my knees, and then turned to the crowd. "It's easy to think these children need to be more like you, behaving, not running through a crowd, but actually you need to be more like them. If you don't receive El Papá's invitation like a little child would, in complete trust, you can't receive it at all. El Papá's family is made of people who become like them."

I placed my hands on the two children and blessed them. "OK, go back to your folks." They ran back into their parents' arms, who had smiles from one side of their faces to the other.

I turned to Mike and spoke in English. "We need to find a place to spend the night. You did put those tents in the back of the van, didn't you?"

FIFTEEN

I was ready to start teaching again by 8:00 a.m. We'd spent the night at the state park by the El Cuchillo Dam, to the east. A long caravan of cars and pickups had followed us from Monterrey. People had slept in their vehicles, or on blankets on the ground, inside the park or along the highway outside. I loved being out here with these people. They wanted what El Papá had to offer them.

"We need to find a more suitable place," I said to Jorge and Pedro.

"What's wrong with this one?" Pedro asked.

"Entrance fees," I answered. "Not everyone can afford that."

We headed back west and found a large roadside park in the middle of nowhere along highway 40. Diego set up a small portable generator and hooked up a mic and speakers to it.

I taught a couple of hours. By that time, several thousand people were crowded into the park. We took a short break, and I turned to Diego, Sebastian, and Jorge standing next to me. "A lot of these people have been following us since yesterday afternoon. They need to eat."

"Tell them to drive back to Monterrey," Diego said.

I shook my head. "No, I don't want them to drive somewhere and back. You give them something."

The three of them stared at me. "Something what?" Diego asked.

"What do we have in the van?"

"A few burritos in the cooler from that taqueria," Sebastian replied. "Some apples. Plus some water bottles in the other cooler."

"Yeah, that'll work," Jorge commented. "Give everyone a crumb."

"Grab the coolers and put them on a blanket right in front here," I instructed them. I walked over to the microphone and faced the crowd. "I know many of you have been with me since yesterday and you're hungry and thirsty. We have some stuff that'll tide everyone over. I want you to sit down in groups of 20 or 30 and come up one group at a time and help yourself."

Sebastian, Jorge, and Diego brought the food and water.

"Great," I said to them. "Bring the first group up here."

The three of them stood there, looking at me like I was crazy. "Well?" I asked.

They motioned to the closest group, which came forward.

"Help yourself to all you want," I told them.

They all got some food and water bottles. The second group came forward. Then the third. By this time, everyone's attention was focused on what was happening up front. People started texting and sharing pictures on their phones like crazy.

More people came to the park. Within an hour, the crowd had doubled. People kept coming forward for food, some of them a second or third time.

"Hey, weren't you guys already up here once?" I heard Sebastian say to three young men.

"Sebastian," I called out to him, "you think we're going to run out?"

After a while, I went to the microphone. "Did everyone get all they wanted?"

"Sí!" they shouted.

"Super. But I want you to understand something. What you

really need to be seeking isn't food that disappears when you eat it, but food that lasts forever. Work for that kind of food."

"¿Cómo le hacemos?" someone asked. *How do we do that?*

"Here's the 'work' that El Papá has given you," I answered. "Believe in the one he's sent. You want food from God? I'm the food he's provided."

"The real enchilada!" someone shouted.

I smiled. "Exactly. I'm the food that comes down out of heaven. I give life to the world. Whoever comes to me will no longer be hungry. Whoever believes in me will no longer be thirsty."

"Keep giving us this food, then!" someone else said.

"I myself am the life-giving food," I responded. "Unless you take me into yourself, you have no life in yourselves. You're a walking corpse. You have physical life, but you don't have life from God."

More and more people at this point were looking intently at me. "How can we take you into ourselves?" someone asked.

"I'm true food," I said. "Whoever receives me, I live in him, and he lives in me. If you take me into yourselves, you have God's life—eternal life. And I'll raise you up on the last day."

My words were difficult for the crowd to make sense of, I could tell. Some people got up and left, grabbing more burritos on the way out. "Who can listen to this?" I heard one of them say.

I was sad to see them go, but it was their choice. A number of other people came up to talk with me. "We want to listen to you," they said, "but these are hard statements."

I felt El Papá's heart toward them. "Don't let what I'm saying cause you to stumble." I looked around at each of them. "What if you saw me suddenly rising up to where I came from? Would you still wonder? I want you to understand: the Holy Spirit is the one who gives life. You can't produce life on your own, through your own efforts. Only he can give you life. Just as El Papá sent me, and I have life because of him, so the one who feeds on me will have life because of me."

I turned to my little group. "You guys don't want to walk away, too, do you?"

"Where are we supposed to go?" Pedro asked. "You have the words of eternal life. We have believed that you are El Único."

I nodded. "I know you have, Pedro. I chose each of you myself. But one of you twelve is a devil."

"People are going nuts online after what you taught yesterday," Sofia said the next morning.

I figured. There were already a million theories about me online. No doubt that number was multiplying. My job wasn't to rein in all of that speculation. It was simply to say and do what I heard from El Papá.

We stayed in northern Mexico six more days. We kept to the countryside, but even in the rural areas, thousands were following us wherever we went. People were coming up from Mexico City, down from Texas, across from Tijuana and Juarez. On the third day, Ana said to me, "People are flying in to join us."

"How do you know?" Mike asked.

"Because I'm hearing South American Spanish."

I was, too.

That same day, we stopped at a market on the outskirts of Saltillo. A man in a folding chair in the market started swearing loudly at Ana, Sofia, and Sebastian as they approached. I walked up a few seconds later, as the man threatened to call his higher-ups to deal with them. He didn't mean human higher-ups, I knew.

The moment he saw me, he flew into a rage, crying out loudly, "Leave me alone! I know who you are, Son of God! Have you come to destroy me?"

"Be quiet, and come out of him!" I commanded. The demon

threw him on the ground and came out of him, without further harm.

Later, Sofia approached me. "That's the fourth time you've done that since we came here. Why are we running into that here, and not back home?"

"We'll encounter it there, too. It's simply more overt here."

"Because …?"

"Black magic practitioners. Worship of ancient gods who are actually demons. People using psychedelics who open themselves up to it. Things that, unfortunately, are growing in the States. The 'sophisticated' convince themselves they can construct a purely secular society. It never works that way. People are drawn to a connection with the supernatural. They'll find something to worship. That something can be very evil."

At the end of the sixth day, I said to Ana, who was driving the next morning, "Tomorrow, let's head toward Mexico City, to Los Bordos."

Sebastian, standing nearby, looked at me in shock. "Manuel, you can't go there."

"Why not?" Emma asked.

"Are you kidding?" Sebastian replied. "That place is one of the worst slums in Mexico. No one is safe there."

He was right. Los Bordos was part of Ecatepec, a city of over a million and a half on the outskirts of Mexico City. Many of its people lived in cinder block shanties, tin shacks, or worse, without running water, without electricity, and without police. Ruled by drug gangs, Los Bordos was a breeding ground of violence, filth, and despair. The fact that people from rural areas would even consider moving to such a place indicated how desperate their lives had become.

I put my hand on Sebastian's shoulder. "Sebastian, I have to go. They can't come to me."

Sixteen

Los Bordos was a ten-hour drive straight through the heart of Mexico. A train of vehicles stretching for many miles followed us all the way down. We stopped only when we had to, and briefly. I wanted to get there before sunset.

On the way, I talked to the ten about how I was doing what I was doing—healing and, when necessary, casting out demons whom people had allowed in. Down in Los Bordos, I told them, they would be doing the same things themselves.

By the time we arrived, we'd lost most of the caravan who had followed us from northern Mexico. People knew what this place was like. We parked the van on a road that climbed one of the shantytown's hillsides. We didn't know a soul there. But El Papá did.

"Let's split up and head out," I said as we got out of the van.

The ten all stared at me like I was crazy. "What do you mean, 'split up and head out'?" Mike asked.

"We need to cover a lot of ground," I answered, "and there are eleven of us. You all pair up. You four ladies, grab one of the men. Stick with each other. We'll all meet back here at the van at 8:00 Monday morning and head north." It was Friday evening.

"What are we splitting up to do?" Diego wondered.

"What you've seen me do. Heal the sick. Cast out any demons you encounter. Tell people El Papá is inviting them to be connected to him."

"By ourselves?" Pedro asked incredulously. "You're not going with us?"

"I'm heading one way. All of you head different ways. In pairs. Like I said in the van, you've been with me. You've been learning from me. Now it's your turn. That's the point: to learn from me. You know how I do this. Now I want you to do it. I've given you authority over all the power of the enemy. Trust me—nothing will injure you."

I could tell they weren't too sure about that last part, but I was sure. El Papá had shown me exactly what he was doing here. They'd be fine.

By this time a crowd had formed around us, both people who had followed us from northern Mexico, and, increasingly, people who lived in Los Bordos.

"But where are we supposed to stay?" Ana asked. "What are we supposed to eat?"

"Eat what people offer you to eat. Spend the night where you're invited to spend the night. When you go inside a place, tell them who you're with and why you're there. If someone refuses to let you in, say to them, 'Realize this, that the kingdom of God has come near you.' And then move on to the next dwelling. Meet back here at the van Monday morning."

"Uh, Manuel." Jorge glanced at the surroundings and then looked back at me. "I don't think there will be a van here by Monday morning."

"Or tomorrow morning," Diego offered.

"It will be here. See you at 8:00 Monday." I put on my baseball cap and headed up the hill, deeper into the slum. The entire crowd came with me, pressing around me. Whenever someone touched me and was healed, I could feel the power flowing from my body into theirs.

At the top of the hill, I looked back at the ten. They were still standing there. I couldn't help but smile. I'd instructed them how to swim; now I'd thrown them into the deep end. They'd figure it out.

For two days I went through the barrio. At times it seemed like every one of its inhabitants was gathered around me. It became hard to walk the streets, much less enter people's abodes.

The people there dressed in simple clothes, but from time to time I noticed a man following who was dressed differently, in much finer attire. A group of men always surrounded him. At one point I asked the people next to me about him.

"That's Rodrigo Jiménez," they answered. "He's one of the chief *narcotraficantes* in the barrio." A drug lord.

After most of a day of following me around, Rodrigo and his men worked their way through the crowd toward me. People let them pass.

When he got to me, I said to him, "Rodrigo, I'd like to eat at your house tonight."

I could hear people murmuring around me. "Doesn't he know who that is?" "How can he eat at the house of a *narcotraficante?*"

I turned to the crowd and said, "I'm not here for people who think they've been good enough for God. I'm here for people who know they haven't been."

That evening, I dined with Rodrigo and his wife, Alejandra. During dinner, he said to me, "I never imagined I would see what I've seen this weekend. Someone who can do the things you do." He paused, looked at Alejandra, and then back at me. "I'm not worthy for you to come to my house. Can God be merciful to me, too?"

I put my fork down. "Rodrigo, El Papá didn't send me into the world to condemn anyone. He sent me to connect people to God. If you believe in me, you become connected. It's that simple. And I'll never throw you out. Ever."

He leaned back in his chair and thought for a moment. Finally, he spoke. "I'll traffic drugs no longer. I'll liquidate my holdings. The women I've made widows, and their children, I'll find them and support them."

"Rodrigo!" Alejandra responded. "They—your associates—they'll kill you!"

"Then I will be killed," he said.

I looked at Rodrigo and smiled gently at him. "You are blessed, Rodrigo. El Papá's salvation has come to your household. No matter what happens, I promise you this: because you've trusted me, you have eternal life. You'll never come under judgment."

Alejandra looked at me with wonderment. "You have authority to say this?"

Rodrigo responded. "If you had seen what I saw—"

"I do," I said to her. "El Papá has life in himself. He gave to me to have life in myself. And I give life to whomever I wish." I turned to Rodrigo. "You've already passed out of death, into life, my friend. I myself will raise you up on the last day."

The next morning, as scheduled, I returned to the van. The ten were all there, waiting for me.

"Manuel!" Pedro said almost before I was within earshot. "You won't believe what happened!"

"What?"

"That was so awesome!" Diego said.

"We killed it!" Mike declared.

"We healed people!" Ana said.

"People listened when we talked about El Papá's invitation," Sofia added.

Sebastian stepped forward. "Even demons went out of several people when we commanded them to in your name!"

I laughed. "Of course they did! While you guys were out there with people, I was seeing Satan falling like lightning from heaven." I put my hand on Sebastian's shoulder. "But don't focus on the fact that the demons were subject to you. Be thrilled with this: that your names are recorded in heaven."

SEVENTEEN

Miles Probst never cared much for social functions, but they came with the job. As CEO of one of America's largest investment management companies, responsible for over a trillion dollars of assets, he had to hobnob with the important people from time to time. But of all the gatherings he felt obliged to attend, the annual Kennedy Cener Honors Gala in DC was his favorite. He enjoyed the luncheon that the president and first lady always hosted, the opportunity to meet artists in various fields (some of whom were actually interesting), and the evening entertainment at the awards ceremony.

He picked up a glass of wine, glanced across the expansive atrium, and then smiled. A familiar face was looking back at him.

"Naomi," he said as he walked up to her.

"Miles! I didn't know if you'd make it or not."

"Where else can I be with the president, Garth Brooks, and Naomi Sato at the same time?"

"Well, I'm usually available," she replied, her eyes sparkling. "I can't speak for the other two."

The two of them had established a certain playful banter since they had met several years before, after Naomi had been appointed First Deputy Managing Director of the International Monetary Fund. Now, every time they saw each other, they fell right back into it. Though both divorced, neither of them ever expected anything to come of it, which made it all the more fun.

They meandered toward the two-story windows that overlooked the Potomac River.

"A little bird told me that consumer demand might be taking a dip this year, Miles."

"How so? Our projections look steady."

"What's happening in Mexico," she said. "Just a possibility."

"You think the guy from McAllen is that serious?"

They stopped at a window. Naomi looked out over the water and sipped her chardonnay. "I think Juan Carlos laid the groundwork. Telling people to share instead of just consume. Invest in heaven, not just earth. This new guy, Gonzales, has upped the stakes. Way up. People are claiming he can heal anyone. In Nuevo Leon they said he fed a crowd of thousands out of thin air."

"What?"

"Combine that with a message of 'invest in God, not in things.' If he gets enough followers, you think that can't influence demand?"

They stood in silence for a moment.

"You think he'll catch on?"

"Videos of him are getting millions of views a day. I know that some people are already calling for him to be president down there."

"He'd have to be a Mexican citizen to be president."

"Not of Mexico. Of Greater Mexico. Mexico plus the Southwest. The half we took from them in 1848."

"That's a pipe dream. It'll never happen."

She looked down the Potomac and pointed at the Washington Monument. "Well, American independence was a pipe dream until George whipped Cornwallis at Yorktown. And George couldn't heal people with a single touch—or feed thousands with a couple of burritos."

She turned and looked him in the eye. "How long before you think he'll have a following of a hundred million? Five hundred million? A billion?"

Across the Potomac, the president's chief of staff, Daniel Holden, was hosting an early evening meeting in his West Wing office in the White House. He poured drinks for himself, Robert Dillon, the Secretary of Homeland Security, Christopher Ottenger, the Director of the FBI, and Alice Paige, the president's campaign manager.

Holden sat behind his desk and looked at Paige. "What's the worst-case scenario, from your perspective?"

A year earlier, Holden wouldn't have brought Paige into this meeting, but with the election 17 months away, political considerations were vital—perhaps paramount. Besides, Holden had always valued Paige's input on any matter. He found her instincts to be exceptional on issues both political and otherwise.

"Worst case?" she answered. "The other party nominates him."

"Unlikely."

"Perhaps. But it should be on our radar. Other worst case, third-party run."

Holden shook his head. "He might take more votes from the other side."

"I'm not worried about him siphoning off votes. I'm worried about him winning."

"Third-party candidates never win."

"We've never seen a third-party candidate like he would be."

Holden realized that was true. Once upon a time, such an outsider would never even be mentioned as a presidential possibility. But politics had changed, and in an internet-dominated world, the impossible was no longer impossible.

The four of them sat for a moment, sipping their drinks.

Finally, Holden spoke again. "He hasn't made any overtly political statements yet. To my knowledge."

Ottenger cleared his throat. "We can put two and two together. Juan Carlos talks for months about a new government. We figured his following would die down if we put him away, which it eventually did. But then this new guy comes along. Juan Carlos was a nobody. If what we're all hearing is true"—he looked around at them, not wanting to say something that might sound foolish—"honestly, I don't know what this guy is, but he's not a nobody."

Dillon chimed in. "We could detain him at the border. Say that we're investigating his meeting with that drug lord."

Holden shook his head. "No. That'd make it worse. The administration can't be perceived as opposed to him. Certainly not until we figure out what he's about."

"But the drug lord meeting issue is legit," Dillon responded.

"Maybe NSA can tell us something about it," Ottenger suggested. "In the meantime, how about if I send someone to ask him a few questions once he returns? Non-threatening."

"What would that achieve?" Paige asked.

"Two things. First, it'll let him know we're keeping an eye on him. Might rein him in a bit. And second, it'll plant a seed in the mind of anyone close to him who has second thoughts later on. It'll tell them we're always an option."

The group pondered that one for a moment. "Let's do it," Holden said. "But it has to be low-key."

Dillon nodded. "I'll instruct my guys at the border to let them pass." He had another sip of brandy. "You know, it would be nice if we actually had someone on the inside." His eyes met Ottenger's.

"You think we're not working on that?" Ottenger replied.

Eighteen

We got swamped at the U.S. border crossing. People had joined the caravan behind us all the way up from Los Bordos, and waiting in a three-hour car line was their chance to get out of their vehicles and approach the van for healing. People with cancer, heart problems, liver failure, mental illness, addictions. The suffering broke my heart. Humanity was never intended to experience all of this. I was thrilled to be able to make people whole again.

Most of the crowd had to turn back when we got to the border patrol station. But on the U.S. side a line of cars was waiting for us and fell in behind us as we headed north. They followed us all the way to Tim's ranch. El Papá had decided our days of obscurity there were over.

When we got to the entrance to Tim's property, I said to Pedro, "Let me off here; you guys drive on up to Tim's house and relax."

Several hundred people got out of their vehicles and joined me at the front gate. More kept arriving. I stayed with them until well after dark.

I finally walked up to Tim's house, exhausted, but not too exhausted to give Justin and Maya big hugs. It was good to be back with them. Tim heated up dinner for me. I hadn't realized how hungry I was.

"I've been following you going through Mexico," he said.

"Online?"

He nodded. "You can hardly get on there and *not* know what you're doing."

I chuckled. "I know. I've seen some of the headlines. I'm not looking for publicity, you know."

"Maybe not, but publicity is looking for you. Speaking of which, I wanted to extend an offer to you."

Tim was extremely well connected throughout South Texas. If he had an offer to extend, it probably involved one of his connections.

"I was talking to a couple of friends of mine in San Antonio," he said. "Lots of money. They want to rent out the Alamodome for a night and have you speak."

"That's a big venue."

"Manuel, after what you did in Mexico, you could pack any stadium in this hemisphere."

"When?" I asked.

"Next week. A concert cancelled."

I finished a bite of meat loaf. "I appreciate the offer. Let me ask El Papá about it."

In the living room, the Twelve were watching a talking heads program on cable news. I was the topic of the segment.

"I guess it was a slow day for politics," I joked as I took a seat.

"No, hardly," Mike replied. "You've become a big deal. You're the possible leader of a nationalist religious movement. The possible leader of a movement to reunite the Southwest with Mexico"—*that's a new one*, I thought—"or a possible presidential candidate."

"Manuel, you have my vote," Jorge assured me.

"Thank you, Jorge," I said. "That's touching."

Tim and Eileen had just served us all some decaf and snickerdoodle cookies when we heard a knock at the back door.

Kiara looked at me. "I thought you sent the crowd home."

"I did."

"Someone must have come down the dirt road out back," Tim said, looking a bit irritated. He walked to the door and stood talking with a man for a moment. Then the two of them stepped inside. I recognized the man's face immediately. "Mr. Morris."

"I apologize for the interruption," Randall Morris said. His gaze fell on me. "Do you have a few minutes?"

Randall Morris was the top guy in the entire religious hierarchy for Texas and Louisiana. That meant he had been to theological school and had risen up in the religious ranks, probably from local supervisor of numerous worship houses, to a subregional head, and now to head of the entire two-state region. He was easily among the 30 or so top religious influencers in the country. I'd never seen him online without his sacramental purple robe, but this night he came dressed in shirt and slacks.

I glanced around the group, most of whom knew who he was and, I could tell, were wary of him. I'd been preaching about the family of God. Here was the region's religious head honcho. What kind of trouble did he represent?

But I could tell from the look on his face: he didn't represent any kind of trouble. He wasn't coming as an authority figure. He had the almost sheepish look of a seeker.

"Absolutely," I said. "Please join us." I got up to grab another chair from the dining room.

He eyed the group and then looked at me again. "Do you mind if we talk privately?"

"Not at all. Would you like some decaf?"

"Yes, that would be nice."

"I'll get some," Tim said as he rose and headed for the kitchen.

Randall and I went outside to the covered porch and sat in two wooden rocking chairs. Thousands of crickets filled the night with their chirping. We heard a loud hoot owl from a nearby tree. I loved being outside with the sounds.

"So, what brings you all the way down here from Dallas?" I asked him.

"I had to come," he said. "I realize the things you're doing are from God. The healings. Feeding people. What you did in Los Bordos."

I sat silently, waiting for him to continue.

"But ... I'm confused about your teaching."

"How so?"

"The claims you're making. What you're saying about coming to connect people to God."

"You find that ... unexpected?"

"Yes. Very." He stared into the darkness of the night, as if contemplating where he wanted to take the conversation. Finally, he leaned a bit closer to me. "Can I be honest with you?"

"That's up to you."

"All my life I've tried to do the things God has told us to do. Obey the commandments. Keep the rules."

"And how is that working for you?"

He sighed deeply and shook his head. "Not that well. I may be doing my duty, but I don't have a real sense of being connected to God. People expect me to tell them how to get to God, and I try to help them ..." He paused. "But ..."

"But you yourself don't really know."

He looked down toward the wood planks of the porch. "Not really. But you do, it seems." He looked back up at me in a plaintive sort of way.

Tim arrived with two cups of coffee and some cream and sugar. I rocked in my chair for a few moments, looking out over the ranch bathed in moonlight. "You can't get to God by keeping the rules, you know."

Confusion enveloped his face. "Then what are they for?"

"They show you how far short even your best effort falls."

"Of God's perfection?" he added.

I nodded. "How well you keep the rules isn't the issue. El Papá's goal has never been for you to get your act together, perform better."

"But that's what everyone believes," he objected.

"I know. They're wrong." I let that one hang for a minute. This was contradicting all his religious training, I knew.

"Then what is his goal?" he finally asked.

"To become one with you. That's the only way you can share in his life, and his love, forever. That's what you were created for, to be joined to him. That's always been his goal. I've come to make that possible."

We sat for a moment, listening again to the crickets. I loved this man. He was searching for the truth, but his religious training was muddying the waters for him. I needed to cut through the clutter. "But your heart isn't ready to be one with God yet."

His shoulders slumped. "It isn't? What do I need to do to make it ready?"

"You can't make it ready. Only God can." I glanced at our coffee cups on the table between us. "Think of it this way. Tim brings you a cup with coffee in it. But instead of good coffee, what's in the cup are used grounds. Would you add cream to it?"

"No, of course not."

"Why not? It's coffee."

He chuckled. "Well, maybe so. But not drinkable coffee."

"Ah. Well. That's the point. That cup with the used grounds—that's how your heart, your human spirit, comes into the world. It's coffee, so to speak, but it's not suitable."

"Not suitable for what?"

"For what it was designed for—to be joined to God. It's messed up. Dirty. Sinful. That's how everyone is. At heart, you're a rebel against God, living for yourself. You can put a religious veneer on it, but underneath, it's still the same." I realized that last statement would cut Randall, in particular, to the quick.

I continued. "God is the cream, so to speak. You are the coffee. They are meant to be one. But if your heart is used coffee grounds, he isn't going to come into the cup and become one with you." I pointed to his cup of good coffee. "He'll only join himself to that."

"But how do I get my heart from one place to the other? I've tried—"

"You can't. Period. No one can. Not even God is going to try to clean up used coffee grounds. He's going to toss them out and start over. He's going to completely take out the old, sinful heart you were born with and replace it with a new, pure heart."

He stared at me for a minute, trying to grasp what I was saying.

"El Papá already told you this," I said. "Haven't you read it?"

He shook his head. "I guess not."

"Go reread the prophet Ezekiel. El Papá said this would be a key part of his new arrangement with humanity. I'm ushering in that new arrangement.

"Here's the bottom line, Randall." He probably wasn't used to strangers calling him by his first name, but I wanted to get personal. "To be in God's family, you have to be born a second time. Your mother gave birth to you, humanly. Now the Holy Spirit has to give birth to a new spirit within you. You have to be born from above. It has nothing to do with you trying to be better. El Papá has to literally give birth to a new you."

"And how does that happen?" he asked.

"It's simple. You put your trust in me. That's how it happens. El Papá loved you enough to send his own Son for you. If you receive me—if you believe who I am, and what I'm about to do for you—El Papá himself will give birth to you. Then he will come live in you. Join himself to you. You'll have his very own life. Eternal life."

Nineteen

The next morning, we all had breakfast early. I wanted to be out by the gate before the crowd tried to descend upon Tim's house. While I was still eating, however, there was a knock at the door.

"Somebody's impatient," Dan commented from the kitchen.

"Or has an emergency," I said.

Pedro went to the door and came back a moment later looking anxious. "It's the FBI. They want to talk to you, Manuel."

"I'll handle this," Dan said, putting down a skillet of eggs.

Five minutes later he returned. "They want to talk to you about the drug lord in Los Bordos, and they want to talk to you about Juan Carlos. You don't have to speak to them at all. I advise you not to."

"I will, briefly," I replied.

Dan wasn't happy with my decision, but it needed to be done. I walked onto the front porch.

"I'm happy to make a brief statement," I said.

One of the FBI agents pulled out a small writing pad and pen to take notes.

I continued. "Tell your superiors this: concerning Rodrigo Jiménez, I have business with anyone El Papá is calling to himself, drug lord or not. Concerning Juan Carlos, no one's ever been born greater than he. That's the man you've arrested. You'd do well to heed what he said. Concerning me, the things I do—the things you've undoubtedly seen—show that El Papá sent me.

And concerning you—personally, I mean—if you're willing to do El Papá's will, you'll know whether what I'm teaching is from him or not."

My eyes met those of the younger agent. He tried not to react, but I could tell my words were penetrating his shell.

"Now, if you'll excuse me," I said, "there are people out front waiting for me. Mi Papá is working today, and so am I."

I walked back into the house. Dan was standing by the front door, waiting for me.

"They'll be back, you know," he said.

"I know." I grabbed a bottle of water from the fridge. "I'll be out by the road."

That evening the twelve questioned me about the FBI.

"Don't you think you should post something on social media to explain what you were doing with Rodrigo Jiménez?" Sofia asked.

I smiled at her. "Well, I'd have to be on social media for that, don't you think?"

"You are."

"Are what?"

"On social media. Last week I set us up accounts."

"On which ones?"

"All of them. I've been tweeting things you say every day. You've got six and a half million followers already."

I couldn't help but be amused. Here I was, intentionally not promoting myself on social media, and my group was doing it instead.

"Anything else I need to know?" I asked.

"Well," Sofia said, "we have a website. And an email account. You keep getting invitations to be interviewed on TV and podcasts."

I smiled and grabbed a dinner roll. "It's good to know I have options. And look, about Rodrigo, I appreciate you wanting to look out for me, Sofia. But I'm not here to respond to rumors and suspicions. Anyone can see what I'm doing. That tells people who I am, and who sent me. That's enough."

She didn't agree, but that was final.

I told Tim that night I would go to the Alamodome. El Papá had shown me he was at work there.

"You're welcome to stay here until then," Tim offered. I accepted.

Every day, from breakfast until dinner, I went out by the road to be with the growing crowd. The state highway patrol had such concern about safety that they finally cordoned off a large section of the road and erected a detour. In the evenings my little group and I would sit in the living room for several hours, talking about El Papá and his family.

"You're all accustomed to living in a world where you have to earn everything," I said to them. "That's not how El Papá's family operates. In his family, what you have, you're freely given.

"It's like the owner of a business that's expanding rapidly. The owner keeps hiring new sales people. When December 31 rolls around, they have a big sales team meeting to announce year-end bonuses. The one hired a month before is announced first. He gets $10,000. Everyone around the room looks at each other, thinking, *If he got $10,000 for working four weeks, I'm going to get a fortune!* But when everyone else is announced, each one gets $10,000.

"After the meeting, the veteran sales people go to the owner's office. 'We worked hard all year generating sales for this company, and now at the end of the year we get shafted. The new guy got as much as we did!'

"But the owner says to them, 'Why are you complaining? I told you if the company kept doing well, you'd get a nice bonus. You got a nice bonus. If I want to take some of my profits and give the same bonus to him, why is that your concern? Can't I freely give any bonuses I want to?'"

Maya, who had worked in sales, shook her head. "But … no. That's not fair."

I smiled at her. "Maya, you don't want fair. You want El Papá's grace. Grace means he gives freely, and you receive freely. In El Papá's family, everything is freely given. You can't earn it, so that's the only way you can receive it. That's how it will always be, in all the ages to come."

Each day provided plenty of opportunity to teach something important. At breakfast the next morning, I could tell Pedro was ticked off about something. "What's bothering you, Pedro?"

He glanced at Diego. "What's bothering me is that Diego keeps setting his alarm for 5:00, saying he's going to go running, and then he presses the snooze three or four times, and by that time I'm wide awake at 5:30 in the morning, for no reason." He looked at me. "I know, you'll say I need to forgive him, but seriously, what's the limit on that? I've had to forgive him three times already."

I chuckled.

"And you think it's funny!"

"I'm not laughing at you being woken up. I'm amused at your question— 'what's the limit on that?' Let me tell you how El Papá sees things, Pedro. Let's pretend you had ten million dollars in the bank."

He snorted. "Yeah, right."

"The FDIC only insures deposits up to $250,000," Jorge noted.

"OK," I said, "Let's pretend you have ten million dollars with Fidelity. An old high school friend who's fallen on hard times needs a place to crash, and you let him stay at your place. While there, he finds your passwords, accesses your account, and transfers all ten million into an investment he thinks will make him rich overnight."

"Idiota," Jorge commented.

"A poor money manager, yes," I replied. "And a thief as well. Anyway, he loses all of your money.

"So, you find out about it. He knows you can have him arrested and ruin his life forever, so he says, 'I'll repay you every penny!'—which is preposterous. Instead of making him repay, or having him sent to prison, you forgive him of the entire debt.

"The next day your teenage son owes your high school friend $10, but your son doesn't have the cash, so your friend punches him and puts him in the ER with a broken nose.

"At this point, you go to your friend and say, 'How dare you put my son in the ER over $10, when I just forgave you of $10 million!' And you have him thrown in prison for years." I paused for a moment. "El Papá is willing to forgive you an unlimited debt, Pedro. What is Diego's alarm clock compared to that?"

Everyone was silent for a moment, and then Pedro finally spoke. "So, I guess I should forgive Diego at least one more morning."

I couldn't help but grin at him. "At least."

TWENTY

A few days later, we drove the van 200 miles to the Alamodome in San Antonio. By the time we got there, three hours early, every seat in the place was filled, with thousands more outside.

In one of the back rooms, I was able to grab a few minutes alone with El Papá. I knew what he was doing here, and therefore what I was saying here, but it was good to simply have a bit of alone time with him.

"Glorify your name here, Papá."

In my spirit, I clearly heard his reply. "I have glorified it, and I will again."

Well before I was scheduled to speak, we were escorted to a suite where we met the two men who had paid for the whole event: Ron Carter and Diego Nolar. I got to know them a bit as we ate hors d'oeuvres.

"When I found out this venue was available," Ron said, "I was on the phone with Tim within 15 minutes. I guess renting this place puts me in pretty good standing with the man upstairs, huh?" He winked at me.

"Ron," I said, "I'm very thankful you made this possible, but I want to make sure you understand: you can't earn points with God."

He took a bite of a spicy chicken wing and washed it down with some Perrier. "Hey, I know this by itself doesn't get me into heaven. But it doesn't hurt, right? In any case, I've always figured

I'm in pretty good shape. Never stole, never committed adultery, never bore false witness." He laughed. "I mean, what else do I need to do?"

I took a sip of water myself. "Here's what you need to do. Liquidate all your assets, give it all to the poor, and follow me."

His face froze and he simply stared at me. "What?"

"You overlooked the first commandment: don't have any other gods before me." I leaned forward and put my hand on his shoulder. "Be sure you listen to my talk tonight, Ron."

An event organizer entered the room. "It's time," she said to me.

Pedro walked with me into a long hallway. "I thought you said that eternal life comes through trusting in you, not through being good enough," he said.

"It does."

"But you just told that guy to sell everything and follow you."

We turned a corner into another hallway. "That's because he's still trusting in his good works to earn him eternal life. He thinks he's keeping God's law just fine. I had to show him that the law's real standards are a lot higher than he thinks. No one can keep them. No one can ever be good enough."

The hallway led to a wide-open area next to the main stage. "Wait here," the organizer said to me.

Pedro and I stood as she walked off momentarily. "It's hard for the rich to enter God's family," I said. "It's like trying to squeeze a jumbo jet into your garage."

Pedro looked puzzled. "Then who can be saved?"

"People can't save themselves, Pedro. But God can save anyone."

I was scheduled to speak at 8:00. At 7:52 the band stopped playing, the road crew broke the set down, and at 8:03 they turned off almost all the lights in the stadium and began playing "Sirius," the famous NBA intro music.

A spotlight shone on an emcee in the middle of the stage,

who spoke over the music. "And now! I know who you've all been waiting for!" The crowd roared their approval.

This wasn't exactly the way I would have scripted my introduction. A bit more low-key would have been my style. But however he wanted to introduce me was fine. El Papá knew exactly what he was doing.

"We've all seen the videos!" the emcee continued. "And I'm sure some of you have already been following him around down south of here." Part of the crowd let out a shout. "And honestly"—he glanced my way—"we have no idea what Manuel may have in store for us tonight!" The crowd roared again. "So, let's give a huge San Antonio welcome to the prophet from South Texas, the one and only, Manuel Gonzales!"

The lights in the stadium went out. Music blared again over the loud speakers. The crowd erupted. I walked out to the single mic on stage. Spotlights beamed multiple colors onto where I was standing.

The music crescendoed and then tapered down and ended. The lights came back up. My visage appeared on the stadium's huge electronic screens. I stepped to the microphone. "Maybe I should have brought a Spurs jersey," I said.

The crowd hooted and hollered.

"We love you, Manuel!" someone shouted from the audience. Then another. Then another. Within seconds, the crowd was chanting in unison, "We love Manuel! We love Manuel!" That lasted for several minutes. I simply waited. Finally, I leaned toward the mic again. The crowd quieted.

I looked out over the huge gathering and smiled. "Let me tell you about mi Papá."

TWENTY-ONE

"A man in Monterrey," I told them, "had a very successful business producing fine custom-leather goods. His clients included some of the wealthiest people in Mexico. He made many millions.

"His oldest two children helped him run the family business. The youngest, however, was just graduating from an exclusive private school, and he and his father didn't get along. In fact, he hated his father.

"In an angry outburst one night, the young man screamed, 'I wish you were dead! Then I could have my money and live anywhere I want!'

"His father turned and went into his study, emerging a few minutes later with a check worth several million. 'You're a grown man now,' he said to his son. 'Here's your share of the family fortune. Live as you see fit.'

"The son took his millions and moved into a swank apartment overlooking the ocean in L.A. He threw around money on partying, cars, and women. He got into drugs. He invested a lot of money in a movie that failed. Within two years, he had spent his millions. The Hollywood crowd turned their back on him. He got a job driving a truck, but because of his drug habit, he ended up on the streets, eating out of trash bins.

"Finally, he thought, 'My father's horses eat better than this! I'll go back to my father, apologize, and maybe he'll give me a job making boots.'

"He hitchhiked back to Monterrey and borrowed a phone to call his father's business office. 'Tell my father I'm walking home and I could use a job in the factory if he has one.'

"He started walking the last 20 miles to his father's ranch. But he'd only walked two when an SUV pulled up alongside him and his father stepped out. The son looked down at his worn tennis shoes and began his speech. 'Padre, I'm sorry I took your money and wasted it all. I know I've been—'

"But his father threw his arms around him. 'My son! You're back! I didn't even know if you were alive!'

"They drove to the ranch house. Over a dozen cars were already parked in the circular driveway, and others were arriving by the minute.

"They walked through the front door. There, above the foyer, was a huge banner that read, 'Welcome home, son!' Balloons adorned the downstairs. Mountains of food and drinks were being served. A crowd of people, both extended family and friends, erupted into cheers the moment they saw him.

"The son was shocked, but the father beamed, tears in his eyes. 'Everyone, my son has returned! I'm so thrilled you all came to celebrate with me!'

"But the son's older brother was furious. 'How can you throw a party for that disgrace of yours!' he said to his father outside. 'You never throw a party for me!'

"The father put his arm around his shoulder. 'Son,' he said, 'we have to celebrate. Your brother may as well have been dead. Now he's alive. And we have him back.'"

The stadium was silent.

"That's El Papá's heart toward you," I said.

I changed the course of my talk. "The son in the story had to do something, of course, to be reconnected to his father. He had to show up. That was the standard he had to meet, so to speak.

"El Papá has a standard to be connected to him as well, both now and forever. I want to make sure you understand El Papá's standard. Because most people think he grades on a curve. If you try to be a good person, they think, you'll be fine.

"Let me assure you: El Papá doesn't grade on a curve. He never has, and he never will. He's a perfectly righteous judge, and he's always true to himself. He will judge every person righteously, and his standard is his own holiness. To be connected to El Papá, you have to be as holy as he is."

I could hear a murmur go through the crowd.

"Some people are saying that I came to announce that El Papá's standards are now more lenient. His standards are not more lenient. They'll never change. I didn't come to change them. I came to fulfill them for you. On your behalf.

"Do you want to know how righteous you're going to have to be before El Papá? Think of the most righteous person you know—that you've ever heard of. You're going to have to be more righteous than they are if you're going to stand before El Papá.

"Let me be specific. A long time ago, El Papá told all the people, 'Don't commit murder. Anyone who does will be subject to judgment.' But understand this: if you're simply angry at someone, you're subject to the same judgment. On earth, if you slander someone, you may have to answer for it in court. But even saying 'You idiot!' on the freeway is enough to get you thrown into the fires of hell.

"A long time ago, you were all told, 'Don't commit adultery.' But here's the truth: if you simply look lustfully at a woman, you've already committed adultery with her in your heart. That's El Papá's standard."

"What about the women?" some guy shouted from the stadium floor.

"Women, too." I continued. "The scriptures say, 'An eye for an eye, and a tooth for a tooth.' That's fine for human justice. But it's not El Papá's real standard. Here's his real standard: don't resist an evil person. If someone spits on you and slaps you on the cheek, offer him the other cheek. If someone sues you for your motorcycle, give him your pickup truck, too. If someone asks you for money, give it to them. Don't expect to get paid back."

The crowd was completely silent. Stunned, probably.

"The old system said: love your neighbor, and hate your enemy. But doesn't everyone love those who love them? Even drug dealers do that. How hard is that, to return good for good? But El Papá is good to everyone, both the good and the bad. He gives jobs to bad people, too! And houses. And cars. If you want to be his sons and his daughters, do good to everyone. Love unconditionally anyone who is your enemy, who hates you, who mistreats you. Put that person at the top of your prayer list.

"Do you want to know how righteous you need to be to get into El Papá's family? You need to be perfect, just as El Papá is perfect."

I paused and then said it again. "You need to be perfect, just as El Papá is perfect. El Papá is the King. He's the Ruler. And sin is the complete opposite of his rule. It violates the moral order of his entire universe. El Papá won't dwell with it. If you want to be with him, you have to be perfect."

I looked out over the crowd. "How many of you can live up to that?"

No one said a word. "Then who can be saved?" someone finally shouted.

"That's a great question," I responded. "Who can ever be saved if you have to be perfect? It's impossible for people, but not for El Papá."

I took the microphone from its stand and walked to the edge of the stage.

"Here's El Papá's love for you," I said. "He is, right this minute, revealing a way to be made right with him—to stand perfect before him—that has nothing to do with keeping rules. This way to be right with him comes only as a gift. It has nothing to do with how good you've been, or how bad you've been. You can't do enough good things to earn it, because it's not available that way. It's only available as a free gift. All you have to do is receive the gift. There's a word for receiving this gift: faith. You say to El Papá, 'I believe what you're telling me, and I receive your gift.'"

I looked around at the entire crowd.

"Do you want eternal life?" I asked.

"Yes!" the crowd shouted.

"Do you want to be connected to El Papá?"

"Yes!" the crowd shouted again.

"Then here's the truth: I am eternal life. You receive me—you open the door and invite me in—and you have the life. El Papá sent me into the world, that whoever puts their trust in me would never perish. Whoever hears what I'm saying, and believes the one who sent me, has eternal life. Right here, right now. He's already passed out of death, and into life."

Twenty-Two

We spent the night on couches and in sleeping bags at the home of a gracious couple north of San Antonio, in a little town called Wimberley. I rose early the next morning to spend some time alone. Their green lawn, dotted with tall oak trees, sloped down to a small river. I sat for a long time, listening to the water as it passed by, and listening to El Papá.

I heard the screen door open and Pedro joined me.

"Chido," he commented, looking out toward the river. *Cool.*

I smiled. "Muy chido." *Very cool.*

We listened together for a few moments. Finally, he spoke again. "I guess we'll be heading back to the Valley today."

I could tell it wasn't just a question. It was a wish. He missed Marta.

"No," I answered. "It's time to take the message to other places. That's what I came for."

"Anyone can see videos of you online, you know."

I shook my head. "It's not the same. We have an invitation to speak at the Cotton Bowl stadium in Dallas."

Pedro fell silent for a moment.

"You know, Pedro, you can return to the Valley anytime you want."

He breathed deeply, shook his head, and turned to me. "No. Marta misses me, but she understands. I must be with you."

I reached over and put my hand on his shoulder. "And I with you, Pedro."

That afternoon, I was sitting at the kitchen table when Maya walked in, grinning.

"What?" I asked her.

"¡Mira!" *Look!*

She handed me her phone. Rachel, who at this point was living with her mother again, had sent Maya a sonogram picture of her baby.

"Tell Manuel it's a girl!" she had texted. "Just like he said!"

I laughed with joy and texted her back.

Congratulations, Rachel! She looks just like you!

DALLAS, TEXAS

I spoke at the Cotton Bowl on Thursday. As with the Alamodome, it was packed, with tens of thousands more standing outside, watching on large screens at an outdoor pavilion on the State Fair Grounds. The music was blaring. The crowd was chanting.

Pedro leaned over to me before I went onstage. "Everyone's acting like they're at a Taylor Swift concert."

I grinned at him. "They should. Someone greater than Taylor Swift is here."

My message was the same as in San Antonio: the incredible love of El Papá. His heart to be united with them. How it was impossible for them to ever achieve that, but that El Papá, in his grace, could do it for them. How he offered this as a free gift.

"Do you want to know how much it thrills El Papá to join you to himself?" I asked the crowd. "Imagine you're married with three kids and you drive up to Yellowstone National Park to go camping. Yellowstone is huge. It has wild animals. They can be dangerous. On day two, your three kids—14, 12, and 8—go hiking in a safe area nearby. But the eight-year-old gets separated and lost. You go looking for him but you can't find him. You start to panic. You notify the park rangers. They implement their missing person protocol, but they can't find him, either.

"Volunteers gather and form search parties, to no avail. He's now spent two days and nights out in the wilderness, without food, without fresh water, without shelter. You're giving up hope of ever seeing your son alive again.

"On the third day, you're still desperately searching. You hike to the top of a hill and then down through the forest to a ravine with a small river running through it. You get to the river, look down the bank to the east, and then to the west. And there, a hundred yards away, you see what looks like a perfectly healthy eight-year-old, standing and tossing rocks into the river. Your son.

"Now, how thrilled do you think you would be to see him? How thrilled would you be to run to him, embrace him, and find out that he seems all right? How thrilled would you be to take him to the medical station and hear the EMT say he's dehydrated but other than that he's fine? How big a celebration will your family have at the park? How big a celebration will your family, and your extended family, and your friends, and everyone else you know, have when you get back home?

"I want to tell you something—and I realize this isn't intuitive because of all the wrong ideas everyone has in their minds about El Papá—but as thrilled as you would be at finding your child, that's but a small reflection of how thrilled the God of the universe is when he finds you, and joins himself to you. Because that's what he's been waiting for, not for two days, but since before the world began.

"And let me tell you, if you all think you can party hearty in Dallas"—whoops erupted from the crowd—"you wouldn't believe how much they party in heaven when El Papá finds you."

At our hotel that night, I called Mateo Hernandez, a man who had been one of Juan Carlos's early followers and who had stayed with him, even after Juan was arrested. He'd become my go-to guy to check on Juan, who had been moved from McAllen to La Tuna, a low-security federal detention facility on the US-Mexico border.

"Juan's doing fine," Mateo reported. "The inmates treat him like a hero. He's glad the violence at the border has stopped."

"How's he handling this—emotionally, I mean," I asked. Juan had, for a time, been the face of El Papá's work. Now he was sitting in jail. "I'm sure this has been hard to adjust to."

"He's good. Honestly. I was talking with him the other day about how you've grabbed everyone's attention, and he said to me, 'That's God's plan. I just came to point to Manuel. Now he's the focus.'"

TWENTY-THREE

SOUTHERN U.S.

When people realized I was willing to come to their cities and speak, invitations started pouring in. A medical society in New York asked me to speak on the science of healing. An exorcism group in Miami wanted me to keynote its annual conference. A UFO group in Albuquerque invited me to speak about aliens. A cruise line wanted to host an exclusive $25,000 Mediterranean cruise featuring me and the Twelve.

"Can we do that one?" Maya asked.

I grinned at her. "Ask them if they have an open soft serve ice cream machine."

"Seriously, how do we decide which of these to accept?" Sofia wondered.

"We accept the ones El Papá tells me to," I told her. "We'll head across the South, and then north."

Organizers would book an open date at the largest available facility in town—usually a football stadium. Shreveport. Jackson. Birmingham. Tallahassee. Plus smaller towns along the way. Sometimes we stayed in hotels. Sometimes we stayed at the homes of supporters. Everywhere we went, huge crowds showed up. And on the interstates, a caravan many miles long followed us. The schedule was grueling, but I was thrilled to tell so many people in person what they so desperately needed to hear.

"I'm here so you can change the way you think about God,

and how you respond to God," I said in every city. "God's kingdom, his government, has come to you, right here."

I talked with them about El Papá's love, and what he was now offering them.

"Two men showed up one Saturday at the worship house," I told them. "One of them was very religious. Not only did he show up every Saturday, but several times a week besides. The other was the owner of a strip joint. When the religious man looked over at the other, he shook his head in disgust. 'God,' he said, 'thank you that I'm not like that sinner. I come here faithfully. I give ten percent of my income. I even lead my children in family scripture reading.' But the other man fell to his knees and said, 'God, be merciful to me! I've got nothing to offer you. But I want to receive your gift.'

"Let me tell you: That man went home right with God. But the religious man missed what God was offering him."

That little story probably didn't endear me to the religious hierarchy. But it didn't matter. According to Sofia, invitations weren't exactly pouring in from religious leaders, who were choosing instead to distance themselves from me. Mike showed me an online interview with one of the country's regional religious heads. His words seemed to sum up the hierarchy's attitude toward me.

"I've heard this—this Mr. Gonzales—say that he and the Father, God himself, are one. He makes himself out to be equal with God! That is blasphemous, and it is dangerous. God himself will bring an end to this nonsense."

I turned to Mike after watching it. "I guess he missed the part in the scriptures where El Papá says a child will be born who will be called Mighty God, that he'll be from eternity past, and that he'll reign forever."

As we traveled, the crowds were such that I had few opportunities to spend time with people individually, though some persistent souls created those opportunities for themselves.

A blind man was standing by the elevator at our hotel in Montgomery. "Are you Manuel?" I heard him ask a man who had walked up to the elevator before we did. "Are you Manuel?" he loudly asked us as we got there.

"I am," I said to him. "How long have you been standing here asking for me?"

"Since lunch." It was 10:00 p.m.

"What do you want me to do for you?"

"I want to see again," he said.

I touched his eyes with my fingers. "Then receive what you believed you would receive."

His sight returned. He looked into my face in amazement. Tears began streaming down his cheeks. "I can see! I can see!" He hugged me as tightly as he could, then he turned and hugged Diego. "I haven't seen since I was a boy! Oh!"

He hugged every one of the Twelve, and then he collapsed onto his knees and simply wept for joy. I knelt next to him, tears of joy trickling down my cheeks as well. After he composed himself, he gazed into my eyes, a huge smile adorning his face.

"Come, follow me," I said to him. "You'll see everything else El Papá wants to give you."

We had rallies in Tampa, Jacksonville, Savannah, and Charleston. In Atlanta, a small restaurant closed for the day and the owner invited us to dine privately. I was sitting by the window. But a woman with a small red dot on her forehead must have found a back way in.

"Manuel!" she cried out as she entered from the kitchen. "My daughter is suffering terribly. Please heal her."

Two employees blocked her from approaching us. "Manuel!" Before I could respond, they forcibly removed her.

Ten minutes later she was standing outside the restaurant, holding a sheet of paper against the window. "Please heal my daughter!" it said.

I smiled at her, pulled out my phone, typed a note on it, and held it against the pane. "Woman," it read, "You have great faith. Go home. Your daughter is healed."

I could see tears well up in her eyes as she nodded to me and then walked off.

At the stadium in Knoxville, I started speaking to the audience at 2:00 in the afternoon. At 2:15, we could all hear the sound of a helicopter approaching. It appeared over the southside bleachers, hovered over the stadium, and then slowly descended onto the center of the field. Most of the crowd, I'm sure, thought this was part of the program, but I had no idea what it was. I looked over at Pedro and Diego on the side of the stage. They both shrugged.

The pilot cut the helicopter engine and the blades slowly wound down. Police approached it from both sides of the field. I motioned to two policemen behind me on the stage. "Whoever's in the helicopter, let them come to the stage," I said to them. They got on their walkie-talkies and passed along my request.

Five people emerged from the side of the helicopter: four of them carrying the fifth on a stretcher. They brought him up on the stage. He was a young man, maybe 20, paralyzed from the neck down. He turned his head on the stretcher and looked into my eyes.

I leaned down toward him. "Son," I said to him, "Your sins are forgiven."

I had inadvertently left my lapel mic on. I could hear a murmur pass through the crowd. Someone not too far away in the crowd shouted out, "Only God can forgive sins!" Another person shouted his agreement. A few people started booing. I wasn't sure if they were booing my statement or the two shouters. It didn't matter.

I straightened up and looked at the huge crowd. "Yes, only God can forgive sins. But which is easier, to say, 'Your sins are forgiven,' or 'Get up and walk'? Just so everyone here knows who

I am, and the authority I have to forgive sins …" I turned to the young man. "I say to you, get up and walk." His eyes grew wide. He looked down at his legs. He swung his feet over the edge of the stretcher, stood up, and walked across the stage.

Getting away by myself to just be with El Papá was often a challenge. I took every opportunity I had. One late afternoon, Kiara, Emma, and Maya found me sitting on a folding chair in the ice machine room down the hotel hallway.

"What are you doing in here?" Kiara asked. "Everyone is looking for you."

"Listening to El Papá."

Maya glanced at the ice machine. "It's a little loud in here for that, isn't it?"

I grinned at her. "We manage."

Emma stepped into the little room. "Manuel, I've been wanting to ask you—can you teach us to pray like you do?"

I'd been wondering when someone might ask me something like that. Five minutes later the thirteen of us crowded into one of our hotel living rooms.

"Emma asked about learning to pray." I turned to her. "What would you like to learn?"

"You seem to actually hear from God."

"Yes, I do."

"I want to, too."

"I'm thrilled that you want to hear from El Papá," I said. "One day soon you will."

"When?"

"When the Holy Spirit comes to live in you. After he does, El Papá will speak to you, Spirit to spirit."

"I thought the Holy Spirit was with us now," she said.

"He is. But he's not in you. Not yet."

"So how are we supposed to pray now?" Sebastian asked.

"Well, tell me some of the things you learned to pray growing up." I looked around the group. "Short prayers, I mean. Kid prayers."

"Give us what we need for today," Justin said.

The others chimed in.

"Have your way in our lives."

"Accomplish your plan on the earth."

"Protect us from being tempted."

"Lord, be glorified," Sofia said. "Well, I guess that's a song chorus."

I smiled at her. "OK, that's good. All of them. Pray those things."

"You're telling us to pray our kid prayers?" Jorge asked.

"I'm saying those are good enough. El Papá knows what you need. He doesn't hear you better if you say a thousand words. Keep it simple.

"Remember, El Papá is never holding out on you. He's happy to give you his kingdom. If your son wanted a soccer ball for his birthday, would you give him a rolled-up ball of duct tape instead? If your daughter wanted a basketball hoop for the drive-way, would you put a trash can out there for her?"

"Pedro would," Sebastian commented.

"Look," I continued, "you were all born with selfish hearts, disconnected from God. But still, you want to give good gifts to your children—or your children-to-be. Don't you think El Papá wants even more to shower you with good gifts?"

They all nodded, understanding what I was saying.

"Think about an inconsiderate boss you might have. You want to take a week off to go visit family. He refuses. 'We're way too busy!' he claims. But you persist. You wear him down. You keep asking, and you keep asking, and finally he says, 'Fine! Take your week off!' This, from a guy who doesn't really care anything about you. Compare him to a heavenly Papá who wants to freely give you all things.

"So ask, and keep asking. Seek, and keep seeking. Knock, and keep knocking. Everyone who asks, receives. Everyone who seeks, finds. To everyone who knocks, the door is opened."

That evening, Maya knocked urgently at my hotel room door. "Manuel! Manuel!"

I opened the door. She was beaming.

"I got a text from Rachel. She had the baby!" She showed me a photo of Rachel holding the newborn, looking tired but happy.

"How big was she?" I asked.

She pulled her phone back and glanced at it. "Eight pounds, three ounces."

And perfectly healthy, I thought.

"You'll never guess what she named her," Maya said.

"What?"

"Emmanuella."

Our celebration was cut short half an hour later when my phone rang. It was Mateo Hernandez, Juan Carlos's follower.

"Juan's been moved to another prison facility," he said.

"Which one?"

"I don't know."

"They won't tell you?"

"They won't tell anyone. He's just not at La Tuna anymore. Some reporter is trying to track him down, but he's got nothing yet."

That couldn't be good news. The charges against him had been bogus to start with. Everyone knew it. And now they'd moved him to an unknown location.

"Can I ask you something?" Mateo inquired. "Something Juan told me to ask you right before he was moved."

"Sure."

"Juan wanted to make sure—are you El Único?"

I couldn't help but smile. Here was a man, a great man, completely faithful to God. He did what El Papá had told him to do. But now what he probably thought would be a brief incarceration was dragging on, month after month. He was having doubts. Anyone would.

"When you find him," I replied, "tell Juan this: the blind see; the deaf hear; the disabled are healed; the diseased are cured. Even the dead are raised. And people hear the good news. Tell Juan he's blessed, because these things don't offend him."

"How could anyone find those things offensive?"

"Trust me. Plenty do."

TWENTY-FOUR

We had rallies in Raleigh, in Charlottesville, and in Richmond. Starting in San Antonio, we'd been on the road for three months. The money I'd put aside from selling my auto shop share had long since run out. We were being supported by some individuals whom El Papá had prompted to assist us. Jorge handled our financial account.

Finally, our prime destination lay before us. Many weeks of preparation by innumerable supporters, including some who were highly connected, had made it possible. I was scheduled to speak at the National Mall in Washington.

"I've never been to Washington," Pedro commented as we drove the van away from the stadium in Richmond. "I wonder what they're expecting from you?"

I shrugged. "I don't know what they're expecting, Pedro. But I know this: they're unlikely to expect what they're going to get."

That night, I had an invitation to attend a posh dinner party at a mansion in the northern Virginia horse country with some of the wealthiest philanthropists on the East Coast. Normally the Twelve and I were a package deal, but I didn't want to impose on the event by bringing a quarter of the guests myself. My companions understood. Sort of.

"Why do you think they invited you?" Justin asked during lunch at the home of two of our supporters.

"Curiosity," I replied. "Show. Influence."

"Influence who?"

"Me. They'd probably like to get me on their side."

"Their side of what?"

"Their side of what they want the world to be. And who they want to keep running it."

"I think they'll be disappointed," Maya said.

"True, but they don't know that yet."

"Manuel, how do you feel being around people like this?" she asked.

"How do you think El Papá feels being around them?" I replied. "Everyone's the same before him."

That afternoon Ana and Sofia picked up a tux for me.

"I've never worn one of these things," I commented to Ana as I tried for the fourth time to tie my bowtie.

She shook her head. "Manuel, you're never going to get that right." She stepped forward, tied it for me, and stepped back. "Muy elegante."

I borrowed a car from our host and drove myself to the event that night. I passed through the gate at the front of the estate, rode down a straight passage under a thick canopy of trees, and came to a circular drive in front of the home. A valet took my keys. I was escorted to an expansive back deck that overlooked an immaculate green, sloping lawn.

Thirty or so people stood on the deck and in the yard, drinks and hors d'oeuvre plates in hand, talking, laughing, and enjoying the music of a string quartet playing under a gazebo. I was introduced to Carl, the host, who in turn led me around, introducing me to all of the guests.

After I'd met everyone, one guest put his arm around my shoulder and led me off to the side. "Manuel, this is a unique group. Very committed to global sustainability. People here would like to explore mutual philanthropic endeavors with you.

You seem devoted to assisting those who are underserved. Tell me your long-term goals."

"Sure, I'd be happy to," I said to him, "Long term, I'll be coming in a cloud with power and glory, with my mighty angels in flaming fire. Those awaiting me will marvel. Those not awaiting me will mourn. For those who have believed the good news, I'll bring my reward. They'll be glorified. Those who haven't responded to El Papá's offer will receive what they've earned."

His hand dropped from my shoulder and he stood looking at me uncomprehendingly.

"Did you mean long term or intermediate term?" I asked him.

At that moment the roar of a motorcycle engine caught everyone's attention. From around the corner of the mansion a Harley raced onto the back green, leaving a long rut in the lawn. The motorcycle swerved around two parties of guests and came to a stop at the edge of the deck. The driver was a woman.

"It's OK, everyone," the host assured the frightened guests. "It's OK. We're calling the police."

"No," I replied to him. "I'll talk to her."

She got off the bike, ran to me, and fell at my feet. She wore a blue leather vest with a Confederate flag on the back and looked to be in her 40s. Her long hair was mangled. Her arms were bare, save for the tattoos that covered them. One tattoo read, "I love my race."

She looked toward the ground and sobbed. "I'm sorry," she said softly. "I'm sorry."

I knelt down next to her and gently raised her chin with my hand. "Have you been following me on your bike?"

She nodded, tears still streaming down her face. "Since South Carolina. But I'm out of money. And gas, almost."

"What's your name?"

"Amanda."

"She doesn't belong here," one of the guests said. He turned to the host. "Carl, look at her. She's a hater."

I stood up. "Is there anyone here who hasn't harbored anger in your heart toward someone? Some group? Despised them? Hated them?" No one said anything. "If so, you're welcome to escort her out."

But no one moved. I knelt back down and looked Amanda in the eye. "Amanda, your faith has saved you. Your sins are forgiven."

She threw her arms around me and sobbed once more. Finally, her crying slowed and she released her hold on me. "They're right," she said in her Southern drawl. "I don't belong here. But I belong with you."

I grinned at her. "Yes, you do. You're welcome to spend the night with my little group." I gave her the address where we were staying and texted Pedro to let her in. She got on her motorcycle and looked at the lawn. "My apologies for the grass," she said to the host.

"I'll take care of it," I said.

She revved up the cycle and drove off. Everyone stood silently. Finally, Carl said, "Let's eat, shall we?"

At dinner, the guests wanted to know my ideas for reform. What did I think should be done about climate change? Systemic racism? Income inequality? Lack of access to health care?

"I don't have any ideas for reform," I replied.

I could tell that the whole group was taken aback. "What do you mean, you don't have any ideas?" one of them asked. "You see these issues all the time in South Texas. And it's clear you want to help people. Surely you have some ideas."

"I didn't come here to reform anything," I answered. "I came to transform. The whole world lies in the power of the evil one. I came to destroy the works of the devil. I'm making all things new."

A man near the end of the long table leaned forward. "Manuel, I've seen a couple of those videos that people are showing on the internet. Supposedly of you. I'm not sure if they're real or not. But either way, how do we know what you're saying is true?"

"I thought that would be obvious," I said to him. "The works El Papá has given me to accomplish—the very things I do—tell you the truth about me. They tell you El Papá sent me."

"But if it's all a fake ..."

"So what will you do to prove it to us?" the woman next to him asked.

I shook my head. "I've already been showing you, and you haven't believed. Look, if I glorify myself, what does that prove? El Papá is the one who glorifies me. When you lift me up, then you'll know who I am. Whoever believes in me, I'll raise him up on the last day."

I looked around at them. Clearly, what I was saying did not compute for this group. "Imagine you're middle class and your credit is bad. One night you go to Main Event to go bowling with a friend."

"What is Main Event?" one of the women asked.

"It's a recreation center. Anyway, you don't have any cash on you, and your friend loans you $30. A month later you come across a house that you'd love to buy, because you're tired of paying rent. But you can't qualify for a loan. So a different friend loans you $300,000 for the house."

"Quite a friend," a man commented.

"Yes. But you soon lose your job and you can't repay either one. So, both of them forgive the loan they made to you. Now, which one are you going to love more—the first friend or the second?"

"The second," Carl answered.

"Of course," I responded. My eyes ran up and down the table, falling on each of them. "That woman who was here earlier, Amanda. She spent her last penny following me up here. She was on her last tank of gas. That's why she interrupted this gathering. It was her last chance. She gave up everything to find me, because she knew that she needed to be forgiven a whole lot. So she loves a whole lot.

"You, on the other hand, got chauffeured here. You were served wine and hors d'oeuvres to hobnob with your friends. You assumed you'd have an interesting and possibly beneficial evening with me. You have many causes that you give your excess money to. You think that because of your good deeds, you have little need of forgiveness. So you love little.

"You think to yourselves, 'I have unlimited wealth; I don't need anything.' But you don't realize that you're wretched, pitiful, poor, blind, and naked. Let me be your investment advisor: Buy the pure gold I'm offering, so you can be truly rich. Let me give you fine clothes, so you can cover your shameful nakedness. Let me heal your blindness, so you can see."

They were perfectly silent.

I leaned forward and put my elbows on the table. "I extend to each of you the same invitation I extend to everyone, rich or poor. I'm standing at the door of your heart, knocking. If you open the door, I'll come in. And we'll dine together forever."

Late that night, Pedro greeted me when I walked into the home where we were staying.

"How'd it go?" he asked.

I put the car keys on the kitchen table. "Well, I don't think I made any friends, if that's what you mean. Except one. Did Amanda make it here?"

TWENTY-FIVE

"There must be a million people here."

Pedro stared in amazement at the massive crowd on the National Mall, extending from the Capitol Building, past the Washington Monument, and halfway along the Capitol Reflecting Pool toward the Lincoln Memorial.

The event's organizers had erected a temporary platform on the Capitol's terrace. Four giant video screens had been placed at equal intervals down the Mall. I'd requested that there be no music on the loudspeakers. I didn't want a party atmosphere. I'd requested that there be no emcee to introduce me. I didn't want someone unfamiliar setting the wrong tone. Fifteen minutes before I was due to speak, the crowd started chanting, "Manuel! Manuel! Manuel!"

When the time came, I simply walked out to the mic on the platform. I turned and took a long look at the Capitol, and then faced the throng. I waited a moment in silence before I spoke.

"I'm here to announce a new government. It's nothing like the government you've been used to. You can't fit this government into the old system. It's nothing like the old system. El Papá is bringing something completely new. As Isaiah the prophet said:

A Child will be born to us,
A Son will be given to us.
And the government will rest on his shoulders.

He will be called Wonderful Counselor, Mighty God,
Eternal Father, Prince of Peace.
His government, and the peace he brings, will never end.
It will be built on everlasting justice and righteousness.
With righteousness he will judge the poor,
And decide with fairness for the afflicted of the earth.
He will strike the earth with the rod of his mouth,
And with the breath of his lips he will slay the wicked.
He will keep on until he achieves justice for everyone.

"Do you think I came to bring peace on earth? Hardly. I came to bring division. Families will be split over me. Your own family will become your enemy. So will your neighbor. You will have to choose your allegiance. Choose wisely!

"Woe to you politicians! You hypocrites! You're supposed to represent the people, but the only people you represent are yourselves. You sell yourselves to the highest bidder and make yourselves rich while pretending to be on the side of the oppressed. Woe to you who pass evil laws, calling them good, and to you who constantly render unjust decisions. You rob the people of their rights, so the powerful can feed on the powerless.

"Woe to you bureaucrats! You hypocrites! You've been given authority to operate government according to the people's will, but you subvert it at every turn, and oppress them. You sit on your little thrones and make the people bow before you—you who are supposed to be serving them.

"Woe to you billionaires! Because you've amassed a fortune, you think you know best what people should do, what people should say, what people should think, what people should want. You use technology to remake society in your own image, but you are fools. You are blind guides leading the blind. The same goes for you movie stars, you athletes, you internet personalities with huge followings. You think you're wise, but the foolishness of God is far wiser than you are. You tell people how to live, but the end of that path is death.

"Woe to you media! You're supposed to inform the public so they can wisely participate in representative government. Instead, you tell them what you want them to hear, and you withhold from them what you don't want them to hear, so they'll be ripe to demagogue. Liars! You're like your father, the devil. He was a liar from the beginning. Lying is his nature. It's yours as well.

"Woe to you corporations! You convince people that they need what they don't. You promise to satisfy them and you cannot. You feed their basest desires. You pretend to be good citizens of the world, while you exploit slave labor and crawl into bed with dictators. The cries of those you have plundered can be heard from their graves.

"Woe to you financiers! You conspire with those in power to rig the game for yourselves, to get what you want, without any thought for the welfare of others. You make sure others pay the price while you get rich. You collude with the government to eat away people's pay by devaluing their money. Do you think you will stay at the top? You will be brought down to the depths.

"And you religious leaders—you legalists. Woe to you as well! Do you think you will escape just because you claim to speak for God? You invent man-made rules that weigh people down, and say people must be as devoted to God as you or they won't make it. Yet you yourselves aren't going to make it! You are dead people, supposedly telling others how to find life. You don't know the heart of El Papá, and you don't have his love in your hearts. Abandon your religious schemes! Come and take freely from me. I'm the only one who can give you true life. And my supply is infinite."

I motioned across the throng with my arms. "All of you who have come here today, you're accustomed to looking at the weather forecast for the next day, or the next week. Some of you analyze stock market trends. Some of you track political fortunes. Some of you bury yourselves in fantasy football projections. You all try to keep up with what's going on around you. But you need to read the real signs of the times.

"El Papá's new government is right here before you, right now. You can't see it with your eyes. You can't point to it and say, 'There it is!' Rather, it's right here, among you. So think in completely new ways. Respond to El Papá in a completely new way.

"The powers that be can't stop the restoration I'm bringing. El Papá's kingdom right now is like successful gene therapy. A person has defective genes. New, functioning genes are inserted, cells are repaired, and these cells, now healthy, start replicating. Soon they spread to more and more of the body, healing it entirely.

"The time of the present world system is almost up! The time for you to choose is now. El Papá's kingdom is like a stock fund manager investing in a stock. After six months, he says to his associate, 'This stock is stagnant. Let's sell it.' But the associate says to him, 'Let's wait another six months. If it doesn't go up, then let's sell it.' El Papá is extending his patience to all of you. He doesn't want anyone to perish. He wants all of you to be a permanent part of his family. Choose that!"

I pointed to the Washington Monument. "Look at that monument, rising into the sky. Brave men fought and died 250 years ago for your liberty. Look at Abraham Lincoln in the distance behind you. He led a war that freed the slaves. But Americans are still slaves.

"I tell you the truth: everyone who commits sin is the slave of sin. There's an ongoing debate in this country over how people are born regarding sex and gender. But that's not nearly as important as this reality: all people are born slaves of sin. And they desperately need to be freed. I've come to set the captives free. And if I set you free, you really will be free. You'll no longer be a slave, but a son or a daughter. Slaves are never a permanent part of a family. Sons and daughters are. Become a permanent part of El Papá's family.

"Look over to your left, to the National Archives Building. It houses the Declaration of Independence, and the Constitution. They're our documents of liberty. But if you want real liberty, come live under my declaration, and my constitution. The liberty I bring will be an unending source of freedom, both for you, and for those around you.

"If you're weighed down with life, come to me! I'll give you rest from the burdens of living. Learn from me. Unlike cold bureaucracies, I'm gracious, and humble, and on your side! Living under my direction isn't heavy. It's easy. I am offering you rest for your whole being.

"El Papá is renewing all things. One day, I will return. On that day, I won't be sitting in the White House over there. I'll come back in all my glory, and I'll sit on a glorious throne as the King. All the nations and all the peoples will be gathered before me to be judged. I'll sort those who are mine from those who aren't.

"That's when inclusivity will really matter. In me, there is no race, or class, or nationality, or disability—not even male or female. Everyone who comes to me, regardless of who they are, will be included. Make sure you're included!"

TWENTY-SIX

The next morning Jorge showed me the lead headline:

Manuel Gonzales calls for government overthrow

"Well," I said, "you can't believe everything you read, can you?"

"A lot of people will misconstrue what you said," he commented. He handed me a cinnamon bagel and looked me straight in the eye. "A lot of powerful people."

Dan walked in. "It's not those who misconstrue I'm worried about. It's those who understand perfectly well what he means."

Someone clomped loudly down the stairs. Pedro burst into the room.

"The internet is going crazy over your speech yesterday," he said. "I think you riled up a few people. Like … everyone."

"People need to be riled up," I replied. "What time are we leaving for Georgetown?"

"Event is at 1:00," Dan answered. "We can either take the van, or we can take the Metro to DuPont Circle and the university shuttle from there."

"Let's take the Metro," I said.

"The crowd around you on the Metro will be horrible," Pedro objected.

I nodded. "That's why I want to take the Metro." I finished my coffee and bagel and excused myself.

"What are you going to do?" Pedro asked.

"Be quiet with El Papá."

We were headed to Georgetown University for an extended Q&A with students, and I needed to hear from him. I didn't expect a friendly reception there, but the students needed to hear the truth. And El Papá would be opening some of their hearts.

We left at 11:00. Pedro was right. The crowd on the Metro was such that we could barely move. People were clamoring to talk to me, to touch me, to take selfies with me. Halfway to Dupont Circle, I felt a certain power flowing out from me. I turned and looked behind me at the people standing there. "Who touched me?" I asked.

Kiara looked at me incredulously. "Manuel, we're like sardines in here. How can you ask, 'Who touched me?'"

"Someone touched me, and I felt power going out of me."

From behind several people came a voice. "I did."

The crowd parted enough for me to see who spoke. It was a woman, maybe 30 years old. Tears were streaming down her face. She pressed through the people in front of her, fell to her knees in front of me, and looked up at me, her face beaming.

"I've had spina bifida all my life." Someone handed her a tissue and she wiped her eyes. Slowly, she rose and stood up straight before me. "This is the first time I've been able to stand up perfectly straight—ever." She sobbed once more for joy. "I knew that if I simply touched you ..." She dabbed her tears again. "I'd be healed."

I felt like taking her in my arms and embracing her as tightly as I possibly could, but I realized the discomfort she might feel with that. So I simply said to her, "Your faith has made you well. Go. Live in El Papá's peace."

We got to Georgetown University's Columbia Hall at noon. The auditorium was already packed with over a thousand students. The format for the event was simple: straight Q&A.

Whatever questions were on their minds and in their hearts, I wanted to answer.

Diego looked out over the many rows of students from behind the stage curtain. "Why are you talking to a bunch of rich kids?" he asked. These weren't the people he was used to being around.

I smiled at him. "Because I came for them, too, Diego."

I walked over to the event coordinator. "Every seat is already taken," I said. "Why don't we start an hour early to give them more time to ask questions?"

"Fine with me," she replied.

An emcee welcomed the audience, and then welcomed me. When I walked onto the stage, some of the audience stood and cheered loudly. Some clapped politely. Some sat silently. *Those are the ones whose questions I really want to answer,* I thought. Students were already lined up behind two standing mics, one in each of the aisles leading to the stage.

I sat in a chair in the middle of the stage with a wireless mic and thanked them all for being there. The emcee motioned to the first questioner, a young woman, on my left. She stepped to the mic.

"In your speeches you seem to be saying that the most important thing is how someone responds individually to God. But don't you think the most important thing is societal injustice? Don't socioeconomic structures affect people's lives the most? I mean, what about something like systemic racism?"

It was the kind of question no one at the auto shop in McAllen would verbalize, though they might think it.

"I know that question's on a lot of people's minds these days," I replied. "It's an important one. El Papá hates racism. All people are created equally in his image; anyone thinking they're better or that someone else is lesser because of their skin color is evil. It's unjust. And El Papá hates injustice."

I leaned forward in my chair. "Having said that, we must

remember: evil flows from inside people, from the heart. That's where racism comes from—and hatred, and greed, and lust, and lying, and envy, and everything else. Unless you change the heart, there's no way to cure that; the evil simply gets repackaged into another form of evil. You can always change who rules over whom on the human level, but the evil is still there. You can't get clean water from the Potomac River. You can send it through different pipes, but it's still dirty water."

The emcee motioned to the other mic for the next question, but the first questioner wasn't quite done. "So what do you see as the ultimate solution to injustice?"

"The solution is that you need a completely new heart. You must be born from above. The love of God must be put within you. That ultimately solves the problem. Love never does wrong to others."

"OK, let's go to the next person," the emcee said.

A young man stepped to the mic. "I saw on YouTube a talk you gave in Jackson, Mississippi. You told a story about sales people all getting the same bonus at the end of the year even though some had only worked for a few weeks. What was the point of that story? That doesn't seem fair at all."

I nodded. "You're right. It's not fair. Fair is, your sin separates you from God. You die in your sin, and you're separated from him forever. That's what your sin earns you. But El Papá doesn't want you to earn that. He wants you to be united with him. That's what he created you for."

"And you're showing us the way to do that?"

"No, I'm not showing you the way," I replied. "I am the way. That's why I'm here, to connect you to God."

A female student on the other side glanced around momentarily and then stepped tentatively to the mic in front of her. "I guess this kind of follows up to what you just said. In your speeches you seem to be saying that you are the only way to

God. But why is your way any more valid than any of the world's religions? Couldn't it be said that they all lead to God? How can there only be one way?"

I smiled at her. "That's a very good question. Let me ask you one in return. If you strip them down to their core, what's the ultimate goal of every world religion? I mean, what are people trying to do?"

She thought about that for a moment. "Well, I guess you'd say that the goal is to ultimately get to a better place. Like, heaven. Or paradise. Or nirvana."

"And how are people going to do that?"

"It depends on the religion."

"At the core of them all."

"You have to become good enough, I guess."

"Meaning …"

"Do enough good things. Be devoted enough. Become enlightened enough …"

"And what if you can't?"

"Can't what?"

"Ever become good enough."

"Then … I guess you have to try harder."

"But you never really know how good you have to get, do you? So you always have to try harder. Ask devoted followers. They'll admit that. It's like being on a treadmill that keeps going faster and faster, and the slope gets steeper and steeper. Do you think God meant for people to have to go through that to get to him?"

She shrugged. "I don't know. Maybe it doesn't make much sense."

"It makes much less sense when you realize this: God's standard is perfection. It has to be, because it's based on his own character. You want to connect with God, be with him forever, you have to be perfect."

"But … no one can do that."

"Exactly. Which is why all religions fall short, because they depend on human effort. How is more religious effort ever going to achieve perfection? How is it ever going to get you there?

"It's like a bunch of people standing on the beach in San Francisco. The goal is to swim to Japan. One guy swims out a hundred yards and then gives up and comes back. A woman swims out a mile before turning back. You could say, 'She's so devoted!' But so what? The goal was to swim to Japan. She has 4,999 miles to go. No one can make it. No one is good enough, no matter how devoted they are. That's why all religion falls way, way, short."

I stood up from the chair, walked to the edge of the stage, and looked right at the young woman. "What I'm offering is the exact opposite of all that. The kind of perfection you need can't be earned. It can only be received as a gift. El Papá sent his Son into the world to offer that gift. Anyone who receives me, who puts their trust in me, El Papá gives them the right to become his child. Because they've chosen to receive the righteousness of God. As a gift. That's why I'm the only way. No one else can gift you with the one thing you need. No one comes to El Papá except through me."

She nodded hesitantly. I'd given her a lot to think about.

A male student was next. "You said in your speech yesterday that in you there is no male or female. Are you saying that you believe gender identity is not binary, that instead it exists along a spectrum?"

"No," I replied. "I'm saying that in me distinctions that seem to separate humanity, like race, class, gender, and so forth, disappear as things that divide. All are one, because all are in me, and I am in them."

"So you're saying male and female are not exclusive as gender identities?"

"No, I'm not saying that at all. Here's what God said about

that in the beginning: 'Let us make man in our image, in our likeness, and let them rule over the earth. So God created man in his own image; male and female he created them.' That hasn't changed."

The crowd grew restless at that statement. Some students booed.

I continued. "But something else hasn't changed, either: our obligation to love people. Genuinely. Because El Papá loves them dearly. But we love in truth."

"OK," the emcee said. He pointed to the next questioner. It was a young woman, who read a question from her phone.

"What would you say to someone who accused you of simply constructing your own narrative—a narrative designed to establish a new power structure—based on traditional Western religious hegemony?"

I resisted the impulse to smile. The question sounded straight out of a class on postmodern philosophy. I gave her a simple answer that got to the heart of the issue. "I'm not seeking anything from you, or anyone else in this room. You can't add to my power, or take away from my power. I'm here to offer you the best possible gift from God. That's all. I'd love for you to receive it."

She asked a follow-up. "But wouldn't you agree that societal structures inevitably produce a system of oppressors and victims—an inequality of power that is inherently oppressive?"

"No social structures can be perfectly just," I said, "because they're built and run by sinful humans. You'll always have inequality with you. That's reality in a fallen world, until I fully establish my kingdom. That's when perfect justice will truly reign. I assure you, in my kingdom, there won't be any victims."

A hush fell over the auditorium. I'm sure they never expected to hear someone say that.

"But don't you think it's worthwhile to try to fight injustice now?" the young woman asked.

"I do, as long as you can do so in love. Otherwise, it's simply retribution, or vengeance, or it becomes repackaged oppression.

"But here's where your question comes up short. The greatest oppression, by far, that you or anyone else experiences isn't external. It's internal. It's sin in your heart. That's what truly oppresses you. And that's why I'm here. I came to free you from that."

I turned to a young man at the other mic.

"I grew up in a pretty religious family," he said. "It seems like, based on what I learned, there's a lot that God is demanding of us. I guess I'm asking—how can anyone live up to that? It seems really burdensome. At least, to me."

I sat down on the edge of the stage. The young man was being very personal; I wanted to be personal back to him. "Yes, I can imagine it did seem burdensome. But if you think what I'm saying is burdensome in any way, you aren't understanding what I'm saying. What I'm telling you about is a completely new life. You can't fit the old way into it. Did you get here today by riding a horse?"

He smiled. "No."

"Of course not. Riding horses for daily transportation doesn't fit today's world. It's not set up for that.

"You can't combine the religious system you grew up with, with what I'm offering. It doesn't fit. El Papá is making all things new. When you come to me, and learn from me, you'll see that what I'm offering isn't burdensome. Just the opposite. What I give, I give freely. I've come to relieve your soul of its burdens, so you can relax and be at peace. Through me, you can be at complete peace with God, and with yourself."

The students asked questions, and I answered, for five hours. No one left. Finally, the emcee said, "All right, we need to vacate the facility so they can clean for tomorrow. We'll do one more question." He looked at a young woman on my right.

"Thank you," she said to him, and then she looked at me.

"What I don't understand about religion is why God would essentially hide himself from us. If he's real, and if he wants us to know who he is, why doesn't he just make that obvious? Why doesn't he show himself?"

"I appreciate your question," I responded. "The answer is this: El Papá wants you to know him more than you want to know him. That's why he made you: to know him, and to know his love for you. The truth is that people have always partially known him. Creation reveals El Papá. So does your conscience."

She responded quietly. "But that's not really, you know, personal. Why doesn't he just appear to us, so that we can see him?"

I slid off the edge of the stage and walked a few feet in front of her. "Can I have your name?" I asked her.

"Grace."

I smiled at her. "Grace. I've always liked that name. Grace, you're asking an honest question. Here's your answer: El Papá is showing himself. To you, right now. When you've seen me, you've seen El Papá. El Papá and I are one."

TWENTY-SEVEN

Late that afternoon, Prisha Mandal's car passed through the security entrance to the White House grounds. Mandal, CEO of one of the largest Big Tech companies in the world, had come to Washington for two events: to testify again in front of the Senate Select Committee on Artificial Intelligence, and to meet with senior administration officials in the White House. The latter event was the far weightier of the two—perhaps the most important meeting of her brief tenure as CEO.

She was escorted to the Cabinet Room. She'd seen pictures of it before, with presidents conducting "vital" business with Cabinet members. Actual vital business, she knew, rarely happened in such photo-op gatherings. This meeting would be different.

A Secret Service agent opened the door and she entered. She recognized every face around the lengthy oval conference table: Chief of Staff Dan Holden, Attorney General Amy Wu, Senior Advisor Elliot Reed, National Security Advisor Michelle Meyer, Chief Strategist Mark Humphries, Secretary of Homeland Security Bob Dillon, CIA Director Glenn Wiseman, FBI Director Chris Ottenger, the president's strongest Senate ally, Allison Davis, rival Big Tech CEO Jeff Cheng, and Ellen Leggett, majority owner of a media conglomerate that Mandal's company had almost bought two years back.

Holden nodded toward her as she entered. "I believe you all know Prisha Mandal."

She sat and the meeting, which apparently had started without her, continued. Ottenger spoke. "The truth is, we don't know exactly what threat he represents."

"Are the words he used yesterday actionable?" Senator Davis asked.

Wu shook her head. "Legally, no. He didn't call for anything that couldn't be interpreted as a simple change in administrations."

Humphries leaned forward. "But did people take it that way?"

Ottenger circled back to Davis's question. "We've had a baseline collection going on him for some time."

As a member of the Senate Intelligence Committee, Davis knew what a baseline collection on someone entailed. The FBI could search government records, conduct interviews, analyze links between online and phone records, and physically surveil.

"Will that be upgraded to an actual investigation at this point?" Davis asked.

"Certainly."

"Which means what?" Reed asked from the far end of the table.

Ottenger, concerned about the non-governmental personnel in the room, glanced over at Wu. But she nodded for him to answer. Everyone had been briefed on and had agreed to the security requirements of the meeting.

"It means wiretaps, email and other electronic intercepts, tracking devices on vehicles, covert searches. Assuming court approval."

"Which shouldn't be an issue," Wu commented.

Bob Dillon cleared his throat. "Do we have someone on the inside yet?"

Ottenger shook his head. "Still working on it."

"Then let's establish what the rest of us will be doing," Humphries said. "We need to start limiting this guy's online footprint."

"Eliminate it altogether," Reed suggested.

"Ideally, yes."

The conversation had ventured into Mandal's realm. "After his statements at Georgetown this afternoon, his social media accounts will be suspended. That's almost certain."

Humphries looked at Mandal and Jeff Cheng. "Can you two make sure that they are? And can you make sure he stays suspended—permanently?"

"Not a problem," Cheng answered. Mandal nodded in agreement.

"Can we direct internet traffic away from him as well?"

"Algorithms can do that, yes," Mandal answered. She glanced at Cheng.

"That leaves media," Humphries said. He looked at Leggett, the media mogul. "We need to get his approval ratings down. Way down. Make people question his motives. Report on possible dirt ..."

"Like the drug lord," Davis interjected.

Wiseman shook his head. "Nothing there. Our contacts said he and Jiménez were just talking about God."

"Doesn't matter," Humphries replied. "It's still dirt." He looked back at Leggett. "Find some more. Write it up. Have the talking heads discuss it. Play up people's natural suspicion of religious stuff."

Leggett nodded. "All very doable. And it won't hurt ratings, either."

Humphries smiled wryly. "Which is always our main goal, Ellen. Improve your ratings. What about the other outlets—cable, newspaper ..."

"Not to worry. They'll follow our lead. News is a more copycat business than football."

Mandal had forgotten. Leggett owned a football team as well.

Michelle Meyer, the National Security Advisor, finally spoke. "I want to remind us all what Manuel Gonzales said yesterday."

All eyes were on her. She continued. "He said he was bringing in a new government, and that he would be the head of it. It would be on his shoulders, he said. We naturally leap to the political ramifications. But I'll be advising the president beyond that. I'm looking at this as a national security threat. We cannot discount the possibility—probability, some on my team would say—that this man intends to bring down our constitutional order. And that he may have the power to do it."

Twenty-Eight

I was sitting at our breakfast table the next morning, drinking coffee, when Sofia and Emma walked in and sat down. They looked glum.

"We've been cancelled," Sofia said.

"Where?" I asked. "Philadelphia? The football stadium?"

"No, social media. All of our accounts have been suspended. We can't post anymore. Well, except on X. Everyone else's videos of yesterday's event have been taken down, too."

The news didn't surprise me a bit. No doubt they'd been looking for an excuse to do just that. "What were we cancelled for?"

"Violating their community standards," Emma answered.

I had a sip of coffee. "What community standards?"

"They say you're engaging in hate speech."

"Oh." I bit into a cheese Danish. "How so?"

"By not affirming the LGBTQ+ community. Because you said there were only two genders."

"Ah." I looked across the table at the fruit plate our host had prepared for all of us. "Pass that over here, will you?"

Emma passed the fruit plate over and I helped myself to some blueberries.

"We still have over a hundred million followers on X," Sofia noted.

"Really?" I had another sip of coffee. "A hundred million followers. We could monetize that, I bet."

Sofia's face lit up. "Absolutely! I could start working on that today."

I smiled and shook my head. "Just kidding. I'm not here to monetize anything."

"Most people would die for a hundred million followers."

"Yeah, well, I'll get around to that," I replied.

Pedro walked in and took a seat. "What are you guys talking about? Something about being banned?"

"We've been banned from all social media except X," Sofia replied.

"You mean I can't watch YouTube videos anymore?"

Emma rolled her eyes. "No, we can still watch things; we just can't post them."

Pedro exhaled deeply. "Whew. For a second there I thought we were in real trouble."

I laughed. "Pedro, El Papá always has your back. You'll never be in real trouble if you only want what he wants." I looked at the time. "Let's get everyone packed up and loaded. We need to hit the road."

"To where?" Emma asked.

"How about Independence Hall?"

PHILADELPHIA, PENNSYLVANIA

Four hours later we were standing in front of the Hall. It was the perfect place for what I wanted to tell the Twelve. Until now, following me around had been easy. Even, in many ways, popular. But after my speech in DC and the Q&A at Georgetown, lines were drawn. Increasingly, it would either be El Papá's way or the world's way. The middle ground was disappearing.

I pointed at the Hall behind me and said to the Twelve

and the crowd that was forming, "The 56 men who signed the Declaration of Independence in that Hall wrote, 'For the support of this declaration, with a firm reliance on the protection of Divine Providence, we mutually pledge to each other our lives, our fortunes, and our sacred honor.'

"They weren't joking. They knew perfectly well that if they lost the war, they'd be captured by the British and hanged as traitors, their property would be seized, and their families would be impoverished. They counted the cost, and they signed the Declaration."

"Amen to that!" someone shouted from the crowd.

"If you want to continue to follow me, you have to count the cost, too. You can't be my pupil and at the same time love other things more than you do me. That includes the people you care about—father, mother, spouse, children, anyone. It even includes your own life. You can't learn from me if you insist on holding tightly to all of these things. Give them to me instead. I'm the only one you can really trust with them."

We stayed in downtown Philadelphia until well past sunset. Finally, about 9:00, we got in the van and headed north. I turned around in my seat and spoke to all of them. "What I said today, did that bother you guys?"

Pedro looked around at the others and then spoke. "Manuel, we *have* left everything to follow you."

I smiled at him. "I know, Pedro. I promise you this: one day, your reward will be greater than you can possibly imagine."

Around 10:00, Jorge came and sat down next to me. He had his phone in his hand.

"Do you have a minute to watch something?"

"Of course."

He turned the screen toward me. "I was streaming this live cable news interview with Carter Lynch, former head of the NSA." He unpaused it.

"I find this deeply disturbing," Lynch was saying. "We've heard this kind of rhetoric before, and we've seen where it leads. You cannot stand in front of the Capitol and call for the overthrow of the government. That is not simply irresponsible, it's illegal. And he's gathering to him hundreds of thousands if not millions of followers who, no doubt, will act as he instructs. Or, maybe more dangerous, just take matters into their own hands."

"What would you have the government do?" the interviewer asked.

"I would have them charge him with sedition."

Jorge paused it again. "Manuel … do you think …" He sighed and was silent for a moment. "Do you think you overdid it in DC? Used the wrong words?"

Clearly, he was afraid. Afraid for me, afraid for himself, or maybe both. I wanted to calm his fears, but I knew I couldn't do it in the way he wanted.

"Look, I know people will misunderstand what I say at times. That's unavoidable. But I must tell them what El Papá wants to tell them. A new reign is coming. It's already here. They need to know that."

"But they think you're talking about establishing an actual government."

"And that's exactly what El Papá has put into motion. He promised everlasting justice and righteousness."

"But that's in the spiritual realm, isn't it?"

"Jorge, it's in all realms."

TWENTY-NINE

Staying anywhere overnight was becoming increasingly difficult. Crowds followed us everywhere, pressing upon us wherever
possible. To get some sleep, or to get some alone time with the
Twelve, I usually had to address the crowd directly.

"I'm thrilled you are all with us," I'd say to them. Which was
true, of course. "But we have to get some rest. I'll see you in the
morning." People respected that. Mostly.

We drove to New York and spent the night at the Westchester
County home of Robert McClennan, a former U.S. Attorney and
a friend of a federal judge in McAllen who had been supporting
us. The next day we took the train into Manhattan.

A crowd was waiting for us when we got off the train at
Grand Central Station. I stayed with them for over an hour
before we started walking south, toward Wall Street, accompanied by the throng.

We walked almost four miles, the crowd growing as we went.
Mounted policemen rode along the edges of the crowd, scanning
for any sign of trouble. From time to time, I glanced with amuse-
ment at the Twelve staring up at the skyscrapers that seemingly
went on forever. They weren't in the Rio Grande Valley anymore.

"A todo dar," Sebastian commented. *Awesome.*

When we finally got to the financial district, it was getting
close to noon. I saw a worker on a ladder repairing an awning in

front of an old hotel. "Go over and see if that guy will let us use his ladder during his lunch break," I said to Justin. A couple of minutes later the man walked up to us through the crowd, ladder in hand.

"Thank you, "I said to him.

He grinned at me. "For you, Manuel, anything."

He carried the ladder the final three blocks and set it up where I told him, on the sidewalk in front of the New York Stock Exchange. I climbed up a couple of rungs and looked out over the crowd, which filled not only the sidewalks but also the street. The police just let everyone be. Sebastian handed me a megaphone that someone had donated. The people grew quiet.

"I want to tell you some things about the kingdom of El Papá," I said to them. "Because it doesn't work like things on earth work. If you're hard up for money, you're in a good spot. You really are, because you're more ready to join his family and depend on him. You see how much you need a loving Father. If you've been going hungry, you're going to be satisfied. If you've been filled with grief, El Papá is going to fill you with laughter instead. If you end up hated and insulted and rejected because of me, you're incredibly blessed. Give each other high fives! A huge reward awaits you in heaven."

I glanced back at the stock exchange building. "As for you who are rich, let me tell you the truth. Your lives are comfortable now, but comfort doesn't await you. You who are well fed, you'll end up being the hungry ones. You who are laughing and living it up for yourselves, you're the ones who will be weeping. People tell you what you want to hear because of your money. That won't last!"

I pointed across the street at a restaurant that had obviously closed down and had never reopened. "Maybe someone here used to work at that restaurant over there. I know times have been hard for many of you. Who is having a hard time making ends meet?"

Many in the crowd raised their hand.

"I know it's easy to be anxious about how you're going to pay the rent. But here's what I want you to know: El Papá cares about you. He cares about you deeply. So don't worry about your life—how you're going to pay for housing, or food, or clothes. Don't you think your life is about far more than those things?"

I looked over at some pigeons sitting on a ledge to my right. "Look at those pigeons up there. Do they look like they're going without? Their bank accounts are pretty low, but El Papá feeds them. Don't you think you mean more to him than they do? You New Yorkers—have you ever seen a rat in this city?"

The crowd laughed and hooted. "Who hasn't?" someone shouted.

"Right," I responded. "Do the rats here look underfed? Who does El Papá care about more—you or the rats?

"So don't worry about what you're going to eat, or how you're going to pay the rent. How many days are you adding to your life by worrying? El Papá knows what you need. Here's what you need to focus on: receiving his righteousness, and letting him have the reins of your life. When you receive the gift of righteousness he offers, and the wealth of his grace, you'll be the one living rich. And nothing—not even inflation, or a market crash—can take that wealth from you."

We returned that night to Robert's house. Everyone was beat and collapsed into their beds, couches, or sleeping bags. The house was dark, but I tiptoed into the kitchen to get some water before going to bed. I turned on the light, and Robert was sitting at the kitchen table, sipping a cup of coffee.

"What are you doing, sitting here in the dark?" I asked him.

"Thinking." He motioned toward the coffee pot. "Decaf?"

"Sure."

I sat at the table and he poured me a cup.

"Thinking about what?" I asked.

"Where I used to work. The Justice Department." He picked up his coffee cup and held both hands around it. "I watched your speech in Washington. And the one in New York today on X." He took a sip. "I have a lot of friends high in the government. Have had for years. I talk with them frequently." He paused. "Why do you imagine you have people inside the Beltway feeling so threatened?"

"They want to fashion the world in their image," I replied. "To their liking, with themselves ruling. That requires convincing the public of certain narratives. I contradict their narratives, so I jeopardize their power. I tell people that genuine meaning comes from beyond this little world. That something higher deserves their allegiance. That they were created to share the life of God himself. Whoever truly believes that, the powerful can't control."

He paused and placed his cup back on the table. "They're not going to let you keep doing this, you know."

I drank from my cup, looked at him, and nodded. "I know."

THIRTY

The next day I spoke at a high school gym in Long Island. Two more large stadiums had cancelled on us; it appeared only smaller venues might be available going forward. But I was content with whatever El Papá provided. Many thousands came to listen, and to be healed.

"Make sure that when God calls, you respond," I said to the crowd. "A wealthy man in the Hamptons invited all of his rich friends to join him for a week-long celebration of his engagement. He rented a superyacht with crew, hired a famous chef, ordered the finest food, and arranged for a live band. The bill for the week was over $250,000. But the day the yacht was supposed to sail, he started getting texts from his friends:

> Have an appt with my financial advisor. Can't make it.
> Meeting an architect for an addition to our home. Next time.
> Our new Samoyed puppy arrives today. Hope u have a nice celebration.
> I was just on another boating trip two weeks ago. A bit worn out. Sorry.

"The man got angry and said to his assistant, 'Drive the limo into the city. Invite whatever homeless people you find on a one-week, all-expenses-paid vacation.'

"The assistant returned with ten people. The man told him, 'Go back and find more, and keep going back, until every bed on the yacht is taken. Let me assure you: not one person that I originally invited is going to be part of this celebration!'"

After I taught, I stayed for questions. A woman from the gym floor said, "I watched your Q&A at Georgetown. I want to make sure I understand. You're saying no matter how hard we try to be good enough, we'll never make it. We can only receive heaven as a free gift."

I walked down off the portable stage and stood level with the crowd on the floor. "You can only receive God's righteousness as a free gift, yes. Heaven just naturally follows. But it goes deeper than that. The main problem isn't that people aren't good enough. The problem is that they're dead. They're dead to God. They don't have his life inside them. And no system of laws, commandments, rituals, practices, special knowledge—no religion on the planet—can give you his life. To receive God's life, you must come to me, because I am the life. So when you put your trust in me, and I come to live in you, you have the life. Forever."

BOSTON, MASSACHUSETTS

Late in the afternoon, we drove to Orient Point on the east end of the island and took the ferry to New London, Connecticut. The next day we drove up to Boston, where I was invited to speak at a large worship house. There was a catch. Several high-ranking officials in the regional religious hierarchy wanted to meet with me afterward. I was happy to do both.

In the worship house, people filled every available square inch, packing not only the aisles but the doorways as well.

"Good thing the fire marshal isn't here," Ana commented.

All the windows to the old building were opened so people

outside could crowd around and listen. Inside, the temperature rose into the 80s. I walked to the front when I was introduced.

"Let me tell you more about the government I've come to establish," I said to them. "Have you ever seen a redwood cone?" I could see a few heads nodding. "They're about an inch long. Each cone can have up to 100 seeds. So redwood seeds are tiny. But plant one in the ground, and years later you have the largest of all trees, over three hundred feet. That's the government I'm setting up.

"My government spreads, little by little, in hidden ways. It's like a ten-year old girl who, for a school project, posted an interview on Facebook she and her dad did with a homeless man nearby. Afterward, the girl wanted to help him so badly that she started a GoFundMe account for him. Every day, the girl went to school, came home, did her homework, played, and went to bed. Meanwhile, the GoFundMe account took off; the girl wasn't sure how. First, she had raised $100, then $1000, then $10,000 for the man."

I taught for about an hour before wrapping it up with this: "There's a debate in this country as to whether citizenship really means anything. Do people coming across the border, or those overstaying their visas, have all the same rights and privileges of citizens? I'm not here to settle that debate. But let me assure you: in El Papá's kingdom, citizenship matters. You're either a citizen, with all of a citizen's rights and privileges, or you aren't, with none of them.

"At the end of the age, the angels will sort out which is which: those who are connected to El Papá, and those who aren't.

"It'll be like the dads of two ten-year-olds. The dads are sitting before a gargantuan pile of Legos. Some of the Legos are authentic Legos. Some of them are those knock-off brands. One dad says to the other, 'Should we go ahead and separate these, the good ones from the bad ones?' And the other dad replies, 'Are you kidding? Let's wait till the kids get here. They'll know exactly which are which.'

"El Papá knows those who are his. Those who have been made righteous on the inside, they'll shine like the sun in El Papá's kingdom forever. Everyone else will be left out in the dark. They'll be miserable, knowing what they missed."

I looked toward the people standing outside the windows. "I came to connect you to God. That's why I'm here. But you have to receive it. You have to put your trust in me."

After my talk, I invited people to form a line for healing. Much of the crowd did. After ten minutes, my attention was drawn to a woman standing in the line, a dozen or so people to my left. Strange, guttural noises were coming from her, and her face was contorting itself into bizarre expressions. I left the front of the line and walked over to her.

The woman looked at me with terrified eyes. "This is not me!" she said in a normal voice.

"I know," I replied.

A low, inhuman voice spoke from her. "What do you want with us, Son of God? Are you here to torture us, before the appointed time?"

"Come out of her," I commanded the demons.

"Let us go into the sewer rats below the building," they pleaded.

"If that's how you want to live, go!" I told them.

They left her, and the woman slumped to the floor. She looked up at me, peace covering her face. "They're gone," she said softly. "They're gone. I lived with them for years." We talked for a few moments. Finally, she asked, "Can I come with you?"

I knelt next to her and took her hands in mine.

"You have loved ones, do you not?"

She nodded.

"Then go home and be with them. Tell them what El Papá has done for you."

I turned to go back to the front of the line, but the worship leader was now standing in front of me. Alongside him were three other men whose robes indicated they were above him in the regional religious hierarchy.

"This house is meant for solemn worship and for the reading of God's Word," the leader said. "You're making a circus of it."

"Really?" I answered him. "Are you unhappy that that woman, whom Satan bound for years, was set free in your worship house? Stop looking at things through your religious paradigm. Look at things the way mi Papá looks at them."

"Who is your 'papá'?" one of the robed men asked.

I shook my head slowly. "You don't know me, and you don't know him. If you genuinely knew me, you'd know him, too." I glanced up at a large banner hanging from the ceiling. "You have a quote from Moses: 'Choose Life.' Do you want to choose life? Eternal life is this: that you know mi Papá—the one you say is your God—and that you know me. He and I are one."

I could see the shock on their faces.

"You're calling God your personal father," one of the men objected. "You're making yourself equal to him!"

"That's blasphemy!" the man next to him exclaimed.

"If I glorify myself," I replied, "it doesn't mean anything. Mi Papá is the one who glorifies me. You don't know him, but I do. If I said I didn't, I'd be a liar, just like you are. But I do know him, and I obey what he tells me. Long ago, mi Papá promised Abraham that all the world would be blessed through him. That promise was made to two people: to Abraham, and to me. Abraham knew that. He was thrilled at the prospect of my coming, and he saw it!"

"What?!" one of the robed men asked. "You're saying Abraham knew you personally?"

I nodded. "Before Abraham was born 4000 years ago, I am."

The worship house leader took a step toward me. "Leave now, or I will call the police."

I felt angry at their obstinance. They refused to see what was literally standing right in front of them—the one whose coming their own scriptures told them to anticipate. Yet there were plenty of people there who were willing to see.

I went outside to the street, where I stayed with the people until late at night. Finally, the Twelve and I piled into the van and headed west out of Boston. I stretched across a pair of seats, exhausted, and closed my eyes.

The sun was shining brightly when I awoke. I sat up and looked toward the front of the van. Ana was driving.

"Where are we?" I asked.

"An hour outside of Pittsburgh," Pedro responded.

Boston to Pittsburgh. That was quite a sleep. "Have we stopped for breakfast yet?"

Pedro shook his head.

"Let's find a place—maybe a truck stop on the edge of town—and see if the manager will let us use the parking lot," I said.

"For what?"

"For people who want to come."

THIRTY-ONE

That week the opposition we faced presented itself in a new form. It didn't surprise me. The Twelve brought to my attention three articles published in prominent national newspapers. The first questioned the motives of our trip to the Mexico City area, highlighting my connection with now former drug lord Rodrigo Jiménez. The second accused me of causing splits in both local worship house congregations and the national religious hierarchy. And the third one connected me to white supremacists.

"I'm connected to Mexican drug lords, white supremacists, and former BLM supporters," I said to Kiara.

She smiled at me. "I think you have most of the bases covered."

In the middle of the week, my brother Felipe texted. He wasn't happy.

Do u know reporters are asking questions about u? Even at Mamá's. Can't u keep them away from her, man?

Two days later he texted again.

Now its the FBI. The FBI!

At one big truck stop I found Pedro sitting in a booth by himself, sipping on a Coke and staring glumly ahead.

"Pedro," I said, slipping into the seat across from him. "What is it?"

He shook his head. "Some reporter came to the house. Marta talked to him. I told her to never do that, but she did."

"What'd she tell them?"

"Only good stuff," she said. "But still …"

They weren't looking for good stuff, I knew. And they had a way of making even good stuff sound questionable.

Three days later the article about Pedro came out. He'd frequently been in trouble as a teen. He'd dropped out of high school. He'd drifted from job to job, until he got fired from his water drilling job and then joined up with me. He'd never even been part of a worship house before. Marta didn't want him to leave her, but he left anyway. With insufficient money, she'd been forced to move in with her parents.

Pedro grew angrier and angrier as we talked about it. "Man, most of this stuff isn't even true! Or it's so twisted around …"

I gathered the Twelve around me before we headed out again. "Things will not be easy as we go forward. You'll be hated. You'll be slandered. You'll be persecuted because of me. You'll be tempted to let it get to you, and get down, and even quit." I looked at them one by one. "Instead, turn it around on them. When these things happen, be glad. I mean it. Let it give you genuine joy, because your reward in heaven will be a whole lot greater than the hardship you experience here."

We crossed the Midwest, a caravan of vehicles many miles long following behind us. We kept to the state highways to pass through small towns, to better interact with people. We continued to be barred from public stadiums. A few small towns let us use their high school gym or football field. One small private college let us use their football stadium.

"Inviting us here isn't very politically correct, you know," I commented to the university president before he introduced me to the crowd.

He smiled at me. "Not much of what we do here is politically correct."

A corn farmer in Illinois set up a sound system for us on a few open acres and invited me to speak. Late in the morning, Sebastian asked me, "How long do you think we'll be here?"

I shrugged. "All day, I would think."

"I'm guessing you're going to have to feed all of these people like you did in Mexico."

"I'm guessing I won't have to."

Sure enough, word got out of a huge crowd with not enough food or water. By noon, pickups and vans started arriving with hot dogs, burgers, pizza, and every drink imaginable for sale.

I took a bite out of a piece of pizza and grinned at Sebastian. "See? El Papá provides."

He laughed. "Or food vendors."

In Chicago, I began speaking on a slope at Lakefront Park, near downtown. Nearby, people were getting on a large excursion boat at a marina.

"The family of God is like that big boat over there," I told the growing crowd. "Make sure you're on the boat. The invitation is for everyone. The plank is down. All you have to do is step across it. But at some point, they'll pull back the plank, and the boat will leave, and then you'll run to the pier, shouting, 'Let us on!'

"People from all over the world will be on the boat—places you never heard of, groups you never gave a thought to—but you'll find yourself left out, fuming and disconsolate. But whose fault will it be? The boat is wide open, right now. You're invited! Walk across! Join El Papá's family!"

"How do we do that?" someone shouted.

I looked in the man's direction. "A very honest question. You walk across by faith. You trust who I am—the one El Papá promised to send."

"But what do we have to do to get ready?" he asked.

"Nothing. Absolutely nothing. You're ready to receive forgiveness, to receive El Papá's life, just like you are. It's a gift. Just reach out and receive it. That's what El Papá wants for you more than anything. Right now, you're separated from him. You're not connected to him, and so you have no real hope. Unless you believe I'm the One, you'll simply stay that way. You'll die in your sins."

"You're just condemning us!" a woman responded.

"No," I said. "I'm doing the exact opposite. El Papá didn't send me into the world to condemn it. He sent me to save it. The world is already condemned. El Papá wants to change that. That's why he gave his Son. Whoever receives me—whoever believes who I am—El Papá gives them the right to become his very own children. They're not born from two people having sex. Rather, El Papá himself gives birth to them. They're his children forever."

By this time the crowd had grown to several thousand. A smaller crowd had formed on the other side of the jogging path, next to the water, holding up protest signs.

Preach Love, Not Hate
Trans Rights Are Human Rights
Libertarians Against Theocracy

Clearly, it wasn't a single-issue protest crowd. Well, in a way it was. They were protesting me. They began to chant, trying to drown me out. In response, the crowd listening to me started booing them.

I stepped away from the mic and walked through the crowd as it parted for me. I crossed the paved running path separating the two crowds and approached the protestors. Their chanting stopped, although several individuals shouted obscenities at me.

I walked up to a young woman who had a megaphone with her. "Do you mind if I borrow that?"

She hesitated, and then gave it to me.

I held it up to my mouth and turned to the large crowd I had been speaking to. "Don't judge," I said to them. "Or you, too, will be judged. However you judge others—whatever standards you set up for them—that's how you'll be measured.

"Don't look at a spot on someone's shirt and say, 'You'd better clean that!' when your whole outfit is a muddy mess. Take care of yourself before you start insisting that others change."

Both crowds were silent. I handed the megaphone back to the young woman. A young man stood on her right holding a sign that simply said, "Resist."

"I like your sign," I said to him. "What are you resisting?"

"Oppression," he answered.

"I am, too," I responded. I held my hands out toward both crowds. "Everyone here is oppressed by sin. I've come to set you free from that."

The young man eyed me warily.

"You're not convinced," I said.

"No."

"That's OK." I leaned forward to where only he could hear me. "Come follow me. See for yourself."

The woman to his right was wearing a scarf on her head, covering her baldness, and was holding hands with a woman next to her. She looked thin and frail and was clearly being treated for cancer.

"Do you want to be well?" I asked her.

She glanced at the people around her, and then looked again at me. "The doctors say my current treatment isn't working. They're going to switch me to an experimental one."

"Do you want to be well?" I repeated.

She nodded slowly. I stepped to her and placed my hands on her head. "Be well."

I stepped back, and she looked at me incredulously. "My body feels totally right! Is that ... what did you do?" She turned to the woman next to her and they embraced and cried. "My body feels totally right!"

"Go back to your doctors and have them do a scan," I told her. "Tell them what happened to you."

She turned back to me, tears still running down her face. Slowly, she removed her scarf and revealed her bald head. "I don't think I'll need this anymore."

I smiled at her. "No, you won't."

She wiped her cheeks and took a moment to fully compose herself. "Manuel," she finally said, "I'm not much into God."

I nodded. "I know. But he's into you."

THIRTY-TWO

We stayed that night at an Airbnb near Dekalb, west of Chicago. Around 9:15, Mike knocked on the door of the room I was sharing with Justin.

"Come see something," he said.

Justin and I went into the next room, where Mike and Jorge were watching a cable news show.

"They're having a roundtable discussion about you," Mike said. The chyron read, "A Theocracy Coming to America?" Needless to say, the commentary was not positive.

"They're completely twisting things you've said," Jorge remarked. "Don't you think we should respond?"

I shook my head. "They're like stock market prognosticators saying a bull market will go on and on when a crash is right around the corner. They just don't know it. Some people will take them seriously. They'll be sorry."

The next night we were invited to stay in a large house on a lake east of Minneapolis. Late that evening, Mike, Jorge, Ana, and Dan were watching the same show.

"Manuel, are you hearing this?" Jorge called out to me.

"Hearing what?" I walked into the living room.

"They have two people on who claim to know firsthand that your healings and miracles are fake."

"Really?" I glanced at the TV. Two women were talking to the host. We listened for a couple of minutes.

"What do you think we need to do?" Dan asked.

"Nothing."

"But people believe stuff like this."

"That may be." I sat down with them. "But I'm here to do El Papá's work. I'm not here to defend myself."

Dan's lawyerliness kicked in. "But you have to counter these things right away. Otherwise, lies become ingrained in the public consciousness. Then you've got a real problem."

I shook my head. "Dan, I don't need their witness. I testify about myself, and El Papá testifies about me. That's enough."

They let the matter drop. But Dan circled back the next morning at breakfast. "They did a snap poll last night. Your approval rating dropped eight percent in one night."

I couldn't help but laugh. "Approval rating? I have an approval rating? Well, I guess that makes me important!"

"Manuel, this is no joke."

I placed my hand gently on his arm. "Dan, if I were interested in people's approval, I wouldn't be doing what I'm doing. I'm only here to accomplish El Papá's will. That's it. That's my food, to do his will. I only seek his glory. And he seeks mine." I gave a slight shrug. "That's just how we are."

Shortly after breakfast, Emma walked into the kitchen, her face pale. Her hand trembled as she stared at her phone.

"Emma," I said, rising to go over to her. "What is it?"

"Juan Carlos—" She looked up from her phone, into my eyes. "Juan Carlos has been killed."

"Killed?!" Dan asked. "In jail?"

Emma nodded. She handed me her phone to look at the news flash. There were no details about the killing. Protestors were already gathering outside courthouses in McAllen, Brownsville, and Matamoros across the border. Violence was feared.

"Who do you think killed him?" Dan asked.

I shook my head. "I don't know."

Jorge and Justin burst into the breakfast room. "Guys, did you hear this? Juan Carlos is dead."

I started getting texts from friends and family in the Valley. Then my phone rang. It was my mother.

"Manuel, estoy muy preocupado por ti. Mataron a Juan Carlos. Tengo miedo de que tú seas el siguiente. Tienes que volver a casa." *I'm worried sick about you. They killed Juan Carlos. I'm afraid you're next. You need to come home.*

If they killed Juan Carlos in the Valley, returning to the Valley was, logically, probably not the safest move. But my mother wasn't thinking that through. Either way, it didn't matter.

"Sabes que debo hacer la obra de mi Padre." *You know I must do the work of my Father.*

"¿Su padre? Él falleció." *Your father? He passed away.*

"Mi Padre celestial." *My heavenly Father.*

"Tus hermanos y tu hermana piensan que estás loco si sigues haciendo lo que estás haciendo." *Your brothers and sister think you're crazy if you keep doing what you're doing.*

By this time the Twelve had assembled. They went into the living room to let me finish the call.

"Mamá, mis verdaderos hermanos y hermanas son los que hacen la voluntad de mi Padre." *Mamá, my real brothers and sisters are those who do the will of my Father.*

She wasn't pleased, but I stood firm. "Te veré cuando regresemos al Valle." *I'll see you when we get back to the Valley.*

We hung up, and I simply sat for a moment, filled with grief. It wasn't so much that Juan Carlos and I were physically related, or that I'd known him growing up. Rather, we were spiritually related. More than anyone on the planet, Juan Carlos had been of like heart with me. And now he was gone.

Finally, I followed the Twelve into the living room. Concern was written across all of their faces. They probably wanted me to sit and talk the matter out with them, but we could do that later,

I told them. Now, I wanted to be alone, to be with Papá. I went back to my bedroom and closed the door.

Fifteen minutes later, Maya knocked. "Manuel, a line is forming outside—people wanting healing. Do you want me to tell them to go away?"

I opened the door and shook my head. "No. I'll go be with them."

I went outside and looked at a line of at least a hundred people, and growing. Among them was a boy of about eight holding a cocker spaniel puppy. He stepped toward me when it was his turn. I knelt down to his level.

"What's your name?" I asked him.

"Jeremy."

"Can I pet him?" I asked, looking at the puppy.

He nodded and I ran my hands through the soft fur. The puppy licked me and started gnawing on my thumb.

"Ow!" I said. "Sharp teeth." I looked at the boy. "He's sick, isn't he?"

He nodded slowly. "The vet says he's not going to make it. He has a bad heart valve." He looked at me with pleading eyes. "Can you help him? I know you're not a vet, but …"

I smiled at him and lifted the puppy from his arms. "That's true, but El Papá knows exactly how this one is put together. What's his name?"

"Roscoe." I held the puppy up to my face and looked him in the eye. He licked my nose. "Roscoe," I said, "Be healed."

I felt power flow out of me into the dog. He gave a little yelp and then licked me again. I looked at the boy. "Roscoe will be fine," I told him, handing the puppy back.

A big smile broke across his face and he hugged the puppy tightly. "I knew you could heal him!"

I reached out and petted Roscoe again. "Jeremy, I bet you've been training Roscoe."

"House training him, and I've tried to teach him some tricks. But he's still kind of young."

"He knows it when you walk into the room, or get home from school, doesn't he?"

He laughed. "He comes running so fast he usually falls all over himself!"

I smiled at them both. "You and I are kind of the same, you know."

He cocked his head a bit. "How so?"

"You teach Roscoe. I'm a teacher, too."

"You train dogs?"

I chuckled. "Well, no. I teach people. I teach them how to get connected to God. And then, once God comes to live in them, I teach them how to let him live through them."

I held out my hands and took Roscoe into my arms one more time. "The people who learn from me are kind of like Roscoe. They're mine, and they know it. They know my voice, and they know I take care of them. No one can take them away from me. My Dad is stronger than anyone—"

"He is?"

"He is. And no one can take them away from him."

I stayed with the crowd all day and into the evening. Finally, around 10:00, I went back inside the house. Dan was waiting for me with some food.

"I figured you'd be hungry," he said.

"Very."

We sat at the dinner table. For a couple of minutes, he simply watched me eat.

"Why do you think they killed Juan Carlos?" he finally asked.

"To send a message."

"A message to whom?"

"Me."

THIRTY-THREE

We resumed traveling westward, stopping in towns along the way. Most people greeted us with open arms. Some protested. In Montana, we tried to cross into Canada. The government denied us entry.

"I think you violated the community standards of a whole country," Dan commented wryly.

A local TV reporter caught up with us in a Browning, Montana parking lot on the way back from the Canadian border. I shocked her by granting a brief interview.

"I just wanted to say a word to the people of Canada," I said to the camera. "We tried to enter your country this morning south of Calgary, but we were denied entry." A chorus of boos erupted from the crowd around us. "I want you to know this: El Papá's offer is for you, too. It's for everyone around the world. Your government can keep me out, but it can't keep El Papá's kingdom out."

"That's right," a man behind me said.

I continued. "El Papá's kingdom is like a thunderstorm crossing the plains. There's nothing you can do to stop it. I say to you Canadians what I've said in every other place: I came to connect you to God. That's what you were designed for. That's what true life is. So change how you're thinking about him. Believe the good news."

As we crossed the Rockies, I found myself gazing endlessly out the window, amazed at what El Papá had created. I felt as if I'd never tire of taking in the peaks.

We finally got to Washington, driving across the state to an Airbnb we'd rented east of Seattle. After spending an hour or so with the crowd who had followed us, we located our bedrooms and crashed.

The next morning, I told Pedro, Sebastian, and Emma to pack lunch in a cooler for the four of us. I wanted to spend time with the three of them, alone. We drove south toward Mount Rainier. Papá arranged for us to lose our caravan at a train crossing. I knew he would.

"What's at Mount Rainier?" Pedro asked on the way. Pedro always wanted to know our specific objective wherever we went.

"Beauty," I responded. "And snow."

That caught Emma's attention. "Snow? I haven't been in snow for a while."

I looked at the other two.

"I haven't been in snow, period," Pedro said.

"Me neither," Sebastian added.

"This will be a totally new experience, then," I said. In more ways than one.

We passed through deep, old forests with majestic hundred-foot evergreens and bridges that crossed over breathtaking gorges. We rode in silence, in awe of El Papá's creation. I broke the silence after we'd crossed a bridge over the Snoqualmie River far below. "The crowds—who do they say I am?"

Sebastian answered from the back seat. "They think you're a prophet, like the ones from way back. Some say Elijah from the scriptures has returned. He healed people."

I glanced around at them. "And what do you all say?"

Pedro looked at me intently. "You're El Único. You're the Messiah, the Anointed One of God."

I smiled at him. "You didn't reach this conclusion on your own, Pedro. El Papá has made it clear to you."

We rounded a bend that opened up to a magnificent view of Mount Rainier straight ahead of us.

"Wow," Emma said.

"Yeah," I agreed. "Wow."

We rode silently for a minute, and then I spoke again. "I need to tell you all something, although it may not sink in yet. Those in power—I don't mean just government, but in all places of power—they're going to reject me."

"I think they already have," Emma noted. "Try pulling up our social media accounts."

"Well, it's going to get worse. In fact, they're going to end up killing me. But I'll rise up on the third day."

"What?!" Pedro responded. "They can't do that! That'll never happen to you."

I applied the brakes, pulled off on the shoulder, and turned and spoke to him forcefully. "Pedro, you're speaking Satan's words. You're seeing things as people would, not as El Papá does. The cup that mi Papá has given me, I must drink. It's what I came to do."

I looked around at the three of them. "Here's the deal. If you want to follow me, you have to stop seeking life your own way. Seeking life that way means you end up sacrificing real life. Why do that? What good does it do you to become a billionaire and have everything at your fingertips if you miss the real thing? But if you choose my way, and let me call the shots, you'll find true life.

"One day I'll come back in El Papá's glory, with his holy angels, and you'll see my real glory." I put the car into drive again. "But you three—to see my glory, that'll come more quickly than you imagined."

"When?" Emma asked.

But I didn't respond to her. We headed toward the mountain,

entering the national park and climbing upward. Forty minutes later we stopped at Paradise Inn, the historic lodge built on the mountain slope over a hundred years before, and started hiking up the trail. Few people were on it, though we could hear faint voices ahead of us. Half an hour later the trail opened into a wide meadow that held a surprise.

"Snow!" Emma exclaimed.

The meadow itself was green, but unmelted snow remained in the shade next to the forest. Emma ran to it and scooped some up. She looked back at us, beaming. "It's so cold!"

Pedro, Sebastian and I joined her, scooping up snow and molding it in our hands. Pedro formed a ball and tossed it at Sebastian, who returned the favor. Emma joined them in a snowball fight, while I quietly slipped over next to a tree and scooped up some snow myself. A moment later, my snowball landed on Pedro's neck, pieces falling inside his shirt collar.

"Oh!" He tried to brush it out, but his movements just made it worse. "It's freezing!" Then he looked back to see where it had come from, and spotted me standing next to the tree. "That's not fair!" he said. "It doesn't seem right to throw one at you."

"Well, you'd better make a choice," I responded before bending down, forming another ball, and throwing it at him. At which point they all threw caution to the wind. And snowballs at me.

Ten minutes later we all collapsed on the green grass nearby, laughing and trying to dry off.

"Let's go higher up," I finally suggested.

We headed up a tiny dirt trail through the tall grass. The air grew colder. We couldn't hear voices anymore. The higher up we climbed, the more snow appeared, not just along the edge of the forest, but in the fields themselves. Finally, we were actually walking through snow, leaving footprints several inches deep.

"How high are we going to go?" Pedro asked, pausing for a moment to catch his breath.

"Just a little further." I wanted to make sure we were completely alone.

We climbed another fifteen minutes before I said, "Let's stop here and pray." As I was talking with El Papá, I could feel my face changing. I looked down at my flannel shirt and jeans. They were transforming into a brilliant white, whiter even than the snow covering the field.

All three of my friends were staring at me. "Manuel, your face …" Pedro said. "It's … it's …"

Finally, all of them turned away, unable to look anymore at the shining brilliance.

"It's like …" Pedro tried to look at me again, and then quickly averted his eyes. "It's like looking at the sun!"

Suddenly two figures appeared next to me. I knew them well: Moses and Elijah, each in splendor as well. The three of us talked about my upcoming departure, and what I was about to accomplish.

The two finally departed, and as they did, a cloud moved onto the mountain with lightning speed, shrouding us all in fog. Then a booming voice came out of the cloud. "Este es mi Hijo, a quien amo. ¡Me deleita! ¡Escúchalo a él!" *This is my Son, whom I love. He delights me! Listen to him!*

The cloud dissipated. I looked at Pedro, Sebastian, and Emma. All three were on their knees in the snow, their hands in their faces, terrified. Slowly, they uncovered their faces and looked at me. My appearance had returned to normal.

"Don't be afraid," I told them. "Let's go back down. Keep what you saw to yourselves until I rise from the dead."

That evening, I told the rest of the Twelve what I had told the three. "I want you all to know—those in power, they're going to arrest me, and they're going to kill me. But after they do, on the third day, I'll rise again."

They were all stunned into silence, their heads shaking in bewilderment.

At last, Ana spoke. "Manuel … no. It's not possible."

"They can't do that, man," Diego said.

"How can that be?" Kiara asked.

"What will happen to us?" That was Jorge.

Mike finally said what they were all undoubtedly thinking. "I thought you were setting up a kingdom, a new government."

"I am. This is how it happens."

Thirty-Four

SEATTLE, WASHINGTON

The next day the Twelve and I drove into Seattle.

"I've heard this place has become an absolute dumpster," Mike commented in the van. "Homeless everywhere. Drugs everywhere. Utter filth."

"Well, don't believe everything you hear," I replied. "El Papá is working here today. That's what I know for sure. So we are, too."

We exited Interstate 5 and drove to the city center. Homeless people were, in fact, on several downtown streets, their tents lining the sidewalks. Some were clearly drug users, some were mentally ill, many were both.

We parked the van. "Let's spread out," I said. "Two by two. Just heal people. Physical illnesses. Mental illnesses. The demonic. As you go, all in my name. You may run into opposition here. Ignore them. Walk around them. You have a job to do, and it's not arguing with people." I glanced at the time. "Grab some lunch from a street vendor. Meet back here at 2:00."

I walked up and down the streets, encountering people, extending them El Papá's love. I couldn't help feeling moved by their condition. Life had completely failed to work for these people. Their need was great, and they knew it. That's why they so heartily welcomed me.

If the Twelve and I had been walking around Seattle's poshest shopping mall, the need would have been just as great, of course. Most of the people there simply wouldn't have known it.

"Everyone here knew about you!" Ana reported when we all met back at the van. "Most were willing to be helped, if we said it was in your name."

We stayed in the parking lot for two more hours, tending to people, before I hopped up on top of the van and said to the crowd, "We're going to the Jungle. You're welcome to join us there."

"The jungle?" Jorge asked in the van.

"The backside of Beacon Hill, south of here, 150 acres," I answered. "The biggest homeless encampment in the city. But first, find the nearest Walmart, will you?"

"What for?" Pedro asked.

"As of now, we're homeless, too. We need two cheap 8-person tents, 13 cheap sleeping bags, and a giant cooler. And someone locate a fast-food place, will you?"

An hour and a half later, we got to the park and set up tents and the portable sound system under the elevated Interstate 5. Word got around. Many of the homeless started drifting over. Supporters from the Seattle area showed up. So did protestors. The crowd grew to several thousand. I finally took a mic in hand.

"I'm here today to tell you that the kingdom of God has come to you. All of you." I looked at protestors standing behind a large, rainbow-colored banner that read: God Includes Everyone. "I see the banner some of you brought here today. El Papá does reach out to everyone: to black, white, Asian, Latino, indigenous. To L, G, B, T, and Q." Some of the crowd broke into applause. "To the rich"—a chorus of boos—"and especially to the poor." More applause. "There's no person I'm not here for. And no person who receives me will ever be excluded from El Papá's kingdom."

"That's right!" someone shouted.

"I want to speak especially to those of you who camp out here in the Jungle. You may think this society has passed you over. It doesn't care about you. You're out of sight, out of mind. And you're right. You are out of sight, out of mind to this world. But not to El Papá. You're very much on his mind, all the time.

"I'll tell you a quick story. Not long ago there was an old guy who stayed in a place like this down in California. But not far away was a rich neighborhood, full of mansions. So, he set up on the sidewalk by the entrance to the rich neighborhood. Every day he'd sit there, begging as the Porsches drove by. But no one ever gave him anything. The only ones who paid him any attention were the neighborhood dogs, who would sometimes pee on him while he slept.

"One night the old guy died and went to heaven. That same night one of the rich people had an unexpected heart attack and died, too. He went to hell's flames. But from hell he was enabled to look into heaven. He saw an angel, and said, 'Please, go warn my family not to come here. I'm in agony!'

"'No,' the angel said, 'they're too preoccupied with the things of earth. They won't listen.'

"'Then send me back, just for a minute!' the man cried. 'I'll warn them! They'll listen to me if I come back from the dead.'

"But the angel shook his head. 'God has already told them the truth in the scriptures. If they won't listen to God, why would they listen if someone comes back from the dead?'

"I tell you plainly: if you are here, homeless, you can be richer than the billionaire across town. Because all of God's inheritance is for you. This world may not offer you anything, but El Papá offers you everything."

I taught and healed people for two more hours, and then I said to the crowd, "I'm guessing some people are hungry." The crowd shouted in the affirmative.

"All right. Give us a minute." I turned to Diego. "Grab the stuff out of the cooler, will you?"

"You mean that one sub sandwich and that single bottle of water?"

I smiled at him. "Exactly."

Diego returned with the sandwich and the water. "I was wondering what we were going to do with this."

"We're all going to eat and drink."

An hour later, I stood up and turned on the mic again. "Did everyone get enough sandwiches?"

"Yes!" the crowd shouted back.

"Great! I'm glad." I paused for a moment. "I want to say one more thing to you all. I said a little while ago that El Papá doesn't exclude anyone. That's true. He loved the world so much that he sent his one and only Son into the world, so that whoever believes in him would not perish, but have eternal life. El Papá wants everyone to be saved. He wants all to be included. But people exclude themselves. They reject what El Papá is offering them. Don't do that. Receive what El Papá is offering. You didn't have a problem accepting those sandwiches, did you?"

"No!" a couple of people shouted out.

"Of course not. In the grand scheme, that was nothing. Make sure you accept the real gift El Papá is offering."

THIRTY-FIVE

We stayed in the Jungle four days. On the fifth, we began a phase of our journey that I'd been looking forward to for some time. The previous five months had been such a whirlwind of traveling around the country that the group and I needed two things: time simply to slow down and rest, and time away together, when I could focus on training just the twelve of them. Now was that time. And El Papá had provided just the place for it.

We drove back north through Seattle, dropped the van with some friends of friends, and successfully traveled by boat, unfollowed, to the expansive vacation home of a supporter on one of the privately owned San Juan Islands.

"Send out a post for me, will you?" I said to Sofia as we got on the boat.

She shot me a surprised look. "You? You want to send out a message? On X? Chido." *Cool.* I'd never asked her to send one before.

"Say this," I said.

I'm spending some alone time with my little group. We'll see you all in six weeks. California, we'll be heading your way!

I'd informed the Twelve what the plan was several weeks before. I think they were looking forward to the time together as much as I was. We had to double up in bedrooms at the house, but the place was delightful, providing all the space and recreation that we could have wanted. Ana, we discovered, was unbeatable at corn hole. Jorge usually won at horseshoes. Dan couldn't be beat at bumper pool. And Emma and Kiara made a dynamite pickle ball team.

For me, our away time provided the opportunity to teach them, day after day, everything I could about El Papá, and about being in his family. Through our months together on the road, they had gradually caught on to many of the things I'd been saying. Now their greater understanding, though still incomplete, began to be evident.

One morning, Maya sat down across from me at the breakfast table.

"Do you remember a few months ago, back in Texas, when Pedro kept getting mad at Diego for waking up too early? And you told a story about forgiveness?"

"Sure."

"Well." She paused. I could tell her mind was churning. "You've been telling us over and over that everything in El Papá's family comes through grace. It's all a gift. But in that story, it seemed like God's forgiveness depended on us forgiving others. Is that what you were saying, or am I hearing it wrong?"

I loved it. Maya was starting to understand the difference between the arrangement El Papá had had with people for thousands of years, and the new arrangement I came to usher in. "The point of that story wasn't about earning El Papá's forgiveness by forgiving others enough. It was about the incredible forgiveness El Papá offers, and what that means for how you treat others."

Kiara joined us at the table, and I had a sip of coffee before continuing.

"But you raise a great point. Under the old system, yes, God's forgiveness is conditional. And it's temporary, so people have

had to ask for it over and over. Which is why I came to bring a
new system. No one could actually make it under the old system.
Who can forgive perfectly? And who wants to live constantly
wondering if they are still forgiven?"

"No one," Maya said.

"Exactly. The Law came through Moses, Maya. Grace and
truth—and El Papá's total, permanent forgiveness—come
through me."

During much of our time there, I focused my instruction on
one thing: El Papá's upcoming fulfillment of his 4000-year-old
promise concerning all of humanity.

"God promised an incredible blessing to all the nations, all
the earth," I told them. "It's been his plan for humanity all along.
Now, that blessing is about to come to pass. The Holy Spirit is
about to be given. God himself is going to come live in people.
The Spirit. El Papá. Me. We are all about to come live in those
who receive me. And when we do, that will change everything."

They had all grown up in a world in which people were
separated from God. Even the religious system reflected that
separation. You had to do certain things to approach God. To
get clean enough for him. To get your heart right so he would
hear you, or accept your sacrifice, or forgive you. You had to work
to get close to God. But it was never enough.

Now, all of that was going away. I would do all those things
for them. I was ushering in a completely new system.

They would have a hard time letting go of the old system, I
knew. It was familiar. It was comfortable. Throwing off its trap-
pings would be challenging. But I was laying the groundwork for
them to do just that. When I said I was making all things new
between God and humanity, they had no idea just how much I
meant it.

Every day, I taught, they asked questions, I answered, they

asked more questions. They learned, and relaxed, and played, and grew together as a team.

Our time on the island provided me with plenty of time alone with El Papá as well. The longer our trip had gone on, the more I found myself missing how much time we used to have together, just the two of us.

"Papá," I said to him one night, "This group—I know they're yours. I love teaching them about what our family is like, what it will be like for them from now on. I love being able to share all my joy with them."

"My joy, too," I heard him say.

One day I was watching Pedro try to feed a chipmunk a cracker when Sebastian walked up.

"Hey!" Pedro objected. "You'll scare him off!"

Sure enough, the chipmunk scurried away. It got me thinking, though. That night, when we were all gathered in the living room, I asked the Twelve, "Has everyone seen chipmunks around here?"

They all nodded.

"Do they come up to you to be petted?"

Ana chuckled. "Hardly."

"Why not?"

"They don't trust us. They're too skittish."

"They don't know your intentions, do they? And you're about a thousand times as big. What could make them trust you?"

None of them seemed to have a good answer. "They're wild rodents, man," Diego said.

I let them ponder a moment longer, and then I said, "What if you became a chipmunk, and hung out with them, and communicated with them? Could they come to understand your intentions? Come to trust you?"

I saw heads nodding. "If we became chipmunks, sure," Ana replied. "They'd trust us."

"Well, that's what I've done," I said. "I became human,

became one of you, so you could know El Papá. Know his heart for you. His love for you. His incredible intentions toward you. I came, so you could relate to him."

We all sat for a moment as they took that in. And then Kiara added, "And so you could relate to us." Which was gold.

I loved our extended time together in the San Juans. I was conversing with El Papá the night before we left. "You're Lord of heaven and earth," I said to him. "The things we've all been talking about here—I praise you for hiding these things from those the world considers wise, and revealing them to little children. That pleases you, I can tell."

In my spirit, I felt his smile. "It does please me."

PORTLAND, OREGON

Our time in the San Juan Islands achieved exactly what I'd wanted it to. Everyone came away refreshed, the Twelve came away better prepared for what was ahead, and we all came away feeling closer than we ever had before.

We picked up the van and drove back through Seattle, heading south toward Portland. Halfway there, Emma walked toward the front of the van and sat next to me.

"Word's gotten out that we're heading to Portland. Protestors have shut down the Columbia River bridge heading downtown."

"Welcome back to the real world," Dan commented from the driver's seat.

I pulled out my phone and looked at our route options. "Then let's take 205 around the east. There's a state park on the south side."

Dan took the 205 exit.

"Manuel," Emma said, "why do you think people protest you like this? Can't they see you're on their side?"

I shook my head sadly. "No, they can't. Not as long as they're believing lies. Lies will enslave them, until they're ready for the truth."

We pitched tents at the state park. Word got out and a crowd joined us, staying there with us for three days. We slipped back into our usual routine. I was up from dawn until almost midnight every day, teaching and healing.

As the sun set on the third day, I told the crowd I was taking a break. I invited Pedro to join me on a small pier that jutted out into the lake. I could tell something was troubling him.

"I miss Marta," he said.

I nodded. "I'm sure she misses you, too."

"She does."

"I know it's hard being apart. It's been seven months."

We sat silently, looking at the sun's rays reflecting off the water. Finally, I spoke. "We'll be back home soon, you know. A month, maybe."

"We will?"

"Well, you will. I wouldn't exactly say I have a home anymore. El Papá's my home. He's where I live."

THIRTY-SIX

We left Portland early the next morning and drove south on Interstate 5 for six hours. Our destination: Mount Shasta in northern California. I was simply following El Papá's lead. I had some things to teach the Twelve, and this was the ideal place to do it. As usual, a caravan stretched miles behind us. We exited the interstate north of Redding and took a road that dead-ended at a one-story gift shop with a sign that read: *Lake Shasta Caverns Tours*.

Maya, who had arranged a group tour for us beforehand, went inside to handle last-minute details. The rest of us stayed outside, attending to caravan people who had managed to squeeze their vehicles into the parking lot.

Fifteen minutes later, Maya returned.

"They're ready," she announced.

The Twelve and I walked through the gift shop, past the adjoining café, and out onto a pier. The boat ride across the lake, to the foothills of Mount Shasta, only took ten minutes. But it was enough time for Pedro and Jorge to get into a heated argument at the back of the boat. Earlier, I'd noticed them arguing in the van.

The boat docked and we stood in a loose circle onshore, waiting for a tour company bus to take us 900 feet up the mountain to the cave entrance.

"What were you two guys arguing about on the boat?" I asked Pedro and Jorge. The two looked at their feet and remained silent.

"Well?"

"They were arguing about who'd be more qualified to be your number two guy when you start running things. Your government, I mean," Kiara said.

Pedro looked at me. "It's gonna take real work. I have the most experience doing real work. Plus, I'm married. That gives me more real-people experience than Jorge. Isn't that what we're about, real people?"

"An operation this size is going to take financial acumen," Jorge responded. "I'm the only one qualified. I have a master's degree in finance."

"Today's world means handling social media," Sofia interjected. "That's me."

Kiara shook her head. "I don't think either one of you guys is qualified." She got a couple of *yeahs* from the group. "Besides, where do you get off making Manuel's decisions for him?"

"And leaving us out," Mike added.

"Exactamente," Ana agreed.

"Stop," I said. The whole group looked at me. "The world—it's all about power. Who controls. Who calls the shots. Who can benefit the most from knowing those who call the shots."

I walked over to some nearby boulders and sat down. The Twelve followed me.

"It's not that way with us," I continued. "It never will be. If any of you really wants to be great, wants to be first, wants to benefit the most—you'll become the servant of all the rest. You're talking about being my number two man"—I glanced at Kiara and Maya sitting nearby—"or woman. That assumes I'm number one. And you're right. I am. But I didn't come here to be served. I came to serve. I came to give my life as a ransom for many."

I looked around at them. All of them seemed to be tracking

with what I was saying. All except Jorge who, I could tell, was still pouting from the argument.

The bus arrived and we rode upward in silence, looking at the magnificent scenery of the deep blue lake and the mountains around us. When we exited at the front of the cave, I could tell the group was still a bit subdued.

"Hey, you guys, perk up," I said. "El Papá made this mountain just for you."

That elicited a few smiles.

The guide gave us some instructions and we followed him into the rock tunnel. It was barely seven feet high, without much room to spare on either side. "These caves were discovered in 1878 by a local explorer, James A. Richardson," he said. He led us to a ladder that disappeared up a narrow passage. "He didn't have the advantage of ladders and stairs. Be prepared—these are the first of over 600 steps up or down." We followed him up the ladder and into the Crystal Room, a cavern filled with stalactites and stalagmites bathed in dim artificial lighting.

I could tell the group was awed by all they were seeing, and they peppered the guide with questions. Fortunately, they seemed to have left the prior conflict behind.

Twenty minutes later we stood in the Basement Room, the lowest cavern. I waited until all of them were inside and then asked the guide, "Are we ready?"

The guide nodded, bent down, and flipped a switch along the side of the pathway railing. Suddenly every light in the cavern went off, and the group stood in complete darkness.

"¡Guau!" Sebastian said. *Wow.*

"I can't even see my hand in front of my face," Diego commented.

I let them experience the total darkness for a minute before speaking. "Men love the darkness. They love the darkness, and they hate the light, because their deeds are evil, and they don't want them exposed. But there's good news."

I reached into my pocket, pulled out my phone, and turned the flashlight on under my face. "I'm the light of the world. The light shines in the darkness, but the darkness never understands it. The light I bring enlightens every person. No one who believes in me remains in darkness. Anyone who follows me, he won't walk in darkness. He has the light of life."

I looked around at them all in the dimness, my heart swelling with love for each of them. "The light is among you for a little while longer. While it is, walk in the light." I turned the flashlight off. "Don't let darkness overtake you. If you do, you'll have no idea where you're going."

The guide switched the lights back on. We all stood staring at one another. And then I noticed the formation on the far side of the cavern room. "I love that cluster of stalactites," I said, pointing. "It looks like a pipe organ."

"Or Thanos's beard," Jorge added. Everyone gave him confused looks. "It does. Can't you see that?"

Half an hour later we were back on the bus, heading to the boat. Mike sat next to me.

"How did you arrange all of this?" he asked.

"Maya did it."

"And how did you know they could turn off the lights?"

"Maya asked them."

Mike thought for a moment. "Sounds like today Maya might be the greatest of us."

I smiled. "Sounds like it."

When the boat arrived, I said to them, "You all get on the boat. I'm going to stay here and be with mi Papá. Tomorrow's a big day."

"How are you going to get back?" Maya asked. "This is the last boat."

"Don't worry, I'll rejoin you."

Pedro glanced across the lake. "What—you gonna swim?"

"Go," I responded. "Get a bite at the café. Then wait for me on the dock."

They walked to the boat and departed. I sat on one of the nearby boulders and talked with El Papá. The next day would start a new phase of our journey. I needed to hear from him.

Two hours later, after dark, I started walking across the lake. As I approached the dock, I could hear the Twelve talking in the distance. Sofia finally spotted me.

"There's someone on the water," she said, her voice carrying across the water.

"What do you mean, someone?" Mike responded.

"Look." She pointed toward me in the dark. "I think that's a person. Walking on the lake."

"Are you loco?" That was Diego.

"Maybe it's Manuel," Ana said.

"How could Manuel be walking on the lake?" Pedro asked, looking in my direction as well. "That's impossible."

I stopped where I was. "Pedro!" I called out.

Nobody said a word. Finally, Pedro responded. "Manuel?"

"It's me."

He waited for a few moments, and then he spoke again. "Can I come out to you?"

I loved it. Pedro, I knew, couldn't swim. Yet here he was, believing God could enable him to do the impossible.

"Come," I said. "And keep your eyes fixed on me."

In the dim light of the dock, I saw him look at the others, and then back toward me. Gingerly, he stepped off the pier and onto the water. He hesitated for a moment, and then he took a step, then another, then another.

The Twelve let out whoops from the pier. Pedro turned and looked back at them, and then he started sinking like a rock. "Manuel!" he cried.

I was immediately next to him, my hand holding his arm,

pulling him out of the water. He straightened up and we looked into each other's eyes, friend to friend.

"How did that happen?" he asked. "I took three steps!"

I laughed. "That's nothing. Next time, be sure to keep your eyes on me."

Thirty-Seven

That evening, David Patterson, FBI Deputy Director, received an email from the director of the Sacramento field office. It was unexpected, but he'd prepared beforehand for just such an email. He poured himself a cup of coffee and took a few minutes to think it through. But the appropriate action was clear. He sent a brief reply that included four directives.

- Tell me what else you know about this source.
- Assure him that we will keep all correspondence confidential.
- Immediately forward me any communications you receive.
- Do not send replies prior to you and I personally discussing and drafting.

Then he sent a cryptic message to his boss, Chris Ottenger.

We have an informant near Manuel Gonzales. Very near. Finally.

Thirty-Eight

I met the next morning with the caravan crowd in an abandoned parking lot on the south side of Redding, California. Diego and Justin set up the portable sound system in front of two old school buses. People sat on the hoods of their cars and on their pickup tailgates to listen.

"Good morning!" I began.

"Good morning!" the crowd shouted back.

"Some of you have joined us here in California because you or a loved one with you is seeking healing. We won't leave without taking care of that."

The crowd whooped and applauded.

"But we stopped here to take care of something else as well. Some of you have been traveling with us a long time—a few of you, all the way back to when we started in Dallas many months ago. And I've come to know many of you personally along the way.

"Here's what we're doing. We're heading to L.A. I'd like to choose 72 of you to go through L.A. this weekend and do what I do. Share the message of El Papá's family. Heal the sick. Cast out demons. You've seen me do it. Now I want you to do it. I'm not going to be around, physically at least, forever. El Papá wants people to be his hands and feet. That's you."

I pointed to the school buses behind me. "We've rented these buses. I'm going to go through the crowd and pick people. You'll ride together on the buses, and on the way down I'll spend time with you, giving more training and instructions. We'll feed you on the way down. If you have to leave a vehicle here, we'll bring you back on the buses."

I paused and grinned. "Is this a little scary?"

"Yes!" the crowd shouted back.

I laughed. "I know. But we have to start somewhere, don't we?"

I handed the mic to Sebastian and started going through the crowd, healing people and selecting others as I went. An hour and a half later, the 72 filled the two buses. The Twelve boarded the van. I walked to the driver's window to give Kiara instructions.

"Head straight down I5. Let's stop every two hours for bathroom breaks." I thumped my hand against the van's side. "See you in LA."

"These people have no idea what's about to happen," she commented.

I smiled. "Isn't it great?"

I hopped on the first bus and we all headed south.

LOS ANGELES, CALIFORNIA

Seven hours later, before dusk, we stopped at the edge of South Los Angeles, a 51 square-mile area of racially mixed, working-class residents. I hopped off the second bus. The 72 huddled around me.

I motioned for quiet. "Look, no one knows who the Son is except El Papá. And no one knows who El Papá really is except the Son—and those I reveal him to. You now know. The people who live here, they need to know, too.

"So don't be afraid. Every one of you can be tracked and seen at all times."

"We can?" a woman asked.

I smiled. "Don't you think El Papá knows right where you

are? And don't you think his security forces are here in strength for you?"

People smiled back at me nervously.

"We'll drop you off two by two every few blocks. Women, be paired with a man. Go to houses. Ask if anyone needs healing. Tell them the good news—El Papá wants to be connected with them, permanently, and I've come to make that happen. There are lots of drug users in LA, to say nothing of other horrors. Some have invited in demons. Cast them out."

I glanced at the van in back of me. "And, before you go, leave your wallets and your phones in the van."

A look of shock swept across the group.

"Our phones?" a woman asked, bewildered.

"You won't need them."

"What if we get lost?" another asked.

"In 48 hours meet at the Exposition Park west side parking lot. Anyone in this part of town can direct you. I'll be there."

"What if we have an emergency?"

"Borrow a phone. Almost everyone has one."

"What if we can't find a place to stay?" a man ventured.

"You will. El Papá provides." I stepped toward the first bus. "OK, drop your things at the van and then let's head out."

Half an hour later, the bus I was on let off its last pair. Ana looked at me from the driver's seat. "I hope this goes OK."

"How did it go for you down in Los Bordos? El Papá hasn't changed."

I had the Twelve fan out around Exposition Park for the weekend, just as they had done in Mexico. I spent the night at the house of a couple who had been supporting us financially for a number of months. The next morning, I borrowed their car to drive to my destination for the weekend: the largest nationwide conference of religious leaders. The attendees at this event, all 3,000 of them, were the people that individual worship house leaders reported to.

After my speech in Dallas, they'd invited me to speak at their annual meeting. Though some present would oppose me, some would listen and, in time, follow. Those were the ones I came for.

I was the second speaker of the morning, squeezed in between a PowerPoint presentation on social media marketing and a panel discussion on proposed amendments to the conference's constitution. A rather odd sequence, I thought, but El Papá often works in tight squeezes.

After the first presentation, the emcee stepped to the microphone. "We have invited Manuel Gonzales from McAllen, Texas, to say a few words to the assembly," he said before walking back off the stage. Not exactly a warm welcome, but probably representative of the attitude of many, if not most, of the attendees.

No doubt, serving God and his people was the priority for many in the audience. But more than anything, religion was this group's profession. It provided their salaries. It provided their identity. It provided their status in the culture—a standing that, however humble in a mostly secular society, they didn't want threatened. I had the potential to threaten it. Most of them probably expected me to threaten it. They were right.

I walked to the microphone and looked out over the crowd. Despite the hard hearts I expected, I was thrilled at the message I had for them—a message far more amazing than what Moses brought down from the mountain. "I have a few words to say, and then I'm sure some of you have questions. A long time ago, through Jeremiah, El Papá promised that one day he would give humanity an amazing gift. He would set aside the law-based relationship he had with people, and usher in a Spirit-based relationship instead. He said:

'One day I'll make a new covenant with you. It won't be like the covenant I made with my people a long time ago, when I led them out of Egypt. Instead, I'll put my law within you, and write it on your hearts. I'll be your God, and you'll be my people. You won't say to each other, "Get to know God!" because you'll all know me firsthand, from the least of you to the greatest. I'll forgive your sins completely; I won't even remember them anymore!'

"Here's what else he said he would do, through Ezekiel:

'I will sprinkle clean water on you, and you will be clean. I will give you a new heart, and I will put a new spirit in you. I will take out your stony, stubborn heart and I will give you a tender, responsive heart. And then I will put my Spirit in you. I myself will cause you to walk in my ways.'

"Now," I said, "did you notice something about this amazing thing that El Papá promised? He does it. He does it all. 'I will,' he says. 'I will. I will. I will.' El Papá does it. You receive it. You receive it all, as a gift. That's the only way it's offered."

I looked intently around the auditorium before continuing. "I'm here to tell you today—the time is fulfilled. I myself am ushering in this new arrangement. From this time forward, how El Papá relates to the human race is forever changed. He has sent his one and only Son to make it happen. Until now, people have been disconnected from God. I've come to connect them to him. Until now, people have lived in spiritual death. I've come to give them life—the very life of God. Whoever receives me, receives this life. Because I am the life."

"Blasphemy!" a man toward the back shouted, jumping to his feet.

"This is what God promised!" another nearby shouted at him.

The entire assembly erupted into heated debate. After several minutes the emcee came to the mic and tapped on it several times. "Ladies and gentlemen." The crowd quieted down.

"Everyone please be seated. Our schedule this morning does not allocate time for impromptu discussion. So, let's have our brief Q &A, and we will move on to the next agenda item. Do we have specific questions for Mr. Gonzales?"

A man near the front stood. "Some people say the things you're doing, you do by the power of Satan."

I stepped back to the mic. "Be very careful, sir. Don't attribute what the Holy Spirit does to Satan. That truly is blasphemy."

A woman near the back stood and waited for a mic to be brought to her. "Why don't I ever hear you telling people to do the rituals and practices that God wants them to?"

"That's an excellent question," I responded. "I'll tell you. Most people do religious things to make themselves feel acceptable to God. That's a wrong motivation. Doing religious stuff doesn't make anyone right with El Papá. Many religious activities are simply the traditions of men. But the ones El Papá actually gave you, they have one overarching purpose: they point to me. They were a shadow; I'm the substance. Embrace the substance."

"But what about things like the Sabbath?" the woman asked.

"I'm the true Sabbath. I will give you rest. If you're worn out and weighed down in life, come to me. Learn from me, and you'll find rest for your soul. Being joined to me isn't burdensome. It's easy. It's how you were meant to operate."

The auditorium was quiet. An older man finally stood. "Who gave you the authority to do the things you're doing?"

"I'll ask you a question," I responded. "Juan Carlos—who gave him the authority to do what he was doing at the Rio Grande?"

The man glanced at those around him, and then shrugged. "I don't know."

"If that's not apparent to you, it won't do you any good for me to answer your question."

A woman in the middle of the room rose. "Can you tell us

plainly—are you the Chosen One, the one people along the border call El Único?"

"I have told you. The works that I do in El Papá's name, these tell you. What else do you need to see? But most of you haven't believed. How can you believe if what you're mainly seeking is other people's approval?"

The emcee walked across the stage and motioned for the mic. I handed it to him.

"OK," the emcee said to the crowd. "Why don't we take a 15-minute break, and at 10:45 we will start our panel discussion on amendments to the association's constitution."

A hand went up along the right side of the auditorium. It belonged to a man of about sixty in a wheelchair. "Yes, the gentleman in the blue shirt," the emcee said.

"I have one last question for Manuel," the man said.

The emcee sighed. "Very well, one more."

The man looked at me. "Can you make me walk again?"

I reached for the mic. "It depends," I said. "Is this a genuine request, or is this a test?"

The man looked around at the crowd. He had known many of the people there for years, no doubt. For me to perform a miracle at their own conference was the last thing most of them wanted. But apparently the man didn't care. "It's a genuine request."

I handed the mic back to the emcee and walked down the stage steps and around to the man. I squatted down in front of him. "Do you believe I'm able to do this?" I asked him.

"I do believe!" He hesitated for a moment. "But if I don't … can you help my unbelief?"

I smiled and gripped his hand in mine. "Then I say to you, get up, and walk."

The man stood up from his wheelchair. And then he started walking.

Thirty-Nine

Early Sunday evening, I reunited with the Twelve, and with the 72. The 72 reported exactly what the Twelve had reported after going through Los Bordos. "Even sickness and disease are subject to us in your name! And the demonic!"

"Of course they are," I replied. "But I'll tell you what I told the Twelve in Mexico. Don't rejoice in that. Rejoice that you receive life from El Papá."

I glanced at the time. "OK, we need to send some of you, and the two buses, back to Redding. The rest of you are invited to follow the van. I want to be preaching tonight by midnight."

"Midnight?" Pedro asked. "Who's gonna be up to listen at midnight?"

I grinned at him. "Trust me, they'll be up at midnight."

I drove the van that night. Most of the Twelve fell asleep, exhausted from the weekend in South L.A. Before sleeping, though, Emma joined me up front, phone in hand.

"The talking heads are speculating about what we were doing in L.A.," she said.

"I know what we were doing in L.A."

"They're saying we were doing field work for next year's presidential campaign. Or for the Reconquista."

I smiled at her in the rear-view mirror. "Is that what you were doing all weekend?"

Near midnight, I pulled the van into a parking lot. "Good morning, everyone!"

The group awoke and groggily looked around them. "Where are we?"

"The Strip," I replied.

Kiara yawned. "What strip?"

"The Las Vegas Strip."

LAS VEGAS, NEVADA

We got out of the van and walked toward the hotel/casinos. Even in the dark, people began recognizing me. By the time we reached the expansive fountains in front of the Bellagio, a small crowd accompanied us. We veered onto the walkway between the fountains and the hotel, and I hopped up on its stone ledge, facing the gathering.

"A man and his wife ran a small chain of postal stores," I told them. "Their two sons helped them run the business. The couple went on a week-long cruise, but before they left, the man instructed both of his sons to inventory the stores while they were gone. The first son said, 'Of course, Dad,' but he never got around to doing it. The second son shook his head and said, 'Sorry, I'm busy this week.' But after they left, he regretted his reply and he himself inventoried all three stores. Now, which of the two sons did what his father asked him to do?"

Someone shouted out a garbled reply: "I would say ... the second one!"

"Right," I replied. "And it's a good thing you're not driving tonight."

The crowd laughed.

I continued. "Let me tell you, a lot of you people are going to get into El Papá's kingdom before the religious leaders ever do."

A few in the crowd whooped.

"Religious people think they're doing El Papá's work, but the real work he's giving people right now is this: to believe in the one he's sent. That's it.

"Make sure you take full advantage of the opportunity El Papá is giving you. Don't harden your heart! If you do, you may lose even the ability to believe. Respond to him. It's like a rich guy who splits his money among three investment advisors. He says to them, 'I'm taking a year off to sail around the world. Do your thing with my money while I'm gone.'

"A year later he shows up. The first advisor shows him a 30 percent gain on his money. 'Great job!' the rich guy says. The second shows him a 20 percent gain. 'Great job!' the rich guy says. The third guy shows him his financial statement and says, 'See, I put all of your money in a savings account. I didn't lose a penny!' And the rich guy says, 'You're fired!'

"El Papá wants you to do something with the opportunity he's giving you. He wants you to be connected to him. Make sure you respond!"

A man in a suit wormed his way through the crowd, to right below where I was standing. "Mr. Gonzales …"

I looked down at him.

"The management of my hotel would like to invite you inside."

"To gamble?"

The man smiled. "No, to use the main ballroom for your audience."

It seemed like an odd invitation from a casino, but in this case, I realized that our goals aligned. The casino's goal was to get as many people as possible through the door, and to generate publicity. My goal was to bring El Papá's invitation to people who go to casinos. What better way than to go inside a casino?

I accepted. Five minutes later, I walked into the ballroom with a crowd that had grown to many hundred. The hotel crew was still setting up chairs and the sound system. More people, hearing of my arrival, kept coming through the door, including a few in their pajamas. When the mic was ready, I stood and faced the crowd.

"Many of you have been gambling a lot of money here in Las Vegas. Some of you have lost a lot of money. Some of you have even lost the clothes off your back, which is why you're now wearing pajamas."

People laughed and looked around at the pajama-wearers.

"But I want to tell you about a for-sure bet. It's like the casino saying you can win at blackjack by drawing unlimited cards and going *over* 21. You can't lose.

"I know people expect me to come to Las Vegas and rail against people gambling and living sinfully. But I didn't come to Las Vegas—or anywhere else, for that matter—to condemn anyone.

"I'll tell you what I'm here to rail against: zombies. I'm serious. El Papá didn't create people to live as zombies—dead people, walking around as if they had life. Zombies have no real purpose. Humans aren't supposed to be zombies. It's unnatural."

Some people in the audience were nodding.

"Did you ever see *The Walking Dead*, or one of the zombie movies? If you did, you were looking in a mirror. Those zombies are you. I'm not being metaphorical here. I'm telling you straight. You were born into this world disconnected from God. Everyone is. You don't have the life of God in you. Until El Papá infuses his life into you, you're a zombie. You're a dead person, walking around, trying to find life."

I had everyone's full attention by now.

"Here's the sure bet. I am the life. When you receive me, when you put your trust in me, I'll come to live within you. You'll have the life. Guaranteed. Just as life comes to me from El Papá, so life will come to you from me. And you'll live forever."

When I finished talking, local reporters, who had been gathering at the back of the ballroom, rushed forward to interview me. A man about my age pushed a microphone in my face. "Manuel, some people might take offense at you speaking to people inside a casino. How would you respond?"

It was a question I was happy to answer. "I'd simply say this: I came for people who don't know El Papá, to connect them to him. Including people in casinos. That's who El Papá wants to be connected to."

HOOVER DAM

The next morning a hit piece appeared in the online version of a local newspaper. *That was quick*, I thought. But not unexpected. Two women claimed I had come on to them at the hotel. I was surprised they hadn't claimed more than that.

The Twelve were indignant. "You were with us the whole night!"

"This isn't about facts," I told them. "It's about managing perceptions."

Sure enough, Dan informed me that in a snap poll conducted later that day, my approval rating, which apparently had been dropping, was down another six points. "But 38 percent said they were with you no matter what."

"That'll go down, too," I said to him. "In the end, everyone will fall away."

"Not everyone," Pedro objected. "At least, not me."

I put my hand on his shoulder. "Especially you, Pedro."

Pedro was so upset that I'd think that about him. "Manuel, I can't believe you'd say that!"

But I knew.

We headed toward the Grand Canyon that day, passing Hoover Dam, where we stopped and took in the spectacular view.

Visitors began to realize who was there and a crowd gathered. A woman walked up and shook my hand. "I've always wanted to visit Hoover Dam. I just didn't expect to see something here even greater."

I nodded to her. "That you recognize who's here with you—that's a gift from El Papá."

We stood looking over the top of the dam, the water cascading down below us. A man toward the back shouted, "Manuel, the town where I live, south of here, is dry as a bone. Do you think you could divert some of this water that way?"

The crowd chuckled at his request. I turned and smiled at him. "I'm guessing that's a zero-sum proposition. Take it from one town, give it to another. But I'll tell you what's not a zero-sum proposition: the water I came to give. I have an infinite supply. If you're thirsty, come to me. Drink fully—as much as you can. Once you do, from your own heart will gush more life-giving water than this dam could ever provide."

"How is that even possible?" another man asked.

"It's simple," I replied. "The Spirit himself will come live inside you. And he never stops gushing life."

FORTY

We arrived at the Grand Canyon's South Rim the next morning. I wanted to spend some more one-on-one time with the Twelve, so Ana had arranged a mule ride for us down into the canyon. The ride would provide a needed respite from the crowds.

The Twelve stood in awe when they walked to the edge of the canyon. Several in the group had been to Big Bend, and in the mountains in northern Mexico. None had seen anything like this. I hadn't, either.

We met with our guides, Jack and Wyatt, who gave us instructions as we mounted the mules. We'd ride for an hour down into the canyon, have a snack break, and then ride back up.

The trail didn't feel too steep, though at an average 15 percent grade, hiking back up on foot would have been a workout. But if the steepness didn't bother several of the Twelve, the narrowness of the path definitely did. Much of it was only wide enough for a single mule, which for most of the trail was fine. In numerous stretches, however, the edge of the trail bordered on cliffs hundreds of feet tall.

"Why don't these mules scoot away from the edge a little more?" Jorge asked nervously.

Jack, at the front of the pack, chuckled. "It only seems like they're about to go over. They know what they're doing."

Jorge was trying to look straight ahead instead of down into the canyon. "Has, uh, has one ever fallen in?"

"Just once since we've been operating," Jack replied, "but that wasn't the mule's fault."

Jorge didn't seem comforted.

Jorge's fears notwithstanding, we all made it down to the rest spot and slid off our mules, stretching sore leg muscles. The guides handed out water bottles and snacks before everyone sat down together.

"Well, we survived," Emma noted. "So far."

Jorge downed a handful of trail mix and looked over at Emma. "Jack assured us that almost everyone survives."

Emma shot a glance at Jack. "Almost?"

"OK," I said. "I have something on my mind. I want you to get a picture of where all this is headed."

"Hopefully back up to the top," Jorge commented.

"I mean long-term," I said, smiling at him. "A long time ago El Papá spoke through Isaiah the prophet about me. He said,

'Look at my Servant, whom I've chosen—my Beloved,
    who pleases me.
I'll put my Spirit upon him, and he'll proclaim justice
    to the nations.
He won't fight or shout or raise his voice in public,
    but those who have been hurt, he won't cast aside.
Those who are barely hanging on, he won't say they're
    not worth it.
He'll cause justice to be victorious, and his name will be
    the hope of the whole world.'

"I want you to understand: one day I'll bring justice to the whole earth. Injustice won't reign. The rich and powerful and well-connected won't be in charge. Until that time, you're El Papá's beacon in the world. Shine brightly, so people can see it, and know it comes from El Papá."

They were all listening intently.

"I won't be walking around on earth with you much longer. After I leave, people will start claiming, 'There's Manuel!' or 'I am he!' Ignore them. When I return, you'll have no doubt what's happening. I'll be like the lightning which flashes from one end of the sky to another. No one misses it. But first, I have to suffer at this generation's hands.

"The day I come back, people will be carrying on like it's just another day: going to work, taking care of the kids, running errands. Then I'll be revealed in glory, and no one will get out their luggage and start packing. It'll happen in an instant. One person will be taken, the person right next to them will be left.

"Whoever tries to hold onto a life that revolves around themselves will end up losing it; whoever gives that up, and trusts me to give them true life, will preserve it.

"I'm about to journey into death. If you trust in me, you're saying no to a life apart from God. You're choosing to go into death with me. Who you've been, someone separated from God, at odds with him, will die. And when I rise, a new you will rise, fused to El Papá and to me. You'll rise to a totally new life. My life—in you."

"So," Pedro said, "what does that mean we should we do?"

"Be like firefighters waiting at the fire station," I answered. "They're ready. They're doing their jobs. They make sure their equipment is ready, and their truck's diesel tank is full. When the call comes, they respond. But if they don't take their responsibilities seriously, and they lay around, goofing off, when the call comes, they're not ready.

"Make sure you're ready. Make sure you're fused to me. I'm coming back at a time when you won't expect it."

Wyatt stepped over from the mules. "We just got a call. A storm's heading this way. Time to head out."

At that moment a gust of wind slapped us all in the face and we looked to the west. Dark clouds were approaching—quickly.

"Maybe this wasn't the best day to do the Grand Canyon," Sofia said.

I smiled at her. "Don't worry. We'll make it back."

We all remounted and headed back up the trail, Jack in the lead, followed by Jorge, me, Emma, and the rest following. At this point we were far more intent on getting to the top dry than on sightseeing. But the storm moved faster than the mules, and the wind kept picking up.

"¡Vaya!" Jorge exclaimed as a gust buffeted us atop a cliff. *Whoa!* He glanced at the steep drop to his right. "Hold on tight everyone!"

I glanced back at Emma, whose face had gone white as a sheet. Behind her, I could see the bank of dark clouds growing ever closer, from the looks of it dropping sheets of rain not that far away.

"Jack—!" Pedro shouted from several mules back. He motioned toward the storm behind us. "Is that going to be a problem?"

Jack nodded. "Yes!"

"Can't we get the mules to go faster?"

He shook his head. "The mules know how fast they can go."

In the next few minutes, the wind picked up even more. The rain was almost upon us. Jack halted his mule and the whole line stopped. Jorge looked over the edge again. "Shouldn't we, uh, get off this cliff?"

Jack shook his head. "No. No time. At least it's flat here."

A few seconds later, the wind roared in, followed by sheets of rain, and then hail. The wind gusts felt like they would blow all of us over the cliff.

Jack turned and shouted over the din to Jorge, "Whatever you do, don't get off your mule!"

"But we're about to be blown over!" Jorge screamed back.

Jack shook his head vigorously. "No!" he shouted. "That mule weighs half a ton and has four legs. It's not going anywhere! That's where you're safe. Stay on it! Just hold on tight. Pass that down to everyone behind you."

Jorge turned to inform me.

"I heard him!" I shouted. I turned to Emma behind me. "Jack says no matter what, stay on your mule!" She looked at me like I was crazy. "Pass it down!"

Reluctantly, she turned and passed it down. I looked behind her. Everyone was holding on to their mules for dear life.

In a minute an even stronger gust hit us. I looked behind me toward Emma again. Her mule shifted his feet. "Manuel!" she screamed.

I looked up toward the sky. "Be still!" I shouted.

The wind died down. The hail stopped, as did the rain. The clouds parted. The sun appeared. The group sat on their mules, dripping wet, stunned. They were all staring right at me.

I looked around at them. "Why were you afraid? Why didn't you trust me? I said we'd make it back, didn't I?"

Jack finally found his voice. "Manuel, what did you … what just happened? Who are you?"

"I'm the one who's inviting you to follow me, Jack." I glanced up at the cloudless sky and then back at him. "But for now, we'll follow you."

We dismounted at the top. I invited Jack and Wyatt to join us for a bite to eat after they took care of the mules. We walked the short distance to a place called the Yavapai Tavern. It was nearly deserted mid-afternoon, but I knew word would get around about us quickly.

We scooted some tables together and ordered.

"Too bad we don't have a video of today's little happening," Diego commented.

"We do," Sofia said. Everyone looked at her. "I pulled out my phone the minute the mules stopped. Never know when you might want a video log. I'll send you guys a copy."

"Yeah, well," I replied. "Let's keep that one to ourselves for now, OK?"

At lunch, the group was unusually quiet. They didn't seem to know what to say about the day's events. But I knew what I wanted to say to them.

"You know the thing Jack shouted to us today—stay on your mule, it's your place of safety?"

They all nodded.

"That was incredibly profound, really. What did everybody want to do? What was your natural instinct?"

"To get down off the mule," Ana responded.

"Right. Because it felt unsafe, raised up off the ground, with the wind and rain whipping around. But actually, it was the safest place. As Jack said, those mules weren't going anywhere. They weren't going to get blown off the path."

The waiter brought some chips and salsa for everyone and refilled all the water that had been chugged. I continued.

"Here's what I want you to remember from today: when everything in your life is blowing crazily, and you're getting drenched, and it looks like you're about to get blown off, I'm your safe place. I'm always your safe place. Nothing's going to blow me over. Hold tightly to me, and when it feels like you can't even do that, know this—I'm always holding tightly to you."

A crowd soon gathered around us, as I knew it would. We finished our meal and then moved outside to the expansive patio, where I started tending to people's needs. While we were there, Jack and Wyatt arrived.

"We wondered where everybody on this part of the rim went," Jack said.

Some people staying at a nearby campsite invited the Twelve and me to stay with them in their tents, campers, and RVs. Around 5:00, we all walked to the campsite, where I continued tending to people. From time to time, I would stop for a few minutes and speak.

"If you're walking around out here at night, you don't turn

on your phone's flashlight and then put it in your pocket. What good does that do anyone? You need the light shining out, to see where you're going.

"In your life, be light to those around you. But make sure the true light is in you. If what you think is light is actually darkness, guess what? You're groping in the dark, and you don't even know it. And those who are following your supposed 'light' are groping in the dark, too.

"I'm the true light. Follow me, and you'll have the light of life.

"You can tell if someone is following me. You can tell they have El Papá's light—his life—in them. They operate as El Papá meant people to. They love their enemies instead of hating them. They pray for those who mistreat them. They don't go to a worship house with bitterness in their heart against someone. If they've wronged someone, they go make it right before anything else. They give to those who ask them, and they don't draw attention to it. They aren't judgmental. They aren't condemning. They aren't gripped by anxiety about the future; instead, they trust El Papá, and live in the present.

"There are lots of routes you can take in life. But only one takes you where you really want to go. Don't follow the crowd down the other roads! Take the road that leads to life. Put your trust in me.

"If you pay attention to what I'm saying, and do it, you're like someone who builds on some inland California farmland. When the storms come—and they always do—his house does fine, and his farmland ends up being more productive from the rain.

"But if you do nothing about what I'm saying, you're like someone who, with tons of money, builds a mansion on a cliff overlooking Big Sur. The view of the Pacific is unbelievable. Everyone envies him, until a fierce storm comes and his mansion disappears in a mudslide."

Well after dark, Pedro walked up to me with a burger

someone had cooked. "You haven't eaten since lunch. You must be hungry."

I shook my head. "Pedro, I have food you don't even know about."

"Someone already brought you something?"

"My food is this: to do what El Papá sent me to do." We looked at each other for a moment, and then I reached for the burger, grinning. "But I wouldn't mind a snack."

FORTY-ONE

The next morning, FBI Deputy Director David Patterson opened his email inbox at 6:25, same as always. He immediately noticed a message from the Sacramento office. It referenced an unexpected storm at the Grand Canyon the day before. A brief video was attached. He opened it and stared unbelievingly at the video. If this actually showed what it purported to show …

He sent a message to Chris Ottenger, his boss.

Got a message from our guy on the inside. We need to meet ASAP. Manuel Gonzales may be an even bigger threat than we thought.

FORTY-TWO

We left the Grand Canyon and drove straight east into the Navajo Nation Indian Reservation—at 27,000 square miles, the largest reservation in the country, covering large parts of northern Arizona and New Mexico and southern Utah.

"Three hours to Window Rock, Arizona," Maya announced.

"What's in Window Rock, Arizona?" Sebastian asked.

"A gathering Manuel asked me to arrange."

We enjoyed the desolate but beautiful northern Arizona landscape until, just shy of the New Mexico border, our van was signaled off the road by a dozen or so people standing next to a sign that read:

TSÉGHÁHOODZÁNÍ
WINDOW ROCK

One of the people motioned Pedro, who was driving, to go past them and pull onto a small intersecting road. He slowly drove the van past the people, who closed ranks behind it, blocking the road. They motioned the caravan following us to continue down the highway. But before they did, I hopped out and spoke briefly with the driver of the lead vehicle before returning to our van.

"They just cut off the road to the whole caravan?" Diego asked me.

I shrugged. "This is their land. They can do whatever they want."

A woman came to the van and stepped inside. "The Diné welcome you to our land," she said with a smile. "You are most honored guests. You can follow the signs to the Navajo Nation Council Chamber."

Pedro drove forward.

"What are the Diné?" Justin asked.

Emma responded. "That's what the Navajo call themselves. *The People*. Navajo was the name the Spanish gave them."

"I'm impressed," Justin said. "When did you become a Navajo expert?"

"When I looked them up on Wikipedia."

Surrounded by magnificent nearby buttes, canyons, and forest, the small town of Window Rock serves as the capitol of Navajo Nation, hosting both governmental offices and the Navajo Nation Council Chamber. We pulled up to the chamber, a beautiful, octagonally-shaped, red sandstone building. From there we could see the Window Rock itself, a large, natural sandstone rockface with a huge circular hole in the middle that overlooked the town.

We were escorted into the Council Chamber, a large, circular room with long, curved rows of ornate wooden seats, encircling windows high up, and large wooden beams leading to the center of a vaulted ceiling. The meeting place of the Navajo legislative assembly, the chamber immediately evoked a sense of reverence and solemnity. Men and women filled every seat.

We were taken to the front of the chamber where chairs awaited us on a platform. A man walked to the podium and turned toward us. "We are most honored to have you here among us, Manuel, as well as your followers. We would call you *tsoh na'nitini*. Great teacher. We come today to hear your words to us."

He motioned for me to take the podium and stepped down to the front row. I walked across the platform, tapped lightly on the mic to test it, and began.

"For generations your people have honored and revered the one you call the Great Spirit. God is spirit. Those who worship him must worship in spirit and in truth. You have taught your children that the universe is meant to be ordered, beautiful, harmonious. It is. But you have also taught your children that the universe has been disrupted. It's been disrupted by violence, by death, and by evil.

"I'm here to achieve what you have always longed for. I'm here to bring the universe back into harmony, to reconnect you with the Great Spirit, to reconnect you to one another. I'm here to make all things new.

"I tell you the truth. In the beginning was the expression of God. He was with God, and he himself was God. He brought everything into being. Life itself was in him.

"The expression of God is the light of men. I shine in the darkness, and the darkness cannot overcome me. Whoever receives me—whoever trusts that I am who I am—to that person God gives the right to be his child. He himself gives birth to them, not by natural, human birth, but by his Spirit."

I stepped out from behind the podium and walked to the front edge of the platform. There wasn't a sound among those who had gathered.

"I'm here to show you El Papá, the Father. I'm here to give you—each one of you—my own fullness. Once upon a time God gave people rules to live by. I'm here to give you the truth, the grace of God—gift after gift after gift.

"You have never before seen the Great Spirit. You've never seen El Papá. Now you have. When you've seen me, you've seen him."

I turned and looked back across the stage. "I understand that from time to time the Diné perform a healing dance here called the Shaker Dance. It must be important. It can last up to nine days, I'm told."

Numerous audience members nodded their heads.

I walked over to my chair on the platform and moved it to the front center, where I had just been speaking. "I would like to join you in your healing ritual. Whoever needs healing of any sort, I invite to come join me on the stage."

The crowd sat motionless, until an old woman sitting on the back row of the chamber got up and, slowly and with great difficulty, walked down the side aisle and onto the stage. She sat hunched over in a chair next to me.

"Woman," I said to her, "how long have you had such difficulty walking?"

"Thirteen years," she responded.

I placed my hands on her shoulders. "Be straightened. Walk upright again."

Tentatively, the woman sat a bit more upright, then straighter still. A beaming smile crossed her face. She rose from the chair, standing perfectly straight.

"Oh, my," a woman in the front row said. An excited buzz passed through the chamber.

"I invite you all to the healing dance," I said. One by one, they began to join me on the stage.

Word traveled quickly through Navajo Nation. The Diné came from across the land. We stayed with them three days.

At the end of our time together, the Nation's leaders gathered around me. Their president shook my hand. "We have no word for 'goodbye,'" he said.

I smiled at him. "That's good. Because one day, soon, after I've finished my mission, I will come live with you." I looked around at the leaders crowded around me. "I will come live in you."

FORTY-THREE

Before leaving Navajo Nation, I had a favor to ask of the president.

"Do you have two minivans that we could use for a week? And we'll leave our full-sized one here."

"You want to escape the crowds," the president replied.

I smiled. I had liked this man from the minute we met. The intervening time had only caused my fondness for him to grow. "I want to spend the time between here and the Rio Grande Valley simply teaching my little group."

He nodded. "Such time is invaluable. Let me see what we can do."

They came up with two minivans owned but rarely used by a couple of their schools.

"Keep them as long as you need," the president said. "You have blessed us beyond measure." And now he was blessing us. *This is exactly how people are meant to live,* I thought.

Our five women all piled into one minivan and closed the door. Sebastian looked at the other van and shook his head. "Eight guys in one van?"

"It has eight seats," Ana said to him out the front window.

"A tiny middle one."

"You'll survive. Hey, we need some girl time, and this is it."

I turned to the men. "Looks like you guys are outvoted. Sort of."

We got in the other van and left Window Rock via a back road. I took the middle seat.

"We're still going to attract crowds," Mike predicted.

I knew otherwise. El Papá was directing us to a certain place for a reason. "Not if we keep to ourselves."

"What about our caravan of followers?"

"I told them I needed to spend time with you guys, and to meet us in McAllen. They'll be there."

Four hours later, we arrived at our destination: Bandelier National Monument northwest of Sante Fe. Covering over fifty square miles nestled between mountains and canyons, the area featured wide expanses of grass, trees, and stony terrain. The land was dotted with ruins of long-abandoned stone Pueblo buildings. And in the canyon walls, accessible via log ladders, cliff dwellings.

This time of year, the number of visitors was small. We picked a campsite close to a stream, pitched tents, grabbed some of the food the Navajo had graciously loaded us down with, and set out on our first hike.

Each day, we took a couple of hikes, cooked meals, and sat around the campsite in camping chairs we'd acquired in Flagstaff. I would select a topic I wanted to instruct them on. Or sometimes one of the Twelve would ask a question that would get us going. I enjoyed the give and take.

The first night, after dinner, we made s'mores. I hadn't had one in years.

"I want to make sure you all understand something," I said to the group, holding my chocolate-filled marshmallow over the flame. "Your devotion to me will constantly be tested. Make sure you count the cost beforehand. Don't be like an amateur mechanic who wants to rebuild a classic Mustang. He gets halfway through and then he realizes, *I don't have enough money for a new engine.* So, what he's got is actually a pile of junk." I looked around at them all. "Make sure that's not you."

I pulled my browned marshmallow back, squeezed it between two graham crackers, and took a bite. Scrumptious.

"This is heaven," Kiara commented as she finished a bite herself.

"Well …" I said. I left it at that.

During our discussions, the group brought up a lot of questions. Good questions. At lunch the next day, Pedro asked, "How often do we have to pray for something that we really want, that we think is important?"

"It's not a matter of how often," I answered. "It's a matter of being persistent."

"Because God is keeping a tally?" Kiara asked, a bit sarcastically.

I smiled. "No. Because it shows you mean it."

I thought for a moment for an appropriate illustration. One of our auto shop customers came to mind. "It's like a mother who thinks her kid has to walk too far to the bus stop. It doesn't feel safe to her. She emails the superintendent. He ignores it. She emails him again. He ignores it. She keeps emailing him, until finally he says to his assistant, 'I'm sick of this woman's emails. Call Joe and have him schedule a stop in front of her house.' He didn't care a thing about her, but her persistence caused him to respond."

"You're saying God is like the superintendent?" Pedro asked.

I couldn't help but smile. Pedro, always so literal, so concrete. "No, Pedro. The point is about persistence. There's one huge difference: El Papá cares for you infinitely more than that superintendent could ever care."

That afternoon, after lunch, I said to the Twelve, "You guys split up and go climb the cliff dwellings. If you're in threes, you're not likely to be recognized."

"What about you?" Maya asked.

I loved how Maya was always concerned about others. She didn't want me feeling I was missing out, I'm sure. But I wasn't missing out. I was doing what I most wanted.

"I doubt I could climb up there unnoticed," I responded. "I'm perfectly happy staying here. It'll give me some good time with El Papá."

That seemed to satisfy her. They all split up and headed out. I relaxed in one of the camping chairs. "Papá," I said. I talked to him, I listened, and I saw what he had to show me. After we'd been talking for a while, I was startled by human voices nearby. Someone was approaching.

Papá spoke to me clearly. "I sent these."

Two young women with backpacks emerged from a trail into the campsite clearing.

"Hello," I said.

"Hello," one of the women responded. "Sorry, we didn't mean to intrude."

"Not at all."

The younger one made a sign language signal to the first.

"My sister says hello."

"Your sister is deaf?" I asked.

"Yes," she answered, and then she looked around at all the chairs. "Either your group went hiking, or you're expecting to make new friends."

I chuckled. "Maybe both. They went to the cliff dwellings."

"We are, too. Would you like to join us?"

"Thank you," I responded. "I'm just taking a bit of alone time to be with El Papá."

"El Papá?"

"God."

"Oh." That was usually a conversation-stopper. She signed something to her sister.

Suddenly a look of amazement crossed the younger sister's face and she furiously signed something back. The first woman turned to me, the same look of amazement on her face. "You're … you're …"

I nodded. "I am."

"What are you doing out here?"

"I'm enjoying creation. And I'm teaching my trainees for a few days, avoiding the crowds. Except El Papá brought the two of you. Which I know was for a reason."

I rose from my chair. "I don't know American sign language. You'll have to translate for me to your sister."

"Of course. What do you want to say to her?"

The words came from deep within me, reflecting everything I wanted for her: to be whole, in every way. "I want to ask her, 'Would you like to hear?'"

The older sister simply stared at me for a moment. "You're … you can do that?"

"Yes."

Tears welled up in her eyes and began running silently down her cheeks. "She's been deaf since she was a child."

Her sister signed her a question, and the first signed back. The sister looked at me and tears began to flow down her face as well. She simply nodded.

I stepped to her, placed my hands on both of her ears, and spoke gently. "Be opened."

I stepped back. The first woman looked at her sister. "Claire?"

Claire threw herself at her sister and began sobbing. "Emily! Emily! I can hear you!" They embraced and cried for what seemed like an eternity. Finally, they loosened their grasp, and Claire, her face soaked in tears, turned to me and said quietly, "Thank you." She stepped forward, embraced me, and kept embracing me, her head buried in my shoulder, tears flowing.

Finally, she pulled back and wiped the tears from her face. "I just … the first two people I can hear again are you"—she looked at Emily, and then at me—"and you."

Her speech sounded strange, her muscle memory simply different from others.

"Would you like me to make your speech sound more normal?" I asked her.

"You can do that, too?"

"Yes."

Her face lit up again. "Please!"

I laid my hand on the front of her throat. "Be changed."

She looked in my eyes. "What did you do? I felt—"

Emily cried out. "Claire—you sound ..." She threw her arms around her and they embraced once more. I was thrilled just to stand and watch them.

In a minute, they separated, wiping the moisture from their faces again, and Claire spoke. "I can't believe this happened, that we came across you. That God, I guess, brought us here. Didn't he?"

I nodded. "He did."

She shook her head almost imperceptibly. "To be honest, I don't know a thing about—" She looked at the circle of lawn chairs. "I feel like maybe we should, like—"

"Talk?"

"Yeah. Are there things you want to tell us about, you know, God?"

The time had come for the real miracle. I motioned toward the chairs and we all took a seat. I leaned toward the two of them. "I'd like to tell you how much he loves you. And how to become connected to him."

FORTY-FOUR

Emily, Claire, and I were still talking when the first three from the Twelve returned. I could tell they were surprised I was talking with two strangers when we were supposedly keeping to ourselves, but I simply introduced them all. The other nine finally rejoined us. Emily and Claire stayed through the evening.

After dinner and some s'mores, we all played a game that someone had picked up at Walmart.

"Shhh!" Ana warned as the game elicited a roar of laughter from the group. "We're supposed to not attract attention!"

Everyone went mum, but the laughter erupted again as soon as we resumed playing. Every time we finished a round, someone would say, "One more!" and we'd go another round. Around 11:30, Emily and Claire said they needed to head back to their tent. They both hugged me and asked, "Will you be here in the morning?"

"We will," I answered, "but these guys might play 'til 2:00 and wake up at 10:00."

They grinned. "Can we come by?"

"Of course. Love to have you."

They departed and the group started another round.

Just after midnight, Emma's phone rang. Hers was one of the only two phones picking up a signal.

She glanced at it. "It's my mom."

Ever since we'd left Tim and Eileen Wright's ranch in the Valley, I'd noticed how closely she kept in touch with her folks.

She got up and stepped away from the group. Ten minutes later, she returned, her face wet with tears, and handed me the phone. "She asked for you."

I went into the tent to talk. Fifteen minutes later I emerged and looked at the silent group. "Emma probably told you. Tim's had a stroke. They don't know if he's going to make it."

Emma stood up. I handed the phone back to her and embraced her as she quietly sobbed. And I knew I would have to tell her the last thing in the world I wanted to say.

She finally stepped back from our embrace. "Manuel, what if …" she turned and looked at Ana. "How long to McAllen from here? Do you know?"

"Fifteen hours straight. So, realistically, maybe 17 hours."

"If we packed up now and drove through the night, we could be there before dinner." Emma turned and looked at me. "We've done it lots of times."

Jorge, who had the other working phone, looked up from it. "There's a flight out of Albuquerque at 6:31, stops in Austin, then arrives in McAllen at 1:43."

"You and I could fly," Emma said to me, "and everyone else could bring the vans."

"Manuel …" Everyone turned and looked at Maya. "It is possible to just, you know, heal him from here? Like you did back at the underpass? Do you have to be there to touch him?"

"It's possible, yes."

Emma gasped. "Really! You can just heal him right now? Then let's … I'll get on the phone with my mom and make sure he's right there, and she can—"

I shook my head slowly.

"What?" Emma asked. All the sudden enthusiasm drained from her face. "You can't? You won't?"

I motioned toward the chairs and she and I sat. I took her hands in mine and looked into her eyes.

"I must do what I see El Papá doing."

"And ... what is he doing?"

"He's drawing people to himself through us in Sante Fe, and Albuquerque, and El Paso, just like we planned."

"But if you can just heal him from here ..."

"He's not doing that now. He's waiting, and so I'm waiting, too."

"But what if my dad dies?"

"El Papá has made it clear to me. What's happening with your father is for El Papá's glory, and mine, so that many will believe."

"So, he'll be OK?"

I squeezed her hands. "Trust me."

Silently, the group put out the fire and went to bed. We got up in the morning, had breakfast, packed up the vans, said good-bye to Emily and Claire, and drove to Sante Fe, where I taught and tended to people at a large park. The day passed somberly. Despite what I had said to Emma, the Twelve didn't get why I was handling things the way I was.

That evening, we stayed at Casa Escondida, a bed and break-fast half an hour north, where we'd reserved all eight rooms. We were having some to-go food when Emma's phone rang. She answered it, listened for a moment, and then burst into tears. We all knew what had happened.

Emma went into her bedroom. A few minutes later, I knocked on her door. She opened it and stood, simply looking at me, and then she slowly stepped toward me and we hugged.

"Manuel, you said to ..." Her voice trailed off and she was silent for a moment. "I don't understand."

"I know. Just trust me."

MCALLEN, TEXAS

Three days later, we parked a couple of blocks away from the largest worship house in the Rio Grande Valley. It held over a thousand people, and every seat was filled for Tim's funeral, with many people standing in the back and along the sides. Tim's and Eileen's families had been known in the Valley for generations. Every local TV station had sent a crew. So had several national news organizations who, undoubtedly, expected me to be there.

Eileen, dressed in black, met us halfway through the parking lot. Her eyes were swollen from tears. She extended her arms and we stood, hugging.

"Manuel …" She was silent for a number of moments. I simply held her. "If you'd been here …" She cried some more, and then she finally took a long, deep breath and relaxed her embrace. "If you'd been here, Tim wouldn't be dead."

"Tim will rise again."

She nodded, but her eyes were listless. "I know. I know he'll be raised again." She sighed and looked toward the ground. "On the last day, when God—at the resurrection."

"Eileen," I said. I waited until she lifted her eyes. "I am the resurrection. I'm the life. Whoever trusts in me, even if he dies, will live. And everyone who lives and trusts in me will never die." I paused for a moment. "Do you believe this?"

She nodded slowly. "I believe you are El Único. The One sent into the world."

A man in a dark suit walked toward us from the entrance. "Ms. Wright, they're just about ready."

We turned and followed him.

"I'd like you to say a few words at the end, if you would," Eileen said to me.

"I'd like to speak at the beginning," I replied.

Normally, that might have elicited a response. Eileen was someone who liked things to happen in a certain order. But at this point, it didn't matter to her. "OK. That'd be fine."

We walked into the foyer. More family members were there, and they gave Eileen and Emma long hugs with tears. I turned away to give them some space and sat on a bench against a side wall, watching them. Their grief was palpable. None of them expected to lose Tim at so young an age, or so suddenly.

I closed my eyes for a few moments and prayed silently. *Papá, this is so wrong. This is all so wrong. They weren't ... people weren't supposed to ...* I didn't know what else to say for a moment. *Papá, make everything new.*

I felt someone sit on the bench. I lifted my head and looked at Maya. She looked shocked. "You're crying."

I hadn't even realized it. She handed me a tissue. "Are you going to be OK?"

I wiped the tears off my cheeks and nodded. "Everything will be fine."

Emma stepped toward me. "Manuel, we need to take our seats."

I spotted my mother and siblings on the way in and gave them all tight hugs. Eileen and I took our seats on the front row. TV cameras and phones were already recording the entire event. The Twelve, less Emma, found a place to stand at the back. The funeral was open casket, Tim's body unembalmed. He lay in front, between our seats and the platform where the worship house leader would stand. Quiet organ music played.

The worship house leader walked to the front and welcomed the audience. "We are gathered to celebrate the life of Tim Wright," he said, "a pillar of the community for many decades and a man whose character and dedication to God, to his family, and to others was respected by all. One couldn't be around Tim without knowing you were in the presence of someone special. We are joining his wife, Eileen, and his daughter, Emma, in our celebration."

He spoke a few more minutes and then said, "Numerous family members want to say a few words commemorating the life of their loved one. I believe Tim's brother, Craig, would like to speak first."

Eileen straightened in her seat. "Actually, our close family friend, Manuel Gonzales, will speak first."

A buzz rippled through the crowd. The leader, who didn't seem all that pleased with the new plan, nodded. "Mr. Gonzales, then."

I went to the podium. The crowd quieted. Every camera in the place was on me, I knew.

"I am the resurrection," I announced, "and I am the life. Just as El Papá raises the dead, and gives them life, in the same way I give life to whomever I wish. The time is coming—in fact, it's here right now—when the dead will hear my voice. And those who hear will live. I'm talking both about those who are physically dead, and those who are dead, but still walking around."

I glanced at Eileen, and then at Emma. They expected, I'm sure, that I would be talking about Tim. That's not what they were getting, but they were listening intently.

I continued. "Don't be surprised at this. An hour is coming when everyone in the grave will hear my voice and come out. Those who have responded to El Papá's call, they'll rise to life. Those who haven't, they'll rise and receive what they've chosen. They've rejected El Papá's invitation, and they'll remain separated from him. This is what El Papá charges you with, this day: believe in the one he's sent."

I looked up toward the ceiling and said, "Papá, thank you for hearing me. You always hear me, I know. But I say it aloud now so these people may believe you sent me."

I looked down at the casket from where I stood. I could see the upper part of Tim's lifeless body. "Tim," I commanded, "rise up!"

The crowd sat in silence, straining to see what would happen. And then, slowly, Tim rose to a sitting position.

Two women near the front shrieked and fainted. The whole crowd burst into tumult, people leaping to their feet, some screaming, some rushing forward. Others froze in their places, many simply videoing the whole spectacle.

"Oh my God!"

"He's—he's alive!"

"Tim!" Eileen cried out, lunging toward the casket. "Tim!"

FORTY-FIVE

FBI Deputy Director Patterson was about to go into a meeting when his executive assistant came to his office door.

"You might want to turn on the news. Now."

They walked to the closest conference room and turned on a TV. Patterson watched for ten minutes and then said, "Cancel my meeting, will you? And see if Ottenger is available."

Five minutes later Director Ottenger walked in, closing the door behind him. "I was watching in my office."

Patterson looked his way. "He heals disease. He controls nature. Now he overcomes death."

"Have we confirmed today's events?"

"We had two agents at the funeral. They witnessed the event. They spoke to the funeral home. The body had been there three days. They verified the death certificate."

Ottenger sat and stared across the room. "Who is this guy?"

"I don't know," Patterson replied. "But I think we're going to need to speed up our plans."

Ottenger nodded, his attention shifting back to the TV screen. "We are, yes," he finally said. Then he looked at Patterson. "At this point, I'm just wondering if controlling him is actually within our power, or not."

"You mean the FBI's?"

"I mean anyone's."

FORTY-SIX

The media at the funeral descended upon Tim within seconds, demanding interviews. Every other reporter and camera crew from Brownsville to San Antonio, no doubt, would soon arrive, adding to the pandemonium. I met with the Twelve briefly in a small side room at the worship house and sent a note to Tim to call me in the morning. Then we slipped out the back, somehow making it to our two minivans without attracting attention. I was glad Tim had temporarily taken the spotlight.

We drove an hour and a half east, crossed the bridge onto South Padre Island, and headed north to the public access beaches, which were deserted at night. We pitched our tents on the sand and retrieved some food from the vans.

"We won't stay hidden for long here, you know," Sofia said to me as we ate. "The internet is going crazy with what you did today. The crowds are going to get even crazier."

I downed some smoked sausage and cheese on a cracker. "I know. We won't be here long. We'll be in DC shortly."

Jorge looked over. "We're going to DC again?"

"For the Passover march?" Diego asked.

Every year, people descended on DC in the spring to celebrate Passover with a long march. It symbolized the exodus of the Jews from Egypt and celebrated all the present-day freedoms God had provided.

"No," I responded. "Not for the march."

"Then why are we going?"

"So those in power can kill me."

Tim called the next morning just after we finished breakfast on the beach.

"I guess I should say thanks," he said.

"I didn't do it for you. I did it for everyone else. You were fine."

He laughed. "You're right—but thank you, anyway."

"Hey, I need your help," I said to him. "Didn't you once say you had a friend that ran offshore fishing charters?"

The beach remained largely deserted through the morning. It was a cool weekday in early March, a few days short of spring break revelers arriving. Besides, we were miles north of the popular beaches where the hotels and condos stood.

We had only one visitor all morning. Rachel came to visit us, bringing her baby.

"How did you find us?" Justin asked.

"Emma texted me."

We all hugged her and crowded around the baby.

"What's the baby's name?" Mike asked. Clearly, he was out of the loop on this one.

"Emmanuella," Rachel said, looking at me and grinning.

Around noon, some people finally discovered us. Word got around, and a crowd gathered. I started teaching and healing right there on the beach.

The crowd grew. TV trucks started showing up. The Twelve set up our portable sound system. By mid-afternoon, so many people had arrived that we needed bigger speakers to reach the throng that stretched down the beach. Pedro and Sebastian drove back toward Brownsville to find an electronics store.

I wasn't surprised. I knew that after events of the day before, a madhouse would ensue. I was thrilled people were coming. They needed what I came to give them.

"The oceans are full of fish, ready to be brought in," I said to the rest of the Twelve. "But the fishermen are few. Pray to El Papá. Ask him to send more and more fishermen."

FORTY-SEVEN

Attorney General Wu glanced around her conference room table at 6:00 p.m. that evening. The working team to deal with the Manuel Gonzales threat had assembled. It consisted of herself, the CIA Director, the Homeland Security Secretary, the White House Chief Strategist, the FBI Director, Deputy Director, and Cyber Operations Assistant Director, and Allison Davis, chairperson of the Senate Investigations Subcommittee.

The meeting was strictly classified. Every person there knew that nothing spoken or agreed upon in the meeting would be revealed for years. Possibly never.

"All right," Wu said after the last attendee arrived. "I believe we all know what we're here to do. Any questions before we start?"

There was silence, and then Homeland Security Secretary Dillon cleared his throat. "I'm just wondering … we haven't even talked to him yet. Heard his intentions. What if they're benign? Should we initiate all of this even before the hearings take place?"

Chief Strategist Humphries leaned forward. "If we let this continue, the government as we know it may not even be here much longer. He's already said he plans to put a new government in place."

"What that means exactly is unclear," Dillon responded.

"That may be. But his followers' intentions seem quite clear. Have you seen the posters in the crowd? Heard the chants? The movement behind him won't be controllable. For all practical purposes, he'll be made king."

"It's already out of control," Senator Davis commented. "You can't get a flight into any airport from Monterrey to San Antonio. Or a hotel room. People are flocking down there from all over the world. I'm told that in Austin and in Houston this weekend, there'll be pro-Gonzales marches—without him even there. I'm sure those are just the start."

FBI Director Ottenger weighed in. "It's not just that." He looked at Duane Larson, in charge of cyber operations at the FBI, and nodded.

"We've uncovered a nascent movement online to set up a world government," Larson said, "with Gonzales as, well, dictator."

"There's some fringe movement online for everything," Dillon responded.

"This is not fringe. It has some big money behind it."

"From where?" Dillon wanted to know.

"Russia. Eastern Europe. The Middle East. Here."

"Are they coordinating with him?"

"We have no evidence of that. Yet."

"It doesn't matter," Wu said. She looked around the table. "We know enough at this point. We know the threat, the chaos he could cause."

"Is causing," Humphries said. "The stock market fell almost three percent in late trading after that funeral stunt. Fear of instability."

"He's a threat to every one of us," Wu said. "I think we'd all agree, and those above us would certainly agree, that it's better for one man to be sacrificed than for the whole nation to be brought down." She paused and gathered her thoughts. "The hearings will come first. But we need to have everything else ready to go for subsequent steps. Is everyone clear on those?"

They all nodded. The plan was clear.

Forty-Eight

I was with the crowd until dark, and then the Twelve and I drove to a nearby marina, where we boarded a 60-foot, deep-sea fishing boat owned by Luis Gutiérrez, Tim's friend. He just happened to have a cancellation for the week. El Papá provided. Tim covered the cost.

For the next several days, I taught and cared for people on the beach during the day, and we slept on the boat at night. The evenings gave me time to simply be with the Twelve, to prepare them for what was to come. Not that anything could actually prepare them.

The first night on the boat, at dinner, I addressed the elephant in the room.

"I know you're all sad because of what I said yesterday." I looked around at them. Heads were nodding.

"But this has been El Papá's plan from the beginning. His Son would lay down his life to pay for the sins of many. He wants a whole host of sons and daughters, for all eternity. This is how it happens. Remember when we had that corn on the cob back in New Mexico?" They nodded again. "I'm like an uncooked corn kernel. You don't get a crop of corn until that kernel goes in the ground, dies, and out of the ground comes a corn stalk that will eventually produce more corn than you can imagine."

They were all so quiet.

"You will grieve, I know. But your grief will become incredible joy. They will kill me, yes. But three days later I will rise from the dead."

"I know you've told us that," Pedro said. "I guess … I guess I didn't believe it would really happen."

"Pedro, it's my choice to lay down my life. They can't take it from me. I'll lay it down. And I'll take it back up again. This is what El Papá has given me the right to do—to take it up again. And when I do, you'll be so thrilled, you'll be doing backflips."

Later that evening, Sebastian and I were sitting on the deck of the stern, looking up at the star-filled sky.

"Magnificent, isn't it?" I mused. And then I became pensive. I turned and looked at Sebastian, and at Mike, who had joined us. "I've come to bring fire on the earth. That fire will come. But how I wish it were already kindled." I was silent for a moment. "I have a baptism to go through, though. And it will consume me until it's done."

The rest of the Twelve slowly wandered out and joined us. I looked around at all of them and smiled. "I want to let you know something. You've all stayed with me. I genuinely call you my friends. You're not just employees who are given instructions. Right? Friends get the inside scoop. That's what you are to me."

By our second day on the beach, the whole thing had turned into a circus. I figured it would. The crowd had probably doubled, to twenty thousand or more. Food vendors set up shop along the road, behind the dunes. The media arrived in force. I was glad to be with the crowd. And now they could all hear me. Our new speakers reached as far north as Corpus Christi, it seemed.

The crowd was even larger on the third day. A helicopter flew overhead, a "Manuel for President" sign trailing behind it. Someone had printed thousands of such signs for the crowd. It was starting to look like a political rally, all of which made me uncomfortable. For the moment, I simply ignored it. I had people to tend to.

During a quick water break, I raised the issue with El Papá. Should I tell the crowd to put their signs down and refrain from political statements? Should I withdraw from the crowd and publicly disavow any political intentions?

No, he told me. Unfolding events would make that unnecessary.

At the end of the afternoon, those events became clear. Two men in dark suits made their way through the crowd toward me. They could not have looked more out of place. When they got close, they asked for a private word with me.

A minute later they walked away, and Dan came up to me. "Who were those guys?" he asked.

"FBI and Department of Justice."

"What did they want?"

"To meet with me. I told them you and I would meet them in an hour on the boat."

"To talk about what?"

"They didn't say." But I already knew.

On the way to the marina, Dan did everything he could to talk me out of meeting with them.

"Manuel, this is not my area of law. I can't adequately represent you."

"I don't need you to. I just need you to listen with me."

Finally, he relented. "Just don't say anything to them."

"Can I invite them to have a seat?"

They were waiting for us at the marina, Special Agent Torres and U.S. Attorney Bartley. The four of us went to the boat and sat at a small table inside the cabin. Luis and his crewmate took a break.

"Mr. Gonzales," Bartley began, "you are about to be charged, among other crimes, with treason under section 2381, title 18 of the United States Code. If you are found guilty, possible penalties include fines, incarceration for no less than five years, or death. You would, under the first two, be thereafter ineligible to hold elective office."

He nodded toward Torres, who pulled out a sheet of paper from a briefcase and then spoke. "We want you to understand the scope of the allegations against you and the breadth of the evidence we've collected."

He glanced repeatedly at the page before him as he explained. "You have made public statements before thousands which call for the overthrow of the U.S. government. You have solicited numerous others to join you in such activities, which is conspiracy to commit sedition. We have evidence that you have spoken numerous times to your own inner circle of followers concerning your intent to establish a new government over the United States.

"In addition, we have financial records showing that you have personally received payments from foreign governments—entities that the U.S. government considers hostile to its interests and even its existence. We have evidence that you have admitted to receiving these enemy funds for the purpose of bringing down the U.S. government. And we have evidence that you are planning, this week, to come to DC to incite the crowds to overthrow the existing constitutional government and install you as the head of a new one."

The four of us sat silently for a moment. I didn't know if Agent Torres actually believed what he was saying or not. It didn't matter.

Bartley leaned forward. "Now, Mr. Gonzales. Given your unique circumstances, the U.S. Attorney's Office would prefer not to bring charges against you at all. It would be in your best interest, your followers' best interest, and the country's best interest not to have to do so.

"So, we are willing to offer you a deal. The Senate Select Subcommittee on Investigations is scheduled to meet this week. If you are willing to testify before the subcommittee in a public hearing, deny any intent to overthrow the government, communicate to your followers that you have no political intentions whatsoever, and commit to continuing your ministry in a purely humanitarian, apolitical manner, we will refrain from pressing charges. You will be free to pursue whatever endeavors you so choose, per the stipulations of our agreement."

Bartley waited for a moment, and then Dan spoke. "I would like a word with my client."

Bartley and Torres left the cabin, closing its door behind them. Dan looked at me. "They have fabricated all of this! They threw in that foreign money allegation so they could accuse you of treason and not just sedition."

"Of course," I replied.

"They're the government, and they can invent whatever digital trail they want," he said. "But there's no legitimate collaboration. They can't prove that. You can fight this. There's no way—"

"Dan, no." I leaned forward, my arms resting on the table. "This is El Papá's cup. I must drink it. I must go to DC. They will do with me as they wish."

"But Manuel—"

"That is final."

He stared at me for a long moment, and then sat back in his chair and sighed. "Very well. So … what are you going to do, testify before the Senate subcommittee?" He looked toward the door where the two men had walked out. "Tell them what they want to hear?"

"I will testify. As for what I tell them …"

He looked back at me and we exchanged a knowing glance.

FORTY-NINE

I could see most of DC from my window seat as we approached Reagan Airport. I'd never seen it from the air. I admired how the city had been laid out with such precision so long before. Still, the beauty was bittersweet.

Justin leaned in from the middle seat to take a look. "It's beautiful."

"It is," I said, still staring at the ground below. "If only they knew what would bring real peace. But it's now been hidden from them. I'd love to gather all of the people here together, under my wings. But they aren't willing. After this, they won't see me again until they declare, 'Blessed is the one who comes in the name of the Lord.'"

The Senate subcommittee hearing was on Wednesday. We'd arrived three days early. I had a lot I wanted to accomplish in those three days.

Senator Blaine from Idaho met us at the airport and walked us to three SUVs that would transport us. I'd become a lightning rod politically, I knew, but Blaine didn't care. Having served four terms, he'd already announced his retirement.

The minute our caravan left the airport, we came upon huge crowds of people lining the streets, waving flags, bouncing their kids on their shoulders, holding signs:

El Único!
Manuel for President
We love you, Manuel!

It was Sunday, the weather was pleasant, and it seemed the whole city had come out to welcome us. Not all were friendly, however. I spotted a fair share of opposing signs in the crowd. *This week could end up getting ugly,* I thought. That was certainly not my wish, but I wasn't here to control that. I was here simply to do what El Papá had set before me.

We turned onto the winding Washington Parkway and, if anything, the crowds grew even larger.

"Is there a sun roof on this thing?" I asked the senator.

"Are you sure that's safe with all these people?"

I smiled at him. "Quite sure."

We traveled down the parkway and on to the National Mall. There we got out and walked to the Washington Monument.

Pedro looked one way, toward the Capitol Building, and the other, toward the Lincoln Memorial. "This place is amazing," he said.

"Enjoy it while it's here," I replied.

The Twelve looked at me. "Are you saying all this is going away?" Kiara asked.

"That's another matter. Everything on earth has its time, and then it passes. As I said before, hold onto the light, while you have it. These things will pass away. My words will not."

People at the Mall began to recognize us and a small crowd formed. Increasingly, they were joined by those who had been on our route. I was talking to people one-on-one and healing those in need.

We stayed at the Mall until dark, when we were picked up by a couple, Ben and Abigail Thompson, in two large SUVs. The

Thompsons had been supporters since we came to DC the first time.

"How are we ever going to get away from the crowds here in DC?" Ana asked me as we hopped into one of the vehicles.

It was a logical question. We didn't have a boat to sleep on. But it was important for the thirteen of us to have alone time during this week, and I knew El Papá would provide. The Thompsons owned a large home on a peninsula that jutted into Chesapeake Bay an hour south of the city. We'd have time away from the crowds, he had assured me.

Sure enough, by the time we arrived at their house, no cars were following us.

"That was a minor miracle," Ana commented.

"I'm not sure it was so minor," I said.

Late that night, though, there was an unexpected knock at the front door. Henry Garcia, our congressman from McAllen, was standing on the front porch. He wanted to speak with me privately.

"How did you locate us?" I asked him.

"Tim Wright," he replied. Who undoubtedly found out from Emma.

I invited him into Ben's downstairs office.

"I want you to know," he began, "that I'm not the only one on your side on Capitol Hill. There are many. They're just afraid of saying so publicly."

That didn't surprise me. I motioned for him to have a seat, but he launched right in.

"You're not safe here in Washington," he said. "Or maybe anywhere. I have a close connection with a White House insider. Very high up. He says the president wants you dead. They're just trying to figure out how to do it without being blamed for it."

"I know," I replied.

"You do?"

"Why do you think I'm here?" I motioned once more toward the chairs, and we sat. "I appreciate you coming, Congressman. But trust me, I'm not in danger. At any point I can ask El Papá to send thousands of angels. I have more protection than you can possibly imagine."

He looked a bit befuddled. This wasn't the response he was expecting, I knew. "But the president ..."

"If your White House friend sees the president this week, have him tell that snake that Manuel Gonzales says this: 'I will do my work today, and tomorrow, and on the third day I will reach my goal.'"

"He can't say that to the president!"

I smiled. "Well, he can leave out the snake part."

After he left, the Twelve came to me with a question in the living room.

"Am I being ganged up on?" I said as they all found a seat.

"Hardly," Sofia replied. "But earlier today you were talking about things that are here now passing away. We were all wondering, when will that happen? Because the way things have been going in the world, it seems closer and closer."

"I don't know," I said. "El Papá knows. I do know this: one day I'll return and set up my kingdom, my government, physically, on earth. In the meantime, be careful. Many will come, claiming to be me, or a savior of some sort. They'll offer salvation through religion, or a political movement, or even technology. Don't be deceived. Trust me, when I come back, there won't be the slightest doubt who it is.

"Before the end, the gospel must be preached to all the nations. You'll be persecuted, and arrested, and hauled into courts. Don't worry about what you'll say to them. The Holy Spirit will tell you what to say. It's not you speaking; it's him.

"The times will be bad. Wickedness will increase, and most

people's love will grow cold. Family members will betray each other. False prophets will deceive. Everyone will hate you because of me, but not a hair on your head will perish. Stand firm, and you'll be delivered.

"When that day comes, there will be incredible distress, more than at any time in history. If El Papá didn't cut those days short, no one would survive.

"People will faint from terror and apprehension. Then everyone will see me coming in a cloud with great power and glory. I'll send my angels and gather those who are mine from every part of the earth.

"So be prepared for that day. Don't let your hearts be pre-occupied by all the pleasures the world offers, and the anxieties of life. Be watching, and pray that you're ready."

I knew these things were heavy, so I concluded with this: "When you see these things happening, take heart. I'm serious. What you've wanted more than anything is almost here. It's like seeing the first trees budding in the spring. They're still bare, and look barren. But soon, they'll be full of life. So be encouraged! El Papá's infinitely good plan for the ages is unfolding right before your eyes."

The next morning, Monday, we toured the U.S. Capitol. Emma had made reservations through Congressman Garcia's office. Our guide did a double take when he met up with us at the Capitol Visitors Center.

"You're ... here for a tour?"

He led us through the Crypt, a vaulted space with imposing statues beneath the Rotunda where, surprisingly, no one was buried. We walked upstairs to the Rotunda and our guide told us to wait a moment. He walked across the room and, his back turned to us from probably 60 feet away, he spoke in a normal voice.

"How many of you can hear me?" he asked. He turned around and we all raised our hands. He smiled and walked back to us. "Incredible acoustics," he commented. "From there, everyone in the entire Rotunda could hear me. Which is why we speak quietly."

He told us the history of the huge circular room, its paintings and sculptures, and its 180-foot ceiling under the Capitol dome.

I looked around while he was speaking. Visitors had begun to recognize me and move our way. Above, a growing number of people—most likely congressional staffers—were looking down on us over the railings, some making their way down to our level.

Our guide finished his Rotunda presentation and then asked if we had any questions.

"I looked up famous sayings scattered about the Capitol," I said to him. "Is it true that over the doorways to the Senate are three sayings: 'God has favored our undertakings,' 'In God we trust,' and 'A new order of the ages is born'?"

"That's right," he replied. "The first and third are in Latin."

"I have a comment about those," I said. I turned and spoke directly to the Twelve. The whole Rotunda, though, was filling. Out of the corner of my eye I could see three U.S. Capitol police looking at me and conversing.

"God favors the undertakings of all who strive for true liberty," I said in a normal tone, knowing perfectly well that people all over the Rotunda could hear me, and video me. "But few in this place trust in God anymore. It's supposed to be a beacon of liberty, but instead it's a den of lies, deceit, corruption, treachery, and oppression. Don't be taken in by what comes out of their mouths here. This is no longer the People's House. It's the house of and for the powerful. But God is not mocked. On the day of judgment, all will give account for every word they've spoken, and every deed they've done. Why do the people who meet here think they'll escape? Their punishment will be most severe. At

the moment, they arrogantly occupy seats of power and promi-
nence. But they are powerless to thwart El Papá's plan."

I motioned around the large room. "This one building took
over three decades to build. But if you tore the whole thing down,
in three days I could build something that provides far more liberty than this building ever represented. And when I set you free,
you really will be free."

I looked at the Twelve and smiled. "They got the third saying
right, by the way. A new order of the ages is about to be born. I'm
making all things new."

FIFTY

"What were you thinking?! Why didn't you arrest him?" Ed Wheelan, chief of the U.S. Capitol Police, stared at the three officers who had manned the Rotunda area earlier in the day. "Well?"

"Arrest him for what, sir?" one of them asked.

"For demonstrating!"

"But he wasn't demonstrating."

"He was giving a public speech inside the Capitol," Wheelan countered. "That's not permitted."

"Sir—" The second one looked at his fellow officers, then continued. "He was talking to his little group of followers. For three or four minutes."

"The whole crowd was listening! There must have been a thousand people in there."

"But … arrest Manuel Gonzales?" the third one asked.

Wheelan glared at him. "Has he taken you in, too? It's our job to protect the Capitol. If he comes here and does that again, I want him arrested. We are not going to have spontaneous mass protests in the Capitol. Is that clear?"

FIFTY-ONE

On Tuesday morning, I began to teach the Twelve on the steps in front of the Lincoln Memorial. A crowd started to form around us, as I knew it would. We weren't able to set up a sound system here, so we started streaming live to enable the people in the back to follow along with me.

Something else started to form as well: an organized protest on the plaza across from us. They started chanting and waving professionally made placards.

**Down with Religion
No to Theofascism
Save our Democracy!**

I ignored them. I had a message to deliver. "Abraham Lincoln was the doorway to a new nation, so to speak—a nation without slavery. It's what this nation was supposed to be, but wasn't for its first 80 years.

"I'm the doorway to something even greater. Enter through me, and you'll be in my country forever. Once you're in, no one will ever force you out.

"But make sure you enter in." I pointed at the White House, to our east. "You want to get into the White House, you need a reservation. You can't just walk in off the street. You walk up there and say, 'Let me in,' and the security guard will look at his list and say, 'You're not on it.'

"Likewise, there's only one way into El Papá's house. That's through me, his Son. He sent me so people would have a way back to him. There's no other entrance except me, because only the Son's sacrifice can pay for your sins and provide forgiveness, and only the risen Son can pour El Papá's life into you. El Papá loves the world—he loves you—so much that he is willing to sacrifice his own Son. Whoever trusts in me won't perish. Instead, he'll share in El Papá's life—and his life lasts forever.

"Those construction workers behind you, on that scaffolding at the Smithsonian, they'll get into El Papá's house much easier than those who don't think they need me. That includes those who are trying to kill me. It's hard to get into El Papá's house if you don't think you need to. One day they'll realize their need, and they'll pound on the door: 'Let us in! We represented the people!' And I'll say to them, 'Go away! I never knew you.' They'll be miserable, knowing what they missed, and furious that they missed it. But they'll be helpless to do anything about it. Don't be like them."

By mid-afternoon, the crowd around the Lincoln Memorial had grown to tens of thousands. The crowd of protestors nearby had grown as well, trying its best to drown me out. A couple of scuffles between the two groups had already broken out. The police had separated people both times.

Shortly after the second, two of the police walked up to where I was teaching. "We'd like to ask you to disperse," one of them said.

"Why?" I asked. "We're not holding an organized demonstration."

"We know."

"But that group over there is," I said.

"We know."

"Probably without a permit."

He nodded. "But we've been instructed to leave them alone. And we're concerned about real violence breaking out."

For the sake of the crowd, that was the last thing I wanted. "Do you have a bullhorn I could use for a moment?"

He retrieved a bullhorn and gave it to me. I faced the crowd, thanked them for being there, and asked them to disperse away from the protestors. The Twelve and I walked back to our vehicles, people crowding around us on the way.

"I can't believe how many people were here today," Pedro said as we got into one of the SUVs.

"The parade on Friday will be ten times as big," Mike commented.

Despite my attempts to convince them otherwise, I knew what the Twelve expected. They imagined the Passover parade on Friday would be some sort of coronation. Not officially, of course, but the time when the huge crowd would call for me to restore the country—and especially the government—to what it was meant to be. To make it a government of the people, not of only the powerful, once more.

El Papá had other, much greater, plans.

That night, the Twelve drew my attention to a talking heads program on cable news. The panel was discussing the statements I had made in DC, and speculating as to what I might tell the crowd to do on Friday.

"What in the world is Manuel Gonzales talking about?" one commentator asked. "Who is trying to kill him?"

"He's completely nuts," another commented.

"He's dangerous," the third said.

Pedro turned to me. "I never realized you were dangerous."

"I'm very dangerous," I replied in all seriousness. "To them."

We went to the Jefferson Memorial on Wednesday morning. A crowd formed around us again. So did a protest nearby. Again, they tried to drown me out. But the police, better prepared this time, set up barricades between the two groups.

"I don't know how long you'll be able to stay here today," one of the policemen commented to me. "We don't want things to get out of hand."

"We won't be here that long," I assured him.

"A very successful entrepreneur bought out a global competitor," I told the crowd. "He expected that the company he bought out would return a profit, but the company's executives hated him and did everything they could to sabotage him. He sent one consultant after another to try to improve their performance, but they treated the consultants shamefully and nothing improved. Finally, he sent his own son to lead the company, but they had the son framed on false fraud charges and he was imprisoned overseas. Now, what do you think the successful entrepreneur will do?"

A man close to me answered, "He'll fire every one of them, uncover the fraud plot, and have them all thrown in jail."

"Exactly," I said. "And he will turn that company over to people who will run it properly.

"I came to seek and to save people who are lost in life. The truth is everyone is lost in life. They just don't know it. They aren't joined to the one who is life. That's why I'm here; I've come to connect them to El Papá.

"When I come in my glory, I'll sit on my throne, and all people will be gathered before me. I'll divide people into two groups: those I'm joined to, and those I'm not joined to. Those who have my life in them, and those who don't. I'll say to the first group, 'You treated me with goodness, and kindness, and compassion.'

"And they'll say, 'When did we do that?'

"And I'll say, 'You did it to me every time you did it to anyone.'

"But to the others I'll say, 'You were unkind, and took advantage of me, and considered me worthless.'

"And they'll say, 'What!? When did we do those things?'

"And I'll say, 'Every day as you did them to others.'

"The first group will receive their rightful place in my kingdom. The second group will be thrown out."

A man close to me asked, "So are you saying I just need to be good to people to get into your kingdom?"

"No," I answered. "I'm not saying that at all. Good fruit comes from good trees. Make the tree good, and the fruit will be good. If you're a good tree, you'll produce good fruit. The greatest commands are these: Love the Lord your God with all your heart, soul, mind, and strength, and love your neighbor as yourself. But how are you going to keep those commands? You need a new heart. You need to become a good tree. I'm the only one who can give you a new heart."

I pointed toward the Lincoln Memorial. "Yesterday we were meeting over there. Beside it there's a reflecting pool. Its water is stagnant. It's dirty. It's not going to quench anyone's thirst. But the one who believes in me, I'll take out his old, dead heart, and give him a new, living heart. And the Spirit, who will then come live in him, will flow out of him like water pouring over Niagara Falls."

At 11:00, I stopped speaking and gathered the Twelve around me. "We're heading to the Capitol for my Senate hearing. I requested that seats be reserved for all of you."

We started walking toward the Capitol. Normally it would have been a fifty-minute walk. With the crowd pressing around us, and with the police forming a moving wall to keep our crowd and the protestors apart, I knew it would take longer.

"We love you, Manuel!" people nearby kept shouting.

"El Papá loves you!" I shouted in reply.

We finally got to the Capitol and climbed its steps. I glanced back over my shoulder. The crowd had grown during our walk.

It had turned into a rally of tens of thousands, stretching back toward the Washington Monument. They were all in Washington, no doubt, for the Passover parade, and they were cheering loudly. To the sides, many others were protesting loudly.

We passed through the security scan at the west entrance. Dan was waiting for me when I went through. "Don't you have any notes?"

I shook my head.

"What—are you just going to speak off the cuff?"

I smiled at him. "Dan, I know exactly what I'm going to say."

"Which is what?"

"What El Papá has told me to say."

FIFTY-TWO

A Capitol policeman escorted me to the hearing room of the Senate Subcommittee on Investigations. At the front, on a raised platform, behind curved wooden paneling, the six senators who comprised the subcommittee were taking their seats. Fifteen feet in front of them were three tables with chairs for witnesses and their attorneys and handlers. Behind these were perhaps 80 chairs for the audience, all already occupied except the back row, where the Twelve took their seats. Television cameras were set up along the sides of the room. They would be broadcasting live.

I walked to the center witness table and sat, alone. Photographers descended upon me until, a minute later, the chairwoman, Senator Davis, struck her gavel.

"The Senate Subcommittee on Investigations will come to order," she said. The photographers scurried to the sides of the room. The crowd quieted.

"Thank you to our witness, Manuel Gonzales, for being here today. I know you've come a long distance. Thank you to the ranking member, Senator Griffin, as well, on a day when many of us have had to fly back. Thanks, too, to all of our audience and to many outside the hearing room and watching on television. We know that the interest in this meeting is high.

"Our goal today is simply to gain a more complete understanding of the events and alleged phenomena that you have been associated with, Mr. Gonzales, and to assess whether implicit in these are any matters of concern to the people. You have been accused by various parties of making serious statements. Very serious statements, some of which could be considered criminal. Would you like to make an introductory statement to set the record straight concerning what you have said?"

I leaned toward the microphone in front of me. "Senator, I've spoken openly all along. I haven't taught in secret. Most of my teaching is on videos online. Men and women who have been following me know exactly what I've been saying. I suggest you ask them."

"I am asking you, Mr. Gonzales."

I shook my head. "No, Senator. I have no statement to make."

"Then we will proceed," the senator responded. "I turn to the ranking member, Senator Griffin."

Mark Griffin, a 24-year veteran of the Senate, began with an air of cordiality. "Thank you, Madam Chairwoman. I want to start by thanking our witness for being here. You've come a long way on relatively short notice. It's my understanding that your family is originally from Mexico, Mr. Gonzales, is that correct?"

I scooted my chair closer to the microphone and straightened. "My father was born in the United States, Senator. My mother is a first-generation legal immigrant who became a U.S. citizen."

"Did your father start the auto repair shop that you and your siblings operate?"

"He did."

"And you went into the auto repair business right after high school, is that correct?"

"I started working there during junior high."

"Did you go to trade school and become a licensed auto mechanic?"

"No. My father taught me."

"So you went neither to trade school, to a community college, nor a four-year college."

"That is correct."

The senator cleared his throat. "Mr. Gonzales, do you have any formal training in religion or religious studies?"

"I do not, Senator."

"Yet you present yourself as an expert in religion."

"I present myself only as the one sent from the Father."

"The father?"

"God."

The senator looked down at his notes. "So, on what basis do you claim that people should believe the things you say?"

"Senator, the things I do testify to who I am, and who sent me. Anyone who's willing to do the Father's will, he'll know whether what I say is true or not."

The answer didn't seem to satisfy the senator, but he simply looked at the chairwoman. "That's all for now, Madam Chairwoman."

The chairwoman turned to her left. "The chair recognizes Senator Klineman."

Geoff Klineman, the youngest of the subcommittee members, dispensed with any pleasantries. "Mr. Gonzales, you had some association with a man named Juan Carlos. He was said by some to be fomenting rebellion. Can you please tell me, what is your assessment of Juan Carlos and what he was advocating?"

"Juan Carlos was introducing people to a new way to connect with God, and, by extension, with each other. His mission was to point people to me. God appointed him to his task. He spoke the truth."

The senator paused for a moment, quickly scribbling some notes. "Mr. Gonzales ..." He looked back up at me. "It is said that you heal people at will, that you calm storms, that you can even raise the dead. Are these things true? And if true, do you believe these abilities could theoretically constitute a threat to democracy?"

"That depends on whether you consider connecting people to God, and to one another, a threat, Senator."

A smattering of laughter passed through the crowd. The senator's brow furrowed. "Mr. Gonzales, some people say that we as humans are children of God. Some might even phrase it that we are sons and daughters of God. You have been quoted, however—videoed, even—as saying that you personally are God's own Son. It seems to me that would make you pretty much equal with God. Is that what you are claiming? Are you saying that you are the one and only Son of God?"

"I am. That will be evident when, one day, you see me sitting at the right hand of the Father, and coming with the clouds of heaven."

The senator leaned closer to his mic and stared unflinchingly at me. "You are making some incredible claims about yourself. What proof would you like to offer this subcommittee as to what you are claiming?"

"I'm not here to prove anything, Senator. As I said, all the things I've been doing, they tell you everything you need to know. I've told you who I am. The Father has told you who I am as well."

Klineman was visibly irritated. "You do not have a monopoly on faith. I believe in God as well. I would even say he is my father, too."

"If God were your father, Senator, you would love the things I'm doing, since I've come from him. But you don't know him. I know him. If I said I didn't, I'd be lying. But I always speak the truth. That's why you don't believe me, because I speak the truth. If you were of God, you could hear his words—the very words I'm speaking to you."

Chairwoman Davis picked up her gavel and pounded it. "Mr.

Gonzales, I am in authority here and I do not permit you to cast insults at any member of this subcommittee."

"Senator, you would have no authority unless it had been given you from above." I looked up and down the row of senators seated in their elevated seats before me. "Which one of you can convict me of saying anything false? Of a single wrongdoing?"

Davis glared at me. "We are the ones asking the questions here today. We do so to arrive at the truth."

"Senator Davis, I am the truth. The truth is sitting right before you. But you cannot see that, precisely because you are not of the truth."

Several in the crowd gasped, and Davis banged her gavel again.

"Mr. Gonzales, if you cannot appropriately honor this sub-committee, you will be held in contempt."

"With all due respect, Senator, what have I said that's in error? If nothing, why would you hold someone in contempt for speaking the truth in a public hearing?"

Davis scowled, paused for a moment, and then turned to her left. "Senator Hart, you have the floor."

Teresa Hart was known as a middle-of-the-road politician, more intent on compromise than making waves. Her face lacked the animosity that Klineman's had shown.

"Mr. Gonzales, you've been reported as saying that if all the government buildings here in Washington were torn down, you could rebuild all of them in three days. If that is true, we could use you as a consultant on the infrastructure subcommittee."

The audience's laughter broke the tension in the room. The senator continued. "Are you advocating that all the physical structures of the federal government be torn down?"

"Is this something you heard me say, or is this what someone reported to you?"

Hart smiled. "Well, I haven't been to many of your rallies."

"I have not advocated that, no."

The senator looked at her notes for a moment. "Mr. Gonzales, you claim to be ushering in a new government. That is an astounding and, to many, a dangerous claim. Is that your intention, to set up a new government?"

"My government isn't of this world, Senator. If it were, my followers would defend me to the death. But my government is not of this realm. Not yet."

Hart looked over at Davis. "Madam Chairwoman, I yield the remainder of my time to Senator Howard."

"Senator Howard."

Blaine Howard, a former Baltimore area district attorney, reveled in his reputation as a no-nonsense interrogator. He bypassed cordiality and began.

"Mr. Gonzales, I will ask you directly. Has it ever been, or is it now, your intention to set up, at any time, a new government in these United States?"

"It is, Senator."

A murmur passed through the crowd. The senator stared at me until the crowd quieted. He asked his remaining questions in rapid fire.

"Is it your intention to set yourself up as king over the people who live in the United States of America?"

"It is, Senator."

"Have you advocated to any individuals that they give their primary allegiance to you as king?"

"I have."

"Will this kingship of yours eventually replace the constitutional republic under which we currently operate?"

"It will."

"And have you conspired with such individuals to bring this kingship of yours into existence?"

"My kingdom already exists, Senator. You cannot stop it. But to answer your question, yes, I have."

I heard gasps again from the audience.

"Manuel, no!" Emma exclaimed from the back of the room.

The senator turned to Davis. "Madam Chairwoman, I believe we have all the testimony that we need. I move that the subcommittee adjourn."

Davis glanced around at the other four senators. "Second?"

"I second," Senator Klineman responded.

"If there are no objections ..."

The senators shook their heads. The chairwoman pounded her gavel. "Then this hearing is hereby adjourned."

The crowd sat in stunned silence.

FIFTY-THREE

Attorney General Wu, FBI Director Ottenger, and Deputy Director Patterson watched in Wu's office as the subcommittee's proceedings ended. Wu powered off the TV and looked at the two men.

"Well." Ottenger leaned back in his chair. "Our job just got easier. I don't think we'll even need to make the overseas financial allegations."

He expected Wu to concur, but she shook her head. "We may think he just hanged himself, but have you seen how large the crowds have been around him at the Lincoln Memorial?"

"Many thousands."

She looked out her window. "More than that. How many are out there on the Mall right now, demonstrating in support of him?" She looked at Patterson.

"Thirty or forty thousand, according to the Park Police estimate an hour ago. Not including the counter-protestors."

"And how many, if we put him on trial, are going to be on the Mall protesting? Several hundred thousand? A million?"

The three of them stared at each other.

"Are you saying we should do nothing?" Patterson asked.

"No, I'm not. We can't do that. I'm saying two things: first, we don't want to pit this as an us-against-him fight. That's a no-win situation for us. We'd lose every voter who supports him. And second, where would we even find a jury to convict this guy? Half of those people out there on the Mall might be local. We would need twelve jurors who are all willing to vote against him. Does either of you think we can accomplish that?"

The two men were silent. "Unlikely," Ottenger finally responded.

"Exactly." Wu thought for a moment. "We're going to have to alter our plans. Get rid of him ourselves."

"The FBI?" Ottenger asked. "We can't—"

She shook her head. "No. It can never be blamed on the FBI. But neither can we take him to trial. That would be a disaster. We have to think of another way."

They sat silently for a few moments before Patterson finally spoke. "I may know a way."

They discussed Patterson's idea for the next hour and a half. At the end, Wu stood and looked each of them in the eye. "I want to be sure we're all clear on something. The main message that comes out of what you're about to pull off—the message that all of his supporters get—is that this movement is over. It will no longer be allowed. Make sure that's communicated loud and clear. Juan Carlos, Manuel Gonzales, this whole thing is done. And it's not coming back."

She turned and left the room. Ottenger looked at Patterson. "You think what you have in mind will accomplish that?"

"Oh, yeah," Patterson replied. "It'll accomplish it, all right."

FIFTY-FOUR

ST. MARYS COUNTY, MARYLAND

After the hearing, the Twelve and I returned to the Thompson's. The mood was somber.

"Should we go back to McAllen?" Mike asked. "I'm not sure we're totally safe here."

"No," I answered. "I must face what awaits me here. It's what I came for."

"But the statements you made at the hearing …"

"And all the protestors out there against us," Ana added.

"I spoke the truth," I said to Mike. "That will be clear soon enough. As for the protestors, I will accomplish exactly the work El Papá sent me to do. That's what matters."

Ben and Abigail had prepared us all a lasagna dinner with salad and French bread. We ate and then gathered in the living room.

"I need some time to myself tomorrow," I said to them. "The Thompsons have volunteered to take all of you sightseeing."

"Manuel," Emma said, concern written over her face. "Are you just trying to protect us?" I started to answer, but she continued. "Will you be here when we get back, or will they …"

"I will be here, Emma. I promise."

They were all silent. Finally Maya spoke. "Manuel, I'm feeling very …" She looked around at everyone, and then back at me. "Troubled. I don't know how else to put it."

I nodded. "I understand. But don't be troubled. Seriously. Trust me, just like you've trusted El Papá. Nothing is happening outside of El Papá's preordained plan."

"It doesn't seem like it's all going according to plan."

I smiled gently at her. "I know. Let me help you refocus. El Papá is building a new temple. It has many rooms. Those rooms are your hearts. I'm leaving you briefly to get those rooms ready. I'll come back, and we will live with each of you there forever. I've told you the way to live with us there."

"What's the way to do that?" Sebastian asked. "I must have missed it."

"Sebastian, isn't it obvious by now? I'm the way. I'm the only way to the Father, because I'm his Son. Religion won't get you to him. Living good enough won't get you to him. Those are man-made methods. How are they going to join your spirit to his? The only way to be connected to him, to become one with him, is through me."

Diego leaned forward. "Manuel, can you just … show us El Papá?"

I was taken aback by his question. "Diego—really? How can you ask that? You've been seeing El Papá all along. If you've seen me, you've seen El Papá. He's in me. I'm in him. We are one. The things you've heard me say, and seen me do, I don't do on my own. El Papá lives in me. He lives his life through me. He does his work through me."

I looked around at them. They were listening intently. Maybe my words were sinking in.

"It'll be the exact same way with you," I said. That didn't sink in at all. "Look, a day is coming—very soon—when you'll know for sure that El Papá lives in me, and I live in you, and you live in me. Everyone who trusts in me, he lives in God, and God lives in him. El Papá, and I, and the Spirit, we will come to you. We will live in you."

I thought for a moment. "Here—follow me." We all walked out onto the large fenced-in patio. On its far end, vines were growing up the sides of a trellis. I walked across the patio and cradled a vine. "I told you this a long time ago, in Mexico. Right now, El Papá is the vine. I'm the branch. His life flows through me. I live because of him.

"In a short while, you'll be the branch. I'll be the vine. You'll live in me. My life will flow through you. You won't be producing the fruit yourself. I'll be producing it through you."

I paused for a moment. "Here's the truth: you're going to do greater things than me, because I'll be living in you."

"But how will we know this is true?" Justin asked.

I smiled. "Trust me. You'll know. And the Holy Spirit, he'll be your teacher. Once he comes to live in you, he'll be with you forever. He'll take the things that are mine, and he'll show them to you. He'll show you all the things you're about to be freely given. That's his job, to show you what you're freely given. He'll guide you. And he'll show you what's to come."

"What *is* to come?" Emma asked. "I'm scared, Manuel."

I nodded. "I know. But you don't need to be. You are my friends. I'm telling you all these things so that you'll be full of joy. I'm full of joy. Have you noticed?" They smiled at me. "I want you to be full of joy, too. Very soon you'll be sad and grieving, because I'm going away. But that'll be short-lived. You'll be like a woman giving birth. It's painful for a brief time, but then she's filled with joy when the baby's put in her arms. I'll see you again soon, and then no one will be able to take your joy away."

I paused again, and then Sebastian spoke. "But … our enemies. Your enemies."

"Don't worry about our enemies, Sebastian. You're not of the world anymore. You're mine. You're El Papá's. The world will hate you and treat you badly, just as they are treating me, because they don't know El Papá."

"Are you saying you won't be with us anymore?" Maya asked. Maya was always the one who sat quietly and thought things through before she spoke.

"I'm going to El Papá," I answered. "But trust me—that's best for you. I'll send the Holy Spirit in my place. You just won't have me walking around physically with you anymore. If I don't go, we can't come live in you. We can't live through you."

I reached out and took the hands of Maya and Pedro, those sitting closest to me. They did the same, and in a moment the whole group was joined together. "All things that are El Papá's, he has given to me. And I give them to you. I can't say much more at this point; it would be too much for you. I'll simply say this: I give you my peace. My peace isn't the same as the world's. It will guard you completely. So don't be disturbed. Don't be afraid. I've already overcome the world."

FIFTY-FIVE

Late the next morning, Ben and Abigail took off with the Twelve.
After they left, I spent some time talking with El Papá, and listening. Then I got out the groceries the Thompsons had picked up for
us. The Twelve would be gone quite a while, but I had a lot to do.

Six hours later, the Twelve arrived back at the house. They
did a double take when they walked through the front door and
glanced into the formal dining room on the left.

"¡Órale!" Diego said. "¿Qué es esto?" *Wow. What's this?*

"The Passover meal," I replied.

Maya walked to the table and looked over the table settings
and the spread of food. "Who prepared all of this?"

"I did."

"For real?" Kiara asked.

I smiled at her. "What—you think I can't host a celebration?
Why don't you guys get ready for dinner?"

They all returned a few minutes later.

"Who picked up the guys' room?" Pedro asked.

"And the women's," Ana added.

"And cleaned the toilets," Emma said. "They're sparkling."

"I did," I answered.

Ana looked at me, surprised. "You spent your day cleaning
toilets?"

"While the lamb was cooking."

We sat down to eat. I looked around at them all, my heart
filled with love for each of them. They were mine. They had stayed

with me faithfully. Now, my time was almost here. El Papá had sent me, and he had put everything in my hands. I was going back to him. But they would remain, and carry on. They had no idea what awaited them, but I loved them for what they were about to do: venture into the complete unknown.

"I have a quick word before we begin," I said. "You call me El Único. Your Lord. And I am. You've served me faithfully on our adventure together, but this afternoon I've had the privilege of serving you. If I, your Lord, serve you like this, I want you to serve one another like this as well. Always.

"I'm giving you a new commandment. Love each other, the same way I've loved you. There's no love greater than laying down your life for your friends. That's what I'm doing for you. All people will know that you belong to me, if you love each other with my kind of love."

I picked up some of the unleavened bread. "I've been looking forward to having this last Passover meal with you. I won't eat it again until it's fulfilled in El Papá's kingdom."

I broke the bread and handed it to them. "Take this and eat it. It's my body. My body is broken for you."

I picked up my wine glass, and they all followed suit. "This is the last time I'll drink wine until El Papá's kingdom comes. The Hebrews had to slay a perfect lamb and put its blood on the doorposts to be delivered from God's wrath on the land of Egypt. The lamb was the sacrifice, to save them. That all points to me. I'm the true sacrifice." I raised my wine glass a bit higher. "This is my blood, ushering in a completely new covenant. Drink it. It's poured out for many, for the forgiveness of sins."

I then cut some of the lamb and passed it around the table. "Before leaving Egypt, the Hebrews needed food for the journey. They had to cook and eat the lamb. It was life to them. It was nourishment. They had to take the life into them. Eat this. I'm El Papá's lamb. When you take me into yourself—which you soon will—you will have the life. My life."

As we ate, I said to the Twelve, "There's a nearby park that Ben pointed out to me. After dinner, I'd like to go there with you all and talk to El Papá."

When we had almost finished the meal, Maya looked at me. "Manuel, you've grown quiet."

I nodded. "The scripture must be fulfilled. One of you sitting here at the table will betray me to the authorities."

They were shocked and all looked around at one another.

"What?! How could any of us do that?"

"Are you sure?"

"Is it me? It's not me."

"Is it Dan? He's the lawyer."

Sebastian, sitting closest to me, finally leaned over and asked quietly, "Manuel, who is it?"

I pulled out my cell phone and texted someone at the table.

Go ahead. Do it quickly.

Jorge glanced at the text, and then at me. He got up and silently left.

"Where is he going?" Mike asked.

All of them wondered the same thing, I knew. But I ignored the question. My next words were hard to say. "I won't be with you much longer. You'll wonder where I am, but where I'm going, you can't come now. Later on, you will."

"I want to come with you now," Pedro declared.

"Pedro, Satan has demanded permission to test you mercilessly. I've prayed for you, though, that your faith won't fail. When you've returned to me, strengthen your brothers and sisters."

"Manuel, I'll never turn away," Pedro insisted. "I'll follow you anywhere—even to death!"

"Will you, Pedro? Within the next 24 hours, you'll tell millions of people you don't even know me."

"I'll never do that!"

Everyone else nodded in agreement. "We'll never do that!"

Before anyone had a chance to say anything else, I said to them all, "The hour has come for me to be glorified. But my soul is extremely troubled."

"We're here for you, Manuel," Emma said.

I smiled at her. "You all have stood with me. One day you'll reign with me. But right now, I have to drink the cup El Papá has given me to drink. Papá, glorify your name!"

The house shook, as in an earthquake, and a loud voice came from heaven. "I have glorified it, and I will glorify it again."

The Eleven looked petrified.

"That was for your sakes, not mine," I said. "Judgment is now on this world. The ruler of this world will be cast out. When I'm lifted up, I'll draw all people to me."

I knew they had many questions, but it wasn't time for that. It was already getting late. "Let's go to the park," I said.

We got into the two SUVs, drove to the park, and sat down together on an old merry-go-round. And then I prayed.

"Papá," I said, "now's the time. Glorify me, that I may glorify you. You gave me authority over all people, so I can give them eternal life. Eternal life is this: knowing you, and knowing me. I've glorified you here. I've done the work you assigned me. Now, Papá, glorify me with yourself—the same glory I had with you before creation.

"I've shown these eleven who you are. I've given them your words. They understand I came from you, that you sent me. What I ask, I ask not for the world, but for them. They are yours, and you gave them to me, and they did what you told them to.

"I'm coming to you now, Papá, but they're staying here, and I'm sending them out into the world. Guard them, as I've guarded them. They aren't of this world system any more than I am. It hates them, just as it hates me. Protect them from the evil one. Set them apart through the truth of your word, that they may be full of joy.

"I ask, too, for everyone who will believe in me through them. Connect them to us. Make them one with us, with no separation between us. You and I are perfectly one. You're in me, and I'm in you. Join them to us the same way—we in them, and they in us. Give them the perfect oneness with us that we have with each other. I want the world to know that you love them the same way you love me. If they're one with us, the world will believe you sent me.

"Cause them all to be with me where I am. Let them see my glory, which you gave me, because you loved me before the world even began.

"Righteous Papá, the world doesn't know you, but I do. These eleven know you sent me, and I've shown them who you are. I'll continue to show them, so your love for me may be inside them. And so I can live inside them, too."

We all sat silently for a moment. The gravity of what awaited pressed down upon me like the ocean depths upon a diver's lungs. I said to Pedro, Sebastian, and Emma, "You three come with me, will you?" We walked across the park and sat on two benches.

"I feel overwhelmed with grief," I told them. "Stay here and pray. I'm going over there to talk to El Papá." I pointed to another bench further away.

I fell down beside the bench, engulfed with dread of what approached. Never before had El Papá and I been separated. Now, we would not only be utterly separated, but I would actually become sin itself. I would become the ultimate horror, and would be completely alone. His righteous wrath against all of humanity's sin, and all the devastation it had caused, would fall upon me. I would fulfill my role. I was the lamb to be slain.

"Papá!" I cried repeatedly. "Is there no other way?"

I stayed there, praying, for at least half an hour. Then I got up to check on my three friends. They were looking at their phones.

"Couldn't you stay focused this long?" I asked them. "Pray to not be tempted. Your spirit may be willing, but the flesh is weak."

I went back and passionately prayed. After fifteen minutes, I looked down at my arms, shocked at what I saw. My soul was in such agony that blood, from tiny burst vessels, was seeping through my skin. "Papá!" I implored again. "Is this the only option?"

I lay quietly, and he spoke to me. Finally, I simply said, "If there is no other way, your will be done."

A minute later flashing blue and red lights approached. Numerous black vehicles converged on the park, sirens blaring. FBI agents leaped out of the vehicles, guns drawn. The eight still on the merry-go-round ran to the four of us in terror.

"How did they know we'd be here?" Sofia screamed above the commotion.

The agents were close behind. One shone a flashlight in our faces, and then stepped toward me.

"Are you Manuel Gonzales?"

"I am."

The moment I said "I am," all the agents were shoved back and fell to the ground as if hit by a hurricane force wind. They struggled back to their feet and the original agent, shaken, approached me again.

"Manuel Gonzales, we have a warrant for your arrest."

"If it's me you want," I replied, "let my friends go. They've done nothing wrong."

He turned me around, pulled my arms back, slapped hand-cuffs on me, and walked me to one of the vehicles. As he pushed me inside, I glanced back. The agents had all returned to their SUVs. The Eleven stood, motionless. I could hear the women crying. Then the door slammed shut, and we drove off.

FIFTY-SIX

We drove into DC, through its deserted early morning streets. I glanced at the Capitol and the White House as we passed by. Fifteen minutes later, we approached a group of non-descript six-story brown buildings that looked like a prison.

It was. We slowed and passed a sign that read "Department of Corrections: Central Detention Facility." We stopped and I was pulled out of the vehicle and led through two doors, to a processing station. The attendant at the station did a double take when she saw me.

"Why is he here?" she asked the agent in charge.

"Federal charges," he replied curtly.

"Then take him to the CTF next door."

"We were instructed to bring him here." He pulled out a folded paper and handed it to her.

She glanced over it, sighed, and shook her head. "All right. We'll handle him from here."

The agents left. The attendant looked at me. "I have to process you in. I have no choice."

I simply nodded to her.

They seized my personal effects, collected my personal information, fingerprinted me, and took mug shots of me. They performed a cursory physical exam, strip searched me for contraband, and issued me an inmate uniform. Once I had it on, a guard read me my incarceration rights and a summary of facility rules.

Two hours after my arrival, in the middle of the night, they walked me into a cell block. Inmates stirred and recognized me immediately. They were silent, watching what was happening to me. I was led into a cell of my own. It had concrete walls, a single bed with a paper-thin mattress, a sink, and a toilet. The door of bars closed behind me. I sat on the bed and looked out at the inmates across from me.

"Hey, man," one of them finally said. He walked to the front of his cell. "If you're really the Son of God, why don't you get yourself out of here. And us, too."

His cellmate agreed.

But one of the inmates in the next cell said to him, "Are you kidding, man? He's done nothing wrong. We got what we deserved." He looked at me. "Manuel, when you set up your kingdom, I want to be part of it."

I smiled at him. "You will be."

After what seemed like a couple of hours, two guards appeared at the entrance to my cell. One of them opened the door.

"Come with us," he said.

"Where are you taking him?" the inmate I had spoken to asked.

The guard turned and shrugged. "Some transfer."

They walked me back through the facility, past the area where I had been processed. We headed toward what looked like a side entrance. Two men dressed similarly to the agents from earlier that night stood at the door. Their jackets read "FBI," but the guards had apparently not dealt with these men before.

"Why are we turning him over at this entrance?" one of the guards asked.

"Enhanced security."

"Where is he being taken?"

"For questioning."

"Don't we need to sign him out?" the other guard asked.

"No."

The two guards exchanged confused looks. "Hold on," the first guard said. He got on his walkie-talkie for a minute, and then turned to the second. "Joyner says to proceed."

The guards handed me over to the two men, who handcuffed me, grabbed me by my elbows, and put me inside the back of an unmarked black SUV parked ten feet from the side entrance. It had no license plate.

We drove away in silence, but increasingly, I became aware of a presence in the vehicle. I hadn't felt it with the agents who had arrested me earlier, nor had I felt it at the jail. All of those individuals, however misguidedly, were simply doing their jobs. But now, a malevolent spiritual presence accompanied us. Its intent was pure evil. The time of the power of darkness had come.

FIFTY-SEVEN

Pedro started when he heard a loud knock at the front door of the Thompson's home. He'd been in the living room all night, awake. Dawn was just breaking. Manuel had been arrested six hours before. *Now they've come for us,* he thought.

He crept to the front window and peeked past the curtains, his pulse already quickening. But it wasn't the FBI. It was a media truck from a national cable news channel. *How did they find out where we were?* He could understand the government tracking them down so quickly. But the media? There was no point in not responding. They would simply keep knocking, and more would arrive. Better to get rid of them quickly. He opened the door.

A microphone was shoved in his face, a live camera recording his every move.

"Pedro Martinez," the reporter immediately asked, "is it true you were at the scene last night when the arrest of Manuel Gonzales went down?"

Pedro felt paralyzed by the abruptness of the question. "I ... uh ... who are you?"

"Were you there last night at the scene of Manuel Gonzales's arrest?"

Pedro didn't respond.

"You are Pedro Martinez, right—one of Manuel Gonzales's closest followers?"

"No, ma'am," Pedro said. He glanced behind him, desperate for someone to step forward and take the attention away from him, but no one did. He looked back at the reporter. "You're confusing me with someone else. Honestly, I don't even know him." He stepped back inside and quickly shut the door. Diego, Sebastian, and Ana were standing at the bottom of the stairs, in the foyer, fear in their eyes. Ben Thompson and Dan McElroy were coming down the stairs.

"How did they find us?" Sebastian asked.

Dan peaked out the front window. The media van was parked on the street. More would soon follow, he knew. He looked back at the others. "I think we have a more important question. How are we going to get out of this? Whatever Manuel is being charged with, we could be charged with conspiracy along with him."

They all stared at him, trying to wrap their heads around what he'd just said.

"So what do we do?" Ana asked.

"We pack up," Dan replied. "Quickly. Before anyone else shows up."

"Like the FBI?"

"Like the FBI."

"Where are we going?" Sebastian asked.

"We'll figure that out on the way. But right now, we'd all be safer back in South Texas. Away from the DC courts."

He glanced at Ben.

"Whatever you need," Ben said.

Dan nodded. Being in this kind of legal jeopardy was the last thing he ever imagined happening to him. But here he was. Here they all were. He glanced at the others. "Get everyone up. We're out in 15 minutes."

NORTHERN VIRGINIA

The vehicle I was in left the Central Detention Facility, drove a mile or so on a wide city street and then got onto a freeway. Daylight had just broken, but the streets were almost entirely empty. The whole city would have the day off for the Passover march. Shortly, I saw the Jefferson Memorial on the right. We crossed the Potomac and headed west on the interstate, away from DC. After what seemed like an hour or so, we exited. Five minutes later, on a side road, we entered a nature preserve.

The preserve seemed deserted. As we drove through the old forest, its trees sprouting fresh spring leaves, we passed neither cars nor people. The driver stopped the SUV in a gravel parking lot next to three other identical vehicles with no license plates. The two men pulled me out of the car, holding me by the elbows as we headed toward a hiking trail to our right.

Still handcuffed, I half-walked, half-stumbled down the trail with the two men. We encountered no hikers, but we did pass an armed lookout every several hundred yards, each dressed in black attire, with a black ski mask. We came upon several old gravesites on our left and crossed two streams on wooden bridges, all the while heading slightly uphill. Finally, after a mile or so, the trail emptied into a clearing that overlooked an expansive forest at least 100 feet below.

On the edge of the overlook, on the ground, were two thick wooden beams. They had been nailed together in the shape of a cross.

FIFTY-EIGHT

Sofia pressed the Purchase button on her phone and looked toward the front of the SUV. "Done," she said to Dan. "Eleven plane tickets."

Dan dialed Pedro's number in the SUV following them.

"Everyone has a ticket," Dan said, putting the phone on speaker.

"And you think they'll let us board?" Pedro asked. "I mean, they won't be waiting for us at the airport?"

"I think if they planned on arresting us today, Ben and Abigail's was the most likely spot."

"But you can't be sure."

Dan sighed. "No. We can't be sure. But we need to get back to the Valley. Some of us, maybe across the border. The only other way to get to South Texas is to rent a car and drive. Which we can't do without using a credit card. Which they could track down. There's no good option, I'm afraid."

Now what David had written in the Psalms so long before about how I would die made sense. I had read about crucifixion, an utterly barbaric form of execution meant to maximize pain for criminals, and maximize deterrence for others. Even the Romans had finally outlawed it. For me, my executioners had brought it back, no doubt for the same two purposes.

Ten or so men awaited us in the clearing, dressed in the same black attire. Several were standing lookout. Two were manning the cross. Two were manning two cameras set on tripods. One had headed back up the hiking trail. One was conversing on a walkie-talkie, one on a cell phone.

Something quickly became apparent: this operation had nothing to do with some extremist movement, or any other amateur group. Each of the men moved far too deliberately, far too professionally for that. They had received orders from someone, and they were each carrying out their assignments with precision. The whole undertaking was intended to deceive. That's what the prince of darkness did best. His agents were simply following his cue.

The two men from my vehicle and several of the others led me, still handcuffed, behind a small wooden shed fifty yards away, hidden from the sight of the hiking path. They surrounded me, and then another man emerged from the trees a few yards away. In his hand he held a long leather whip, entwined with what looked like pieces of barbed wire. Two of the men removed my handcuffs and tied me to one of the trees, my back facing outward. And then they started flogging me, each lash tearing off pieces of flesh. As they did, the men laughed and cried out "Hail! King Manuel!"

When they finally stopped, the one clearly in charge stepped forward and spit on me. "No one's going to save you now," he said.

They untied me from the tree and returned me to the others. My shirt and much of my skin had been ripped off my back. Blood dripped profusely from my cheeks on down.

The man with the walkie-talkie did a double-take when he glanced in my direction. "What did you do to him? He didn't start screaming? We didn't hear a thing."

"He didn't say a thing. Look, we were just prepping him. Blood loss. They want this over as quickly as possible. Are you ready?"

The man nodded, and they began leading me toward the cross.

As we approached it, I became aware of something descending toward us. I couldn't see it at first, but I could feel it. My body shuddered. I was filled, not with fear, but with revulsion. And then it came into view. Above me—above all of us there—hovered a cloud of what could only be described as pure evil: a demonic horde that had come to torment me, and to triumph over me.

They were a living blackness, the gathering of darkness itself to take claim of all the earth, and beyond, for all eternity. Humanity had been the heir, but had surrendered that claim. I had come to reclaim it, but now was their chance to do away with me.

The demonic swarm descended upon the clearing, howling in delight at my suffering. They mocked me and hurled the vilest insults at me, spewing the utmost hatred from the depths of their beings.

And then creation itself hid. Though still low, the morning sun had been rising in a cloudless sky. But suddenly the sky had blackened.

"What's going on?" one of the men said. "What happened to the light?"

I glanced at the sky, where the largest, blackest cloud bank I'd ever seen now obscured the sun, bringing an eerie darkness over the whole landscape.

We got to the cross. At the top of the longer beam, someone had affixed a wooden sign that had the hand-painted words, "King Manuel." The man standing there looked at me, shaking his head. "I've seen a lot of horrible stuff, but nothing like this."

They stripped me of my clothes and laid me on the wooden beams. I didn't resist. I could see my blood staining the horizontal beam. Two of the men grabbed hold of my right arm and stretched it out. I opened my palm against the plank. One of them pulled out a large hammer from a tool kit, and some steel spikes at least a foot long.

"Papá, forgive them. They have no clue what they're doing."

The man next to him took the hammer, grabbed a spike, placed its point against my skin, and struck it as hard as he could, plunging it through my wrist and into the board behind me. Blood squirted everywhere. My head started spinning. I almost passed out from the pain.

They did the same with my left wrist, then they repeated the process with my ankles. I struggled to stay conscious.

Several of them positioned the bottom of the vertical beam near a square hole in the ground. They lifted me and the cross and slid it in. It landed with a thud. It felt as if my wrists and ankles would rip clean through the spikes.

I faced out over the valley below, toward the cameras on the tripods.

"Clear the field of vision," a man at one of the cameras instructed the men closer to me. "Streaming live in five, four, three, two, one."

I glanced over toward one of the men who had crucified me. He wiped his bloody hands on his shirt and reached for his cell phone.

"It's done," he said to someone on the other end. "He can't last long. The pain has to be unbelievable."

It was. But I knew the physical pain would be the least of it.

FIFTY-NINE

The Eleven passed through security at the airport and walked to their gate.

"Let's split up," Dan suggested. "Not all sit together."

He, Mike, and Diego were heading for some seats on the other side of the concourse when he heard a shriek behind him. He spun and looked. It was Emma.

The three of them rushed to where she and the others stood, eyes fixated on the television news. Strangers were walking closer to the TV and looking as well. Dan glanced up at the screen, and then immediately turned away, aghast at what he saw. He forced himself to slowly turn back.

The chyron at the bottom read "Live video stream of Manuel Gonzales." Above that, two images shone: a closeup of Manuel's head and chest on the left, and a wide angle shot on the right, blurred below the waist. After a moment, the images moved to the upper left of the screen and the newscaster spoke. "Officials are still trying to determine where these images are coming from, to verify that they are authentic, and to attempt to rescue Mr. Gonzales."

All the women in the group were sobbing. So was Diego. Dan tried to move the group to a side area. "We need to stop making a scene. Mike, can you get a couple of the women? Sebastian?"

They all moved to a corner area and started to collect themselves.

"I just can't believe it," Pedro kept repeating.

"How are they showing such graphic images?" Ana said to no one in particular. She turned to Dan. "How can they do that?"

Dan sighed, looking toward the TV screen across the concourse. "I think the graphic images are the whole point."

"Where could they be coming from?" Justin asked.

"Couldn't be that far away," Kiara said. She looked at Ana, the police officer. "Can they reach him in time?"

Dan looked back at them and shook his head. "I don't think there's anyone in charge who wants to get there in time."

The men in the clearing quickly gathered their equipment, except for the cameras, and departed.

I was alone.

My body was quickly losing its battle. I agonized to take each breath. My throat was parched. My blood loss was beginning to produce delirium. I knew, though, that my physical suffering wasn't—

And then the moment came. The moment I had dreaded for months. No forewarning could have sufficed. Nothing could have prepared me. El Papá departed. He with whom I had been one from all eternity—for the first time, we were separated.

The vacuum in my spirit staggered me. I was thrown to the cosmos, untethered to my Source, the one I had been united with for all of time, from before time. All hope fled. Nothing would now deliver me.

"My God! My God!" I cried out. "Why have you forsaken me?"

And now came the transformation. No! my heart screamed. No! I, who had known nothing but perfect purity, perfect righteousness, perfect beauty, perfect glory, perfect beingness as the Origin of all creation—I was instantly, hideously made the opposite.

I was made to be sin itself: the cancer of creation, the ruin of humanity, the rupture in the universe's entire moral order, the utter opposite of El Papá's glory.

I became everything he hated.

And then, what had to happen, what I came to bear, what I'd chosen to suffer from before the world began, finally became reality.

All of El Papá's wrath against sin, against the ruin of his creation, against the horror of human suffering, all of the judgment of God stored since the beginning, descended.

Upon me.

El Papá's judgment—the judgment due to all of humanity—poured upon me in all its fullness.

I let myself be crushed.

When it was finally over, when his wrath had been spent, when the infinite penalty had been paid, with my last ounce of energy I managed to raise my head.

"It's done," I said. "The payment is made."

I took my last breath and said, "Papá, I commit my spirit into your hands." And I bowed my head.

Sixty

Shortly after 1:00 that afternoon, Ben Thompson called Congressman Henry Garcia's cell phone. They talked for a few minutes until Ben finally asked, "Can you make that happen? This afternoon?"

"Government offices are closed," Garcia answered. "And the city is in chaos. The whole Passover parade has turned into a giant protest march."

"People will answer their cell phones," Ben said. "People you know."

There was silence for a moment from the other end. "I can make it happen. I'll call you to let you know when and where."

"I'll be near the Capitol."

Two hours later, the two of them met at the district morgue. Too late, the FBI had tracked where the images of Manuel Gonzales had been live-streamed from. They took his lifeless body down and transported it back for identification. Ben and Henry performed that task for the coroner.

"Where do you want the body sent?" the technician asked once all paperwork had been filled out.

Ben pulled out several sheets of paper and handed it to him. "Funeral home at Cottonwood Creek Memorial Cemetery. They're waiting in front."

"That was awfully quick. How'd you manage that today?"

"It was pre-arranged," Ben answered.

"Pre-arranged?" the man responded. "I thought he was killed."

"He was. He told me to prepare for his burial beforehand."

The man stared at him, for a moment speechless, and then glanced at the paperwork. "All right, everything's in order."

Ben had arranged for the funeral home to quickly clean and dress the body, exactly as Manuel had instructed him.

"Don't you want to be flown back to McAllen for the burial?" Ben had asked Manuel.

"No. Bury me immediately. Above ground, in a mausoleum. Same day, in DC. You'll need to pay them extra to do it on Friday. And get the cheapest casket you possibly can."

"Why?"

Manuel had smiled. "Because by the third day I won't need it anymore." He had written Ben a check to cover the expected cost.

Ben accompanied the body to the funeral home. After prepping it, they placed the body in a casket and took it to the cemetery's mausoleum. Ben laid a hand on the casket and prayed before they pushed it into the vault and sealed it. He and the cemetery employees walked out of the mausoleum, and then Ben approached the four FBI agents who had accompanied them.

"It's over," Ben told them. "I guess you're done here."

The agents shook their heads. "A 24-hour, four-man watch has been ordered," one answered, and then he pointed to a camera set up about fifty feet away. "Plus video surveillance."

Ben was taken aback. "For how long?"

The agent shrugged. "Indefinite, for now."

"Well," Ben said, looking back toward the vault. "I guess he'll be safe, then."

"You can be sure of that."

MCALLEN, TEXAS

The Eleven's plane landed in McAllen just after 5:00. The group arrived grief-stricken. During a brief layover in Houston, Dan had contacted Ben and verified what they most feared: Manuel had been found dead. Burial details had been handled.

Marta met them all with the van. She and Pedro cried in each other's arms. The whole group decided to go to Dan and Tiffany's home and figure out what to do next.

"Do you think I should go straight to Monterrey?" Diego asked on the way.

Dan shook his head. "I've changed my mind on that. If the feds want us detained, they'd flag it at the border. Trying to flee to Mexico would only make it worse."

At Dan's, they all went to the living room and turned on cable news. Gradually, they pieced together the story being reported. Manuel Gonzales had been arrested on charges of treason. He had been processed into the DC jail, and then was being transferred to another location for FBI questioning. But extremists posing as FBI agents, in concert with two conspirators at the jail, abducted him, secreted him off to the nature preserve, and executed him on live video stream. Two guards at the jail had been arrested, but none of the other conspirators had been identified. Gonzales was quickly buried without a service at a local cemetery.

Once the narrative became clear, Ana turned to Dan. "How much of that do you actually believe?"

"I believe Manuel was arrested, because we were there. And I believe he's dead and buried, because Ben confirmed that for us. Everything in between is complete nonsense. No ragtag group of volunteers could pull that off. Especially with such short notice."

Nonsense or not, that's what the public was being told. It didn't really matter, Dan thought. Whatever hopes they had placed in Manuel Gonzales were over. He wasn't ushering in a new system. He wasn't establishing a new government. He wasn't setting up the kingdom of God. None of them were going to exercise power with him. They'd be lucky not to be imprisoned. Nothing could change any of that.

All of them had plenty of questions, but none of them had answers. They met for three hours at Dan's, commiserating about their dashed hopes. Toward the end, Dan was honest with them.

"You guys are welcome to stay if you wish. But I don't see much point. Everyone might as well go home. There's no next step for us. We're done."

The group dolefully concurred. The women shed a few more tears. They all hugged one another. Despite all that had happened, they felt a bond that wouldn't soon go away.

Finally, Maya asked, "Can we just … get together again? In a couple of days maybe?"

They all agreed—they didn't want to say goodbye yet. They'd gather again at Dan and Tiffany's Sunday night.

SIXTY-ONE

Normally, Alice Paige, the president's campaign manager, didn't warrant Secret Service protection. On this day, however, even for a one-mile drive from the White House to Charlie Parker Steak, she requested it. Too much had happened in the previous 24 hours, starting with the kidnapping and execution of Manuel Gonzales, then the morphing of Friday's Passover parade into a demonstration march, over 300,000 strong, followed by sporadic outbreaks of violence between pro- and anti-Gonzales demonstrators.

She stepped out of the government SUV, entered the restaurant, and walked straight to a private room where she and Daniel Holden, the Chief of Staff, and Mark Humphries, the Chief Strategist, regularly met for lunch.

"A lot of protestors still on the Mall," she commented to the two of them as she took her seat.

"The Park Police estimate fifty or sixty thousand," Humphries responded. "But that will abate."

"You think so?" Holden asked.

Humphries nodded. "Most of these people are from out of town, here for the parade. They'll go back home tomorrow. Besides, religious people are notoriously hard to organize politically."

"They did it in South Texas with that Juan Carlos guy."

"That was their home turf. They could virtually walk to those protests. DC is a different matter. Trust me, this will blow over."

"It had better," Paige commented. She had picked up her menu, but she placed it, unopened, in front of her. "The election is seven months out. We have some wiggle room in the polls, but we can't take a huge hit from the FBI's handling of this."

"We won't," Humphries said. "Our position needs to be one of sympathy for Gonzales's family, friends, and supporters. This morning's press release was a good start. Is the president planning a press conference?"

"He'll say a few words from the Rose Garden," Holden answered. "No questions."

"Good. The less interaction about it, the better. Wu will launch an investigation. With something this big, somebody will get fired. She probably already has a scapegoat picked out. Congress will hold hearings for a day or two. Pro forma."

"What about his key followers?" Paige asked.

"Ottenger had every one of them checked out," Humphries replied. "A bunch of nobodies. They'll fade back into the woodwork."

"No trials?"

"No trials. The less attention we pay to this whole thing, the better. We'll let it peter out on its own. Which it will."

Humphries picked up a breadstick and tore off one end. "Honestly, I don't think this could have gone better. The threat's been neutralized. Everyone will move on. Seven months from now, nobody will be talking about Manuel Gonzales."

SIXTY-TWO

Jon Mason sat in the front seat of his FBI vehicle outside of Cottonwood Creek Memorial Cemetery plot #782: the public mausoleum. He and his partner, Ethan Cole, were seven hours into an eight-hour shift that began Sunday morning at midnight. Guarding gravesites was not exactly what he'd signed up for with the FBI. But he and Cole were low men on the totem pole. So were the other two special agents in the nearby vehicle. Hence, graveyard duty.

It made sense, he figured, guarding the casket. Rumor had it that this Manuel Gonzales had claimed he would come alive again. Having someone steal the body and allege that had happened was the last thing officials wanted.

As daylight broke, Mason took a break from all the file work on his laptop and randomly scrolled through his phone.

"Find anything interesting?" Cole asked.

Mason shook his head. "Nothing we don't already know. Unless you consider—"

Suddenly, in front of them, a light so brilliant appeared that Mason immediately looked away and shielded his face. "Whoa! What in the …?"

He glanced at Cole, who was averting his eyes as well. The brightness gradually lessened. Mason stole a glance toward the mausoleum. He could finally make out something.

Two beings of superhuman size and beauty stood in front

of the entrance. Their bodies shone with dazzling white light and they moved with unparalleled grace. One of them motioned toward the doors. The ground shook and the doors opened.

Cole looked at Mason. "Do you think we should get out and—"

"Absolutely not."

Mason glanced at the two agents in the other vehicle. They were glued to their seats as well.

The beings walked inside, removed the casket from its vault, and set it on the ground. Then they exited the structure and sat on the tall stone ledges on each side of it.

A moment later, a blinding light burst from the entrance, and a force like the wind of a hurricane. It blasted past the two FBI vehicles, sliding them back several car lengths on the gravel. Mason and Cole eyed one another in terror. Neither could look at the entrance itself.

Finally, the light abated. And out from the mausoleum walked a human—Manuel Gonzales. But he was not like any human Mason had even seen. He radiated light and power, and looked completely ageless. And somehow, Mason knew, indestructible.

Manuel Gonzales slowly stepped onto the gravel, glanced up at the angels behind him, and nodded toward them. His gaze turned to Mason's vehicle, and he looked the agent directly in the eyes. And then he disappeared.

The brightly shining beings continued sitting on the ledges. The FBI agents remained in their vehicles. In a few minutes, out of the corner of his eye, Mason noticed two men and a woman approaching, carrying flowers. As they approached the entrance, the shining beings stood before them. The people looked terrified. Mason quickly pulled out a directional microphone and rolled his window down.

"Don't be afraid," one of the beings said to the three. "Emmanuel isn't here. Why would you look for the Living One among the dead? He's risen, just as he told you he would. Look inside. See for yourself."

The three cautiously put the flowers on the ground and stepped inside. They came back out, the woman crying, the men clearly shaken.

"Can we see him?" the woman asked the being. "Will he come back to us?"

"He will appear again in the Valley. Go back home. Tell the Eleven what you have seen."

Mason sat motionless. His phone rang, and he glanced at the other vehicle. One of the agents was calling him. "Should we question those people? Take them in?"

"With those beings out there? Are you kidding?" He realized how lame that sounded, but he wasn't about to change his mind. "Besides, what would they tell us? We saw everything they saw."

The three people left. Then the beings disappeared as well. Mason opened his car door and walked toward the mausoleum. Cole and the other two agents joined him. They stopped in the entrance and looked. There, on the ground, lay the open casket. There was no body. But the graveclothes had been neatly folded and left inside.

SIXTY-THREE

At ten hours a day, including stops, Washington, DC to Corpus Christi took three days to drive. To Hank Murray and Jeff Atkins, it seemed like three weeks. They didn't say much on the road. After what had happened in DC the last 48 hours, they didn't know what to say. Or think.

Many months before, the two of them had driven from Corpus to the Valley to check out Manuel Gonzales for themselves. They'd been traveling in the caravan behind him ever since and had been selected to be two of the 72 in LA. They'd gotten to know Manuel. They'd believed in him. They'd been part of his cause. They'd even driven to DC to be part of the Passover march with him. But now there was no more cause.

They got off Interstate 10 in Lake Charles, Louisiana for gas. On the entrance ramp to get back on, they passed a hitchhiker. Hank looked at him in his sideview mirror.

"Go back and get that guy," he said.

"The hitchhiker? Why?"

"Just … because."

Jeff pulled onto the shoulder, started backing up, and looked over at Hank. "You just feel like putting our lives in danger?"

"I feel like we should pick him up. Besides, how do you know we're not already in danger?"

They stopped and invited the hitchhiker to join them. He seemed normal enough. They filled him in briefly on where they were going. He filled them in briefly on hitchhiking. The car fell silent.

After a while, the hitchhiker spoke again. "I appreciate the ride and all, but this car seems a bit, well, glum."

Hank and Jeff glanced at each other.

"Yeah," Jeff responded.

"Why?"

Hank turned back to him. "We were just in DC."

"And?"

"And we were there with everything that happened."

"What happened?"

Jeff looked at him in the rear-view mirror. "Have you been under a rock? Haven't you heard about Manuel Gonzales?"

"What about him?"

"Congress subpoenaed him to testify, and then the feds arrested him, and then they—or someone—conspired to murder him. We were part of his ..." Jeff stole a glance at Hank, who shook his head almost imperceptibly. "His fans, I guess. We— a lot of people in South Texas, actually—thought he was the Promised One. El Único, they call him."

"And now?" the hitchhiker asked.

Jeff shook his head. "It's over. We supposed. But there's a rumor out there that maybe he's not dead anymore." He turned back toward the hitchhiker. "Honestly, I don't know what to think at this point."

The hitchhiker sighed and leaned forward. "Don't you guys realize that El Único had to suffer all of this?"

They both looked back at him, unsure what to say.

"Do you want to know why?"

"Yeah, I do," Hank replied.

They passed a "Welcome to Texas" sign on the interstate and a billboard advertising the Ten West Diner up ahead in Orange, Texas.

"Let's get a bite to eat there," the hitchhiker suggested.

They exited the interstate and grabbed a table at the diner. The hitchhiker picked up the conversation right where they'd left off.

"Here's why El Único had to suffer," he said. "Listen closely. Four thousand years ago God made a promise to bless the whole earth. That blessing would be this: God himself would come to live in people. They would forever be connected to him as closely as they could possibly be.

"But God knew that people's hearts weren't ready to be joined to him. So he promised that one day a Messiah would come. And through his death and resurrection, God would get people's hearts ready. He would completely forgive them. He would completely cleanse them. He would take out their old heart and give them a brand new one, and put his own desires in them. Then, when all of that was done, he would come live in them.

"Do you understand what this means for your life? I mean, here and now?"

Hank looked at Jeff and then at the hitchhiker. "I'm not sure."

"It means that, if you've believed in the one God sent, your relationship with God has been taken care of. You and God are completely OK. Forever. That's the only way he could come live in you. You're forgiven. You're clean. Your heart is new. Deep down, you want what he wants. You know him now, because he lives in you. You never have to do anything to get right, or stay right, with God again. You *are* right.

"You can stop focusing on yourself, and instead focus on him living in you. Because if God himself lives in you, it changes everything.

"You're not trying to be good enough anymore. You're not

trying to perform. You're simply letting him live his own life, in you. You're trusting him to do it. Because he himself will cause you to express his life.

"That's what he promises. That's the whole point. The God of the universe lives in you! Through his union with you, he expresses his own life to the whole world. And beyond."

The server brought water and a basket of rolls to the table.

"It's like this," he continued. "Imagine you've been told you're competing for the world chess championship in six months. You're not very good at chess. Even if you did everything you could to improve, you still won't be nearly good enough in six months."

"Or six years," Jeff said.

"But what if the reigning chess champion came to live inside you? Now how ready are you?"

Hank and Jeff looked at each other. "Really ready," Hank said.

"Right. You're completely ready, because he lives in you. You're not trying hard anymore. You're not trying to make yourself good enough. You're just trusting in him in you."

The hitchhiker picked up a roll and looked at them both. "You're free now. You're free to simply be El Papá's vessels, vessels of his love." He broke the roll in half and handed it to them. "Take me inside you. I'm the bread of life. I come to live in you. I pour out through you. And so you share my life with others."

Suddenly, their eyes were opened, and Hank and Jeff recognized him.

And then he disappeared.

SIXTY-FOUR

Late Sunday afternoon, everyone (less Mike, who was running late) met again at Dan's. Dan and Tiffany served them all refreshments. Dan could read in them the fear that he expected. Despite having been back in McAllen for 48 hours without incident, they all knew perfectly well that the FBI could come through the door any moment and arrest every one of them.

But now a different mood had crept in as well: confusion. They'd received texts and a call from Ben and Abigail, describing some strange events at the cemetery. Clearly, they and Congressman Garcia had experienced something. The question was, what exactly? Angels? Manuel rising from the dead? All the Eleven knew for sure was that his body was no longer there. That's what Ben had reported.

So where was it? The FBI had posted a four-man watch on the burial vault. They were there when the Thompsons and Congressman Garcia had shown up. What, if anything, did the FBI know?

Adding to the confusion was a news report saying that Jorge had been found dead in a hotel room—of an apparent suicide.

The group sat in the living room, mystified. The truth was, none of them really believed what they'd heard. Manuel alive? How could that possibly be? And yet …

"So what do we do now?" Sofia asked. "Just wait around for ... what?"

"I'm applying for my old job tomorrow," Ana said.

Dan nodded. "That's exactly what we do. Return to our old lives. And hope that will cause the authorities to leave us alone."

"Some of the 72 want to keep the movement going," Emma said. "I've heard from a couple of them."

"I have too," Kiara said.

"No," Dan replied. "Absolutely not. That's the last thing we can do. Restarting the movement would almost certainly land us all in jail. Or worse." That silenced everyone for a moment.

"But the protests have started again down here," Kiara finally said. "They expect us to join them."

Dan shook his head. "It's too dangerous. The protests will die down, like they did before. The government wants all of this to go away. We need to cooperate with them."

"But what about what Ben and Abigail said?" Emma asked. "What if ..." She seemed hesitant to finish the thought, as if reluctant to verbalize something that seemed so far-fetched.

"Look," Dan replied, "I appreciate all that Ben and Abigail did for us. But we weren't there. We don't know what they saw. And, really, neither do they."

Sebastian's phone notified him of a text. He glanced at it, and then looked up slowly at the group. "You're not going to believe this. That was Hank Murray of the 72. They picked up Manuel hitchhiking at the Texas-Louisiana border. He was with them close to an hour."

"What?!" the group cried out.

"That's what he said."

"When did they see him?" Maya asked.

"Just now."

"They're sure it was him?"

A knock at the front door gave them all a start.

"Who's that?" Kiara whispered.

Dan shrugged. "I don't know." He got up, walked to the entryway, opened the door, and stood, looking through the screen door, speechless.

"May I come in?" the man asked. He was clearly himself, but his physical body—somehow was different. Very different.

"Y ... yes," Dan stammered.

He reached for the screen's handle, but the man passed right through the screen as if it wasn't there at all.

The man continued through the entryway and stood at the edge of the living room. And then Dan heard someone scream.

"Manuel!" Sebastian shouted. "You're alive!"

"It can't be you!" Ana cried out. "It can't be!"

Dan followed me into the living room, just in time to see everyone rush toward me.

I laughed heartily. "It's me! Here, feel my wrists. Look at my ankles."

We all reunited with loads of hugs, tears, and laughter. I had never seen so many beaming faces surrounding me at once.

"Manuel," Maya finally said, trying to wipe her moist cheeks, "how did you ... how is this possible?"

"I told you I would rise from the dead. Why didn't you believe me?"

"We just thought ..." She shrugged and smiled at me. "I don't know what we thought."

I couldn't help but grin back at her. "Well, now you can know. I was dead, but now I'm alive. Forever."

"I know what we thought," Dan said. The group got quiet. "We thought we'd lost. That you'd lost."

I shook my head. "That's what the forces of evil thought, too.

But they've been defeated. Disarmed. Sin, death—they've been overcome. The victory's been won, for all time."

My eyes landed on Ana. "You told us once that you came to reclaim what humanity lost," she said.

I nodded.

"You've done that, haven't you?"

I smiled at her. "I have. Everything El Papá has is now yours, Ana." I looked around at the group. "It's all of yours."

I extended my arms and we all had a huge hug. Except one of us.

I looked to my right. Pedro. He was standing a little apart from the group, obviously unsure what to do. I walked over to him and embraced him tightly.

Finally, he spoke. "Manuel, how can you ever forgive me?"

I kept holding onto him, but looked into his eyes. "Didn't you see the scars?"

He nodded, tears beginning to trickle down his cheeks.

"It's done," I said. "You are totally forgiven. Who do you think I died for?"

"But, I—"

"No buts, my dear friend. What happened is forgotten. You and I are completely fine, and always will be."

We hugged tightly again, and then I gave him one simple instruction: "After I go back to El Papá, feed those who are hungry for me. Especially those who think what they've done is unforgiveable."

Pedro leaned back. "You'd trust me with that?"

I smiled at him. "There's no one more qualified."

We stepped back to the group. Sofia took out her phone and texted Mike.

Manuel is here!
   He is not!

Come and see for yourself.

Right. I'll believe it when I touch his nail wounds.

Five minutes later Mike walked through the door. "What is this about—" And then he froze when he got to the living room.

I stood before him, holding out my scarred wrists. "Come put your finger in my wrists, Mike. Don't be unbelieving, but believing."

Mike fell to his knees. "My Lord and my God!"

I walked over to him. "You're blessed because you saw and believed." I turned to the whole group. "I'll tell you who's really blessed: those who won't see with their eyes, yet they'll still believe."

And then I noticed the seven-layer dip on the coffee table and an empty chip bowl. "Well, it looks like I missed half the party. Do we have any more chips?"

SIXTY-FIVE

The government went ballistic over my disappearance from the burial vault. Investigators questioned the four FBI agents endlessly, and forbade them from talking to the media. They identified and interrogated Ben, Abigail, and Congressman Garcia, but their stories matched those of the agents.

Rumors spread that I had appeared to various individuals. Social media went crazy with a million theories. Since it couldn't produce my body, the FBI finally admitted that I was missing. The mausoleum was locked down for weeks. Forensics experts combed every inch of ground. Press conferences were held to leak fake stories. The FBI finally settled on a narrative that its four agents had been knocked out with isoflurane gas, security cameras had been disabled, and someone stole my body. People weren't buying it.

Fewer and fewer people were believing the government's account of events surrounding my crucifixion as well. The more evidence emerged, the less it added up.

The FBI did track down and question each of the Eleven. Yes, they'd been selected by me to be my trainees, they admitted. Yes, they'd seen me alive again. No, they didn't know where I was at any given time. I came and went whenever and wherever I chose.

The Eleven didn't just have the attention of the government, of course. The media hounded them relentlessly.

"Don't run from it," I told them. "Play into it. Do interviews.

Tell people what you've seen. Be completely honest. We have no secrets."

The government, the media, and Big Tech did its best to convince people that the Eleven had agreed upon an invented story to tell. When I started appearing to a few others, that narrative became less believable. When I appeared to a gathering of most of the 72 and their friends and family—more than 500 people—at Westside Park in McAllen, it fell apart completely.

FBI stakeouts were posted at all of the Eleven's houses and apartments in case I returned. They had remote listening devices which would reveal my presence. I didn't want the Eleven to endure people kicking down their doors—not yet, anyway—so we simply bypassed all of that. Every couple of days, the Eleven drove the van to South Padre and boarded Luis Gutiérrez's sixty-foot fishing boat. They would head out to sea, where I'd meet with them.

The FBI tracked us with helicopters, but we spoke of little that the FBI would have deemed important. As if upending the entire world was unimportant.

"El Papá has given me authority over everything in the universe," I told them. "So I'm sending you, just as he sent me. Preach the good news to everyone on the planet."

"What exactly do we say?" Pedro asked. Always so practical.

"Tell them what I've told you. They need to change their minds about God. They can freely receive his forgiveness. They can stop trying to earn their way to him. I've done away with that."

"By dying to pay for their sins," Ana said.

"Yes, by dying for their sins. But not just that. When they put their trust in me, I'll not only forgive them completely, I'll make them totally new on the inside. I've removed every obstacle to them being one with us. El Papá, and I, and the Spirit—we will come to live in them. We will live our life of pure love through them."

"This is going to happen to us?" Emma asked.

"Yes, you all first."

"But ... how? I mean—"

I smiled at her. "This life is about to become really simple, Emma. I'm going to come live in you. And you'll live by trusting me. I'll be your guide. I'll be your wisdom. I'll be your love. I'll be your patience, and self-discipline, and strength, and goodness. I'll be your perfect everything. You'll live by depending on me, in you."

"So what exactly do we do?" Pedro asked.

"You live as the branch. You make yourselves available. You tell me you're willing. You hear from the Spirit, and follow his lead. And as you step out, I'll do it through you. It's as simple as that."

I looked around at them all, my heart overflowing with love for each one of them. "I'm the life in you now. I'm all you need. This is what you were made for. Teach people to live this way. Baptize them in Our name. That'll show we've already removed the old from them, and made them completely new."

We met on the boat over a period of almost forty days. On our last day, I had Luis drop us at an isolated marina miles north of any crowds. We walked out onto the beach. As we stood in a circle on the sand, I said to them, "I'm going to leave you now. I won't be coming back to you physically, not until I return to set up my kingdom on earth."

Maya gasped and started crying. Others did, too.

"But it's good for you that I go," I assured them. "I'm serious. I'm going to come live in you, just as I told you. In just a few days, I'll give you the gift El Papá promised—the promise he made four thousand years ago, to bless the whole earth. Now is the time. The promise is for you, and to coming generations, and to everyone, near and far, who puts their trust in me. I'll pour out the Holy Spirit, and we will come live in you, and you'll be filled with power. Everyone will see it.

"You're my witnesses now. Spread the message here in the

Valley. Across the country. Around the world. The opposition
can't stop it. They can't stop you. Through me, people will unite
with God. And they'll unite with one another.

"But stay here in the Valley together until you receive my gift.
And then ..."

"And then they ain't seen nothing yet," Sebastian said.

In spite of their tears, everyone laughed.

"You're right, Sebastian. They ain't seen nothing yet. But
they're about to."

We all hugged, said our goodbyes, and cried some more. I had
everyone gather in a tight circle. We all held hands.

"Remember, I'll always be with you," I said to them. "Even
when this age comes to an end."

I squeezed Pedro's hand to my left, and Emma's to my right,
and then I released their hands and rose from the beach, looking down on them all as I ascended, until I disappeared into
the clouds.

The Eleven waited for ten more days in McAllen.

And then I gave them what El Papá had promised so long
before. We—all three of Us—came to live inside them. We and
they became one. Forever.

*Because God's children are human beings—made of flesh
and blood—the Son also became flesh and blood. For only
as a human being could he die, and only by dying could
he break the power of the devil, who had the power of
death. Only in this way could he set free all who have
lived their lives as slaves to the fear of dying.... Therefore,
it was necessary for him to be made in every respect like
us, his brothers and sisters, so that he could be our merciful
and faithful High Priest before God. Then he could offer
a sacrifice that would take away the sins of the people.*

—The Letter to the Hebrews, chapter 2,
verses 14-17, New Living Translation

*Though he was God, he did not think of equality with
God as something to cling to. Instead, he gave up his
divine privileges; he took the humble position of a slave
and was born as a human being. When he appeared
in human form, he humbled himself in obedience
to God and died a criminal's death on a cross.*

*Therefore, God elevated him to the place of highest honor
and gave him the name above all other names,
that at the name of Jesus every knee should bow,
in heaven and on earth and under the earth,
and every tongue declare that Jesus Christ
is Lord, to the glory of God the Father.*

—Paul's Letter to the Philippians, chapter 2,
verses 6-11, New Living Translation

A NOTE TO MY
SPANISH-SPEAKING READERS

If you speak Spanish, you may have noticed a couple of unexpected language choices in *One of Us*. The first is the use of "El Papá" as how Manuel refers to God the Father. Spanish speakers typically use the word "Señor" when speaking to God; if they are referring to God as Father, they use the word "Padre." However, I chose "El Papá" as a way to convey the sense of intimacy that Jesus communicated when he called God the Father "Abba" (Mark 14:36).

"Abba" is an Aramaic word that Jesus used to address his Father. It is also a word that the Apostle Paul says is natural for us to use with God now, too—we who have become his children through faith in Jesus (Romans 8:15). It is a word that children use today in that part of the world. For us, it conveys both a sense of loving intimacy (like "papa" does) and also of reverence for who God is. Many of us struggle with believing God really wants to be close to us. But he does. That was the whole point of Jesus becoming human, to enable us to be closely connected to God. If we have placed our trust in Jesus, God is now our Abba.

The second language choice was the use of "El Único" to refer to Manuel. It means "the one." I realize that a more accurate and descriptive Spanish word to use here would have been "El Elegido," which means "the chosen one." I used "El Único" not for Spanish-speaking readers, but for English-speaking readers. To an English-speaking reader, the words "El Único" *look* like they mean "The One," and it's easy for such a reader to *remember* that they mean "The One." "El Elegido," on the other hand, means nothing to an English speaker; it is simply an unknown Spanish word. So I chose to go with "El Único." For the Spanish language version of the book, "El Elegido" is used.

Some Important Notes

Readers' Guides
On my website, FreeWithGod.com, you can download free readers' guides for personal growth or for group discussion. The guides are a great way to interact with the story and its truths, either for an evening, for several weeks, or for an extended period.

Translations
I am currently working on making *One of Us* available as an e-book and audio book, in Spanish and Portuguese, in all of Latin America *for free*. If you would like to partner financially with me in this endeavor (and in producing free translations in other languages), you can do so at FreeWithGod.com. I would love to welcome you to the *One of Us* team!

Speaking Engagements and Contact Information
I am available for speaking engagements at churches, at conferences, and for organizations. All such requests can be sent to me through FreeWithGod.com, as can all messages for me. You can also follow me on social media at:

facebook.com/DavidGregoryAuthor

twitter.com/davidgregorybooks

Acknowledgements

This book was ten years in the making. No one engages in a project of this size without considerable help.

I would like to thank Vanessa Vallejos, my Spanish-language consultant, who helped me navigate the subtleties of a language I don't speak that well; my son, Truett Smith, who not only provided invaluable editing help, but believed that God would do something big with this book; Barbara Rolen for her constant enthusiasm for the manuscript, priceless feedback, and unwavering support; Rick Richards for helping me create a fictional world that made better sense to the reader; Mike Mason, whose critique helped me craft the novel's opening and whose great enthusiasm for the book helped enlarge my vision for it; Ralph Harris for helping me think through how best to express some passages from the gospels; Diana Sollars for her invaluable copy editing and proofreading contributions; Bob Atkins for his role in making this book possible; and, finally, my editor, Steve Parolini, who, as before, helped make this novel so much more readable.

ABOUT THE AUTHOR

DAVID GREGORY is the author of a dozen fiction and nonfiction books. His novel *Dinner with a Perfect Stranger* was a *New York Times* extended bestseller. David has been the recipient of the ECPA's Gold Book Award and his novel *The Last Christian* was a Christy Award finalist. Three of his novels have been made into feature films. A native of Texas, David holds master's degrees from Dallas Theological Seminary and The University of North Texas. He was formerly on the ministry team of Insight for Living, the Bible-teaching ministry of Charles Swindoll.

www.ingramcontent.com/pod-product-compliance
Lightning Source LLC
Chambersburg PA
CBHW052020240626

47153CB00006B/1887